"Do you even remem[...]

"Freedom," the capt[...]
that the word had mean[...]
to him long ago.

The necromancer shrugged emaciated shoulders.
"Does that mean anything now?" he asked. "Are you
free? Are they? No, there is no freedom left," he said,
answering his own question. "Your leaders sacrificed
your freedom and theirs along with everything else for
their *one desperate chance at victory*." He spat bitterly.
"Their one sacrifice." He shook his head wearily.
"Some sacrifices should never be made. Some sacrifices corrupt and destroy everything you're trying to
save."

"*You* could have left us in peace. *You* came to *us*.
You made war on us. We simply defended our
homes."

"Defense is only defense so long as it does not destroy what it defends and a decision is not truly made
once if it must be remade over and over again."

His words unsettled the captain and he turned his
yellow eyes on the man's face. "Some things are worth
sacrificing everything for," he said, "they're worth
dying for." He turned back to the battle, feeling what
was left of the necromancer's original glyphs drawing
him back. "And worth killing for."

—From *The Captain of the Dead* by Fiona Patton

In The Shadow of Evil

EDITED BY

MARTIN H. GREENBERG
AND JOHN HELFERS

DAW BOOKS, INC.
DONALD A. WOLLHEIM, FOUNDER
375 Hudson Street, New York, NY 10014

ELIZABETH R. WOLLHEIM
SHEILA E. GILBERT
PUBLISHERS
www.dawbooks.com

First Printing, August 2005
1 2 3 4 5 6 7 8 9

DAW TRADEMARK REGISTERED
U.S. PAT. OFF. AND FOREIGN COUNTRIES
—MARCA REGISTRADA
HECHO EN U.S.A.

PRINTED IN THE U.S.A.

ACKNOWLEDGMENTS

Contents

INTRODUCTION

John Helfers

"All that is necessary for the triumph of evil is that good men do nothing."

—Edmund Burke

WHAT IS YOUR definition of evil? Is it the world-shattering power of a nation or ideology that perpetuates evil for its own gain, like the Third Reich? Is it a despot oppressing his own people for completely personal gain, like Louis XVI, who strengthened his nation at the cost of alienating his own countrymen? Is it personified in a creature that sums up the complete opposite of good, like Satan? Or is it a monolithic corporation pursuing profits no matter what the cost to other companies or even its own employees?

As the examples above show, evil has taken many forms throughout history, and often has been able to advance its agenda, no matter what or where or how, because, as Mr. Burke so astutely observed during the eighteenth century, good men do nothing. Well, except in fantasy literature, apparently.

While I have explored a similar theme in a previous anthology (*Villains Victorious*), this one struck a more personal chord simply because it isn't seen very much in fantasy fiction. Indeed, one wonders if it could even be attempted, as the conventions of the genre would certainly seem to state that evil must be punished and

good triumph. Granted, there have been notable examples of the oppressive, all-powerful dystopia in science fiction, with probably the best-known one being
Nineteen Eighty-four by George Orwell.

But it seems that this is not a theme that is explored
in fantasy fiction; rather, the tomes topping the best-
seller list often tackle the elementary theme of good
versus evil and then make their plots as complicated
or simple as necessary. But whether it be a trilogy or
decalogy or an open-ended series, although the heroes
may suffer hardships and sacrifices and all kinds of
trials, in the end good's victory, even if it is just a
stopgap measure, is practically assured. Current multi-
volume sagas, including *Harry Potter* and others, show
no sign of reversing this trend, although in George
Martin's *Song of Ice and Fire* series, the good guys
drop like flies throughout, so that those books may
play a bit against type before the saga's conclusion.

Therefore, I decided to invite authors to explore the
other side of the coin; fantasy worlds where evil has
already won the epic final battle, where the side of
good is now forced to hide, to slink about, to be the
underdog, and maybe—just maybe—not even survive
to fight another day.

Good certainly doesn't win in the real world all the
time, so why should it in fantasy? This was the question posed to fourteen of today's brightest authors,
and they answered my question with very unique vi-
sions of worlds where everyone lives in the shadow of
evil. So turn the page and prepare to enter worlds
where good and evil are still fighting their eternal
struggle, but the tide has turned against the light, and
now hope, courage, and valor are forced to strike from
the very darkness that has overtaken them.

Fantasy of all kinds is represented here, from Tim
Waggoner's story of a man struggling to provide a life,

any kind of life for his family under the rule of implacable alien masters to Gregory Benford's urban combat fantasy about a place so steeped in evil that even the animals take sides. From acclaimed Canadian author Julie Czerneda comes a tale that asked "what does evil do when it has subjugated everything under its power?" And finally, Fiona Patton creates a nightmarish fantasy world whose inhabitants only know killing and death—until two of them dare to search for something more.

Fourteen tales of good still striving to overcome an evil that has all but vanquished it. In here there are no easy answers, no magical sword or all-powerful wzard that can set things right with one blow or spell. Those committed to good must make hard, sometimes impossible choices to see their cause succeed. For if they do not, then they will forever remain in the shadow of evil.

TO EMBRACE THE SERPENT

Tim Waggoner

Tim Waggoner has published more than eighty stories of fantasy and horror. His most current stories can be found in the anthologies *Civil War Fantastic, Single White Vampire Seeks Same,* and *Bruce Coville's UFOs.* His first novel is *The Harmony Society,* and he is currently working on projects for both White Wolf and Wizards of the Coast. He teaches creative writing at Sinclair Community College in Dayton, Ohio.

BROGAN PULLED out the wax stopper and held the vial before him. He didn't do anything to waft the scent of the yellowish liquid toward his customer, for there was no need. The perfume maker simply stood and tried to keep his hand from shaking. No matter how many times he had been to the palace, he was always nervous in the presence of Asthyrian.

The Naga's great bulk was coiled upon a large marble dais surrounded by burning braziers. The flames helped regulate the giant serpent's body temperature, and their orange light glittered off golden scales as large as serving platters. Clustered around Asthyrian, curled up against him and gently stroking his smooth hide, were a dozen Nawat. The egg layers' naked skin glistened with the same golden hue as that of their sire and lover. They were bald, but otherwise appeared human enough. They were all young and beautiful, and when they weren't attending their god-husband, it was reputed that they lived in luxury that even the highest ranked among Asthyrian's other servants could only dream about.

Though Brogan knew Naga couldn't hear, he said, "Perhaps you will find favor with this scent, my lord. It's a mixture of cinnamon, thyme, eyebright and some odds and ends." One of those being pig's blood. He often used blood of various kinds in the scents he created for the serpent-god. The smell of blood—any kind—was something none of the Naga or their inhuman servants could resist.

As the scent of Brogan's latest perfume drifted toward Asthyrian, the great serpent lifted his triangular head, and his forked tongue flicked out and tasted the air—once, twice, three times in rapid succession. This was the part Brogan hated the most: waiting to find out what the Naga's reaction would be. Whether he loved or hated them, the serpent's response to Brogan's scents was always unreadable.

Asthyrian's gaze turned to the Chu'a standing next to Brogan. Though the perfume maker was unaware of any communication passing between the Naga and the half-human, half-snake priest, the Chu'a nevertheless turned to Brogan.

"Our god finds this scent intriguing," the priest said in a whisper-hiss. "But he wishes to sample the scent applied to flesh."

Brogan bowed his head toward the Naga. "Of course, my lord." It was a normal request, since Asthyrian's Chu'a and Pakwa would be the ones wearing the scent—and a good sign. It meant the Naga was seriously considering this one.

Brogan pushed his shirtsleeve up and made ready to put a few drops of perfume on his wrist.

Asthyrian shifted his great bulk upon the dais, and the Chu'a said, "Hold, Master Brogan."

Brogan froze, the vial not yet tipped far enough for any liquid to spill out. Though the use of the honorific "master" was an indication of how highly the Naga and his servants valued Brogan's craft, he had no illusions regarding his status. If he displeased Asthyrian in any way—such as failing to respond to a command quickly enough—he would be instantly slain. Or worse.

The Chu'a's serpentine eyes narrowed. The priest's face was more snake than human, and though the blue robe he wore concealed the rest of his body, Brogan knew his limbs were scaled and supple as serpents.

"Our god prefers that you put the scent on *her*." The Chu'a pointed at the young woman standing at Brogan's side.

Rheda looked at him with wide, frightened eyes. "Father?" she said softly.

He put a finger to his lips to shush her. This was only the third time he'd brought his daughter with him to the palace, and she was still terrified to be in the Naga's presence. Not that he could blame her. Along with the great serpent's size, Asthyrian projected an aura of deadly power that made the very air around him seem to crackle with foul magic.

Brogan executed another head bow. "Of course, my lord." He turned to his daughter. "Bare your wrist, my love."

Rheda hesitated, trembling from head to toe.

"Do not be afraid," Brogan said softly. "Asthyrian will only smell the perfume. I guarantee it." Brogan had no way of knowing what the gigantic serpent would do to his daughter, but he couldn't very well tell her that. If she became too upset, Asthyrian might lose patience and slay them both. Compliance with the Naga's wishes did not always result in survival, but noncompliance always brought death. If one was fortunate, that death would be swift. If one was not . . .

Brogan gripped his daughter's hand and turned it over to expose her wrist. He tilted the vial over her skin and allowed three drops to fall. No more, else the smell would be too strong and Asthyrian would be displeased.

There was silence in the Naga's throne room as they all waited for the perfume to blend with Rheda's natural scent. After several moments passed, the Chu'a whispered, "Step closer to our god."

Rheda shook her head. "Father, I ca—" Before she could finish, Brogan slapped her face. Hard enough to sting, but not hard enough to do any real damage.

"Remember in whose presence you stand." His tone was stern, but his gaze was pleading. *Just do as they want, my love. Please!*

Though tears burned in her eyes, Rheda nodded and stepped toward the Naga's dais. Brogan was relieved to see that she kept her gaze at the right angle—not so high as to actually face Asthyrian, but not so low that she was looking at the floor.

She seemed so much like her mother at that moment that it made Brogan's heart ache. Curly black hair, high cheekbones, creamy-white skin . . . and even the fala, the baggy gray tunic than all humans were required to wear, couldn't conceal her lovely shape.

As Rheda approached the dais, the Nawat fixed her with jealous glares, and a few of the egg layers even hissed at her, baring long, curved fangs. But Asthyrian rippled the muscles along his great length, and the Nawat grew silent, though they continued to glare at Rheda.

When she reached the base of the dais, the Chu'a said, "Stop."

Rheda looked relieved—*Probably glad she doesn't have to go any closer,* Brogan thought—and did as the serpent-priest commanded.

Then, moving with slow grace, the giant serpent extended his head toward Rheda. The Naga came within a foot of her wrist and then released his tongue. It flicked toward her wrist and almost touched the skin as it tasted the air.

After several more flicks, Asthyrian pulled the tongue back into his mouth, but the Naga did not immediately withdraw his head. Asthyrian kept his serpentine eyes—each as large as a man's outstretched hand—trained on Rheda. For a horrible moment, Brogan thought the giant snake was considering devouring her, but then the Naga pulled back and settled down upon his coils once more.

The Chu'a looked at Brogan. "Our god finds the scent pleasing. He would have five gallons of it delivered by the next new moon." The serpent-man smiled, displaying a mouthful of sharp teeth dominated by a pair of curved fangs. "And he would like the girl to accompany you when you deliver the scent."

Brogan bowed from the waist this time, going as low as his old back would permit. "Thank you, my lord. I shall."

Asthyrian—gaze still focused on Rheda—hissed an acknowledgment, and Brogan knew this audience was over. The perfume maker straightened and motioned for his daughter to rejoin him. He fought to keep his face expressionless, but inside he was giddy with elation. This couldn't have gone better if he'd planned it himself.

But if Rheda felt anything positive about what had

just happened, she hid her emotions most effectively. Her face was expressionless, gaze unreadable.

Brogan decided not to worry about that right now. All that mattered was that she'd done well. Surely she'd come to see that in time.

They turned and together walked out of the throne room, leaving the presence of the monster that had become their god.

No one seemed to know for sure where the Naga had come from. Some said the old gods had imprisoned the Naga deep within the earth long before humankind was created, and that some foolish sorcerer had accidentally freed them. Others believed the Naga had come to this world after laying waste to their own, draining it dry of all resources and then casting it aside like a hollowed-out piece of fruit. Still others believed that the serpents had been sent by the old gods to punish humanity for forsaking the ancient ways. And some thought that there wasn't any reason, that the Naga had come simply because they had.

When Brogan considered these various explanations—which wasn't often—he decided that it didn't matter why the Naga were here. They were, and there was nothing a humble perfume maker could do about it. At such times, he recalled something his own father had told him, not long after the Naga's armies had swept across the land and changed it forever.

We must learn to live in the world the way it is, my son. However much we might wish otherwise, it is the only world we have.

Not much comfort to be taken from those words, perhaps. But that didn't make them any the less true.

"Father?"

"Hmm?"

It was later that night. The sun had set and curfew was in effect. Curfew for humans, that is: Chu'a and Pakwa could roam the city at will. Since Brogan, despite his status as a "Master Perfume Maker," didn't have special permission to be out after dark, he and Rheda sat at a wooden table in their home—a small shack on the eastside in the human quarter—a single candle burning between them.

Rheda's voice was hesitant at first, but it gained strength and conviction as she spoke. "I don't want to go back to the palace. Ever."

Brogan took a sip of vegetable broth, then put the half-empty clay mug down on the table. He noticed that Rheda's mug was still full. He tried to think of a detailed and cogent argument why Rheda couldn't avoid going to the palace. But finally, it came down to one simple reason.

"You don't have a choice." He took another sip of broth while Rheda looked at him in disbelief.

"Of course I have a choice," she said, anger creeping into her voice. "I can choose to stay home, and that's exactly what I intend to do the next time that overgrown worm summons you."

Brogan cast a frightened glance about the room.

"What are you looking for?" Rheda demanded.

"Snakes. Asthyrian's eyes are everywhere." Luckily, he saw none.

Rheda started to laugh, but then she realized he was serious, for she said, "Asthyrian has never spied on us before."

"That you're aware of," he pointed out. "Besides, Asthyrian has never had a reason to keep an eye on us—until now."

Rheda scowled. "And just what do you mean by that?"

Brogan couldn't keep the smile from his lips. "He asked you to try on the perfume for him, didn't he?"

"More like commanded me to," she muttered.

Brogan ignored her. She was doubtless still upset that he'd been forced to hit her in the Naga's throne room though, by doing so, he'd likely saved both their lives.

"That means you found favor in his eyes."

Rheda looked aghast. "Father! What are you saying?"

Brogan took another sip of broth to give him time to think.

"You know things are different since the Naga came," he said, his voice growing wistful. "Very different."

"So you say. As you've pointed out on more than one occasion, I'm too young to have ever known a world without the Naga."

Brogan smiled with sad affection. "Not so young anymore, I'm afraid. You're a woman now, Rheda. If things were as they used to be, you'd be wearing your mother's courting scarf by now and selecting from among a slew of suitors."

"The Chu'a assign mating partners," Rheda said. "And since they do so only when the human population in the city drops low enough, I may never get one."

Brogan was surprised to hear the sadness in his daughter's voice. They had never spoken of such things before. They hadn't spoken much at all—at least, not about anything important—since the deaths of her mother and brother.

Brogan decided to try a different tack. "I'm not as young as I used to be, my love."

"Don't talk like that! You're barely halfway through your fifty-first summer."

"That's old enough as far as the Naga are concerned. You know they . . ." He trailed off. He couldn't bring himself to complete the thought aloud. *You know they don't like the taste of human flesh when it gets too old.*

"But you're a perfume maker," she protested. "The best in the city! As long as you continue to make new and pleasing scents, Asthyrian will never allow you to . . . retire."

Brogan started to take another sip of broth, but he no longer had any taste for it, and he put the mug back down on the table.

"Of the four scents I managed to develop in the last month, Asthyrian rejected how many today?"

"Three," she answered, not looking him in the eye.

Brogan nodded. "What's to say that I'll be able to create any new ones for next month? Or if I do, that Asthyrian won't reject them all?"

Rheda didn't say anything for a time, and Brogan began to think that they were done talking. He was just about to get up from the table when Rheda finally spoke once more.

"I have served as your assistant since I could walk. Perhaps the time has come for you to finally take me on as a full apprentice."

Brogan's heart overflowed with love for his only surviving child. "Nothing would please me more than to have you one day take my place as master of our forefathers' craft. But it is a parent's duty to provide for his child's future, and as much as it pains me to say so, there is no future for you in perfume making."

"Are you saying that I am incapable of learning the craft?"

"Of course not."

Though the truth was, while Rheda was competent enough, she didn't have a strong talent for making perfume and scented oils. Her sense of smell wasn't as acute as it needed to be, and as hard as it was to create scents for humans, it was devilishly difficult to do so for the Naga and their servants. Some smells that humans found pleasing only nauseated serpentkind, and vice versa. Brogan was forever experimenting with strange combinations—rose hips and sheep's brains, lemon and maggots—and only rarely did he meet with any kind of success. Rheda was a good assistant, but she lacked the creative spark that would allow her to develop the unique scents that Asthyrian craved.

"What I should've said is that there is no future in the profession at all. I may be the city's best perfume maker, but what good has it done us? We still live in a rundown shack in the poorest section of the city. The *human* section. We sleep on straw-filled pallets instead of mattresses and are forced to eat half-rotted vegetables. I can't remember the last time we had any meat on this table. Do you?"

She didn't answer.

"Before the Naga came, a man of my talent and skill could've lived almost like a king. And his children would've enjoyed the same luxury."

"But the Naga did come," Rheda said gently. "And they aren't going to be leaving anytime soon. We might not live in what was called luxury when you were young, but we have our own house while others are forced to fit three and sometimes four families into a place this size. Perhaps we don't get to eat meat, but at least we eat regularly, and we do occasionally get vegetables—fresh or not—while others have to make do with gruel and stale bread. You have provided for me better than any other human father could have. Considering the circumstances, you should be proud of what you have accomplished."

Brogan understood what his daughter was saying, but she had been born into a world ruled by Naga. No matter what she said, she couldn't truly imagine any other way of living.

"I once hoped to accomplish much more," he said. "I might be a timid old man now, but there was a time when I considered using my skills to fight the Naga. Since the serpent-gods are so sensitive to smells, I thought if I could develop a scent that repelled them, or perhaps even one that was poisonous to them . . ."

"Why didn't you?" Rheda asked.

"Odds are that I would've been found out and executed before I succeeded. Besides, your mother became pregnant with our first child—your brother. If Asythrian caught me plotting against him and his fellow Naga, I wouldn't be the only one killed; my entire family would've paid the price for my crime." He shook his head and smiled ruefully. "No, it was a foolish, dangerous dream, one that I was well rid of. That we *all* were. But back to the topic at hand. There is no future in perfume making. Not a good future, nor a secure one."

"Is that why you've taken me to the palace these last three times? In the hope that Asthyrian will select me to be one of his servants? What would you have me become? A Pakwa?"

Pakwa were a step below Chu'a. While they possessed some serpentish traits—slitted eyes, fangs, snake-fast reflexes—they were the most human of the Naga's servants. While it was the Chu'a's task to tend to Asthyrian's needs, it was the Pakwa's to oversee the humans. And, when necessary, go to war if a conflict developed between their master and other Naga.

Rheda's voice grew softer. "Would you have me do as my brother did?"

Brogan avoided her question. "I remember the first time I ever saw Pakwa. I was six summers old when Asthyrian's forces came to claim our city for their master. The Pakwa wore silver-plated armor and helmets wrought to resemble serpent heads. They marched through the city streets, thousands of them . . . I'll never forget the sound of so many boots striking the ground in unison, nor the clouds of dust they raised as they went.

"Most of all, I'll never forget all those serpents' eyes staring coldly out from their human-looking faces. There was no pity in those eyes, no mercy. No pride or joy in their victory—no hint of emotion at all. That scared me more than anything else that day, I think."

"Yet you allowed your only son to become Pakwa." Rheda said this matter-of-factly, as if she were merely mentioning a change in the weather, but Brogan knew that it was still an accusation.

"Cinric had no love of perfume making." Nor did he have any talent for it, but Brogan saw no need to mention that now. "And he wanted a better life than what he had known as a boy. He thought he could find that life as a Pakwa."

"And what did he find instead?" Rheda said, her voice rising in volume. "One day Asthyrian decided to go to war with another Naga for reasons we will never know and probably couldn't understand even if we did. Cinric marched off like a good little snake-soldier to do his god's bidding, but he never came marching back."

Brogan was silent for a few moments before responding. "There are worse fates than that which your brother chose."

Rheda's face grew red with anger. "I love you, but you are a stubborn, blind fool. I would rather live here with you in these conditions than trade my humanity to serve the Naga! Or have you forgotten what happened to Mother?"

She stood up, grabbed both their mugs, and stormed off to the tiny alcove in the rear of their shack that served in place of a kitchen.

"No," Brogan whispered. "I haven't forgotten."

Come dusk, Rheda was still mad at him, so she took to her pallet early. For once, Brogan was grateful for her anger. He had work to do and it was work he needed to do alone.

The plot of land he had been assigned was not quite an acre, but it was more than most humans were allowed, especially considering that his family now consisted only of two people. Surrounding the land were clusters of ill-made shacks set so close together that there was no telling where one ended and another began. But Brogan and Rheda not only had room for their living quarters, but also for a workshed and even a small garden where Brogan could grow the plants and herbs necessary for his work. But no fruits of vegetables—growing food without a permit was a punishable offense. And twice a year Brogan enjoyed the rare privilege of being allowed to venture beyond the city walls—in the presence of Pakwa guards, of course—to search the surrounding lands for plants that grew best in the wild.

Perhaps Rheda was right. Perhaps he should appreciate what he had.

But as he stepped out of their home, guttering candle in hand, and began to walk down the narrow stone path to his workshed, the stench of the human quarter hit him as it always did. It was the stink of too many bodies crammed into too small a living space. It was the stink of urine and feces, blood and vomit.

It was also the stink of desperation and hope-lessness, of a people that had lived like penned-up animals for so long that they barely remembered they were human.

As he often did, Brogan held his breath and hurried to his shed, only daring to inhale once again when he was inside and had shut the door. The mingled scents of dried herbs and plants helped to leaven the smell of the human quarter, though they could never mask it completely.

Brogan put the candle into a clay holder in the middle of his worktable. Burning a candle at night was almost sinfully wasteful when there would be plenty of daylight to work by tomorrow. Candles were hard to come by, even for a master perfume maker. But night was the only time he could work alone, and for his plan to have any chance of succeeding, he had to do this without Rheda's knowledge.

From among the dozens of jars and vials that cluttered his worktable, he chose a very special container, one that he had never opened in his daughter's presence. He pried out the stopper and gently, almost reverently, shook out the contents. Three small patches of dried snakeskin fell upon the table, the scales whitish and so thin as to be almost translucent.

Brogan sat staring at the dry skin for some time, careful to breathe shallowly lest he risk blowing the scales off the table and perhaps contaminating them. He tried to detect an odor, but he smelled nothing. That didn't necessarily mean anything. Naga's sense of smell was far stronger than humans, and the scales might well exude a scent that only serpentkind could pick up.

Brogan had rewarded the Pakwa street guard who had brought the scales to him most handsomely with a quart of scented oil that was a particular favorite of

Asthyrian's and that had an intoxicating effect on Naga and their servants. If the Chu'a ever learned of this transaction, Brogan had no doubt that he'd be immediately executed. But the risk was more than worth it.

Of course, there was also the chance that the Pakwa had tricked him, and this was only ordinary snakeskin shed during molting. The city was crawling with snakes of all kinds, had been ever since Asthyrian's arrival. Brogan supposed he'd find out when it came time to deliver the serpent-god's order later in the month.

He picked up a small knife and with deft, practiced motions began cutting the patches of snakeskin into ever-smaller pieces. And as he worked, his mind drifted.

A pounding at the door, loud and insistent.

Brogan glanced at his wife, who was sitting on the dirt floor next to their little girl. Rheda had been playing with a doll Brogan had made for her from dried reeds. But now the doll fell from her hands, forgotten.

"Papa? Who is it?" Her voice was hushed and afraid, but there was also a note of hope in it. "Is it Cinric? Has he come back from his visit to the temple?" Rheda jumped to her feet and started toward the door, but Ellina grabbed the girl's arm before she could get far.

"It's getting late, child. Time you were abed."

The pounding came again, so loud this time that Brogan could feel the ground shudder beneath the soles of his bare feet. He tried to speak, found he couldn't, swallowed, and tried again.

"Take the girl to her pallet and cover her ears with your hands." His voice was strained by fear, but at

least he was managing to get the words out. "Do your best not to listen."

"Why do I have to have my ears covered?" Rheda asked, but her parents ignored her.

Ellina gave her husband a look that was filled with love and sadness. "No, Brogan. I think you'd best help her get to sleep tonight. And you should sleep as well, for you have much work to do tomorrow if you are to fulfill Asthyrian's order this month."

The pounding started up again, and this time it didn't stop. It continued regular as a drumbeat: thud-thud-thud-thud-thud-thud-thud!

Brogan tried to shut out the sound as he walked over to his wife. She had been chosen for him by a Chu'a breedmatcher, but that didn't matter. Over the years, they had come to love each other as much as if they'd married by choice. In some ways, perhaps even more.

"We agreed on this," he said. "I will be the one to open the door."

Ellina held onto Rheda with one hand, and with the other gently stroked her husband's cheek.

"I only agreed to prevent further argument between us—and to spare you the pain of worrying about me. I always intended to be the one."

"But you can't! Rheda will need you! She can't . . ." He lowered his voice in the hope that his daughter wouldn't be able to hear his words over the pounding. "She can't do without a mother."

"What she can't do without is a parent who provides for her future. Once you were gone, how long do think it would be before she and I ended up in one of the Chu'a's flesh-pits?"

Brogan didn't answer. He didn't have to.

Ellina lifted Rheda and placed her in Brogan's arms.

She kissed the squirming girl on the cheek, then kissed her husband on the lips.

"I love you both," she said, tears welling in her eyes. "Never forget that."

Brogan's own tears blurred his vision, distorting the last view he would ever have of his wife's face.

"I won't. And I'll make sure our daughter doesn't forget either."

"Forget what?" Rheda whined. "Put me down, Papa! I want to see who's at the door!"

"No," Brogan said softly. "You don't."

And then without another word to his wife, he started toward the back room where their sleeping pallets were kept, while Ellina went to answer the door.

Brogan wiped away his tears with an old rag. He knew better than to use his hands. He didn't want to risk getting the smell of his tears on the precious scales, and thereby perhaps ruin them.

When the skin had been reduced to a collection of tiny dry pieces, Brogan considered them for a time. The hardest part of perfume making for him— especially when it came to creating a new scent—had always been getting started. First, he had to choose a method: distillation, enfleurage, or maceration. If he had a large enough supply of ingredients, he could experiment with all three, but he only had a small amount of scales to work with, and therefore could only use one method. This meant he would have one chance and one chance only.

After a time, he reached for his mortar and pestle. He'd decided on maceration so that he might preserve as much of the scales' original scent as possible. He scooped the pieces into the stone bowl and began grinding them. And this time as he worked, he would be careful not to allow his mind to wander.

*　　*　　*

Almost a month later, early in the morning of a day that would end with the advent of a new moon, Brogan crept over to his daughter's pallet and, while she slept, applied several drops of his greatest creation on as much of her exposed skin as he could.

When he was finished, he gazed down upon Rheda and smiled sadly. He remembered Ellina's words from so many years ago.

What she needs is a parent who can provide a future for her.

Brogan hoped he'd done just that, but only the next several hours would tell.

He sat alone in the dark, sawing at a piece of hard cheese with a paring knife, when there was a knock at the door. It was a gentle knock, so soft that he might not have heard it if he hadn't been listening for it.

He put down the knife, stood, and went to the door. He hesitated only a moment before opening it.

Standing framed in the doorway against the night was the silhouette of a young woman.

Brogan managed to force a weak smile. "It's about time you returned home. You've been gone nearly three days." He tried to inject a lighthearted tone into his voice, but it came out strained.

"Why did you do it?"

The question was less accusatory than he'd imagined it would be. Rheda's voice was breathy, almost a whisper. *Like a serpent's hiss,* he thought, and immediately wished he hadn't.

"Come in, my daughter. This is still your home, after all."

"Is it?" But she did as Brogan wished, moving across the threshold with silent, liquid grace. Despite the darkness, she crossed straight to the table and sat down. Of course, she didn't need to see—she'd lived here all her life, and it wasn't as if they had an abundance of furniture to get in her way. But Brogan couldn't help feeling that she'd been guided by something other than memory, senses that there were no human words for.

Brogan closed the door and took his time shuffling to the table. He lifted the flint and striker, but his hands were trembling so much that it took him several tries to light the candle.

The flame's meager glow made Rheda's golden skin seem to pulse with its own internal light. Her eyes—which were still mostly human—glistened, and Brogan knew they were now covered by transparent scales. Her skull was hairless, smooth and golden as the rest of her. She no longer wore a fala, but instead was garbed in a robe of crimson silk that would have cost a ķing's ransom back in the days when there had been kings.

Brogan sat across the table from his daughter, and they looked at each other for a time without speaking. He didn't bother to offer any cheese to Rheda. He knew she no longer ate such things.

"You still haven't answered my question, Father. Why?"

Brogan found it difficult to look into those new eyes of hers, so he focused on the candle flame instead.

"So you would have something better to look forward to than a life in the Chu'a's flesh-pits after I was gone."

"I am now Nawat—an egg layer. A concubine to Asthyrian. How is that any different?"

"You are not a piece of meat for the Chu'a to use as they please. You are the bride of a god, and you will be treated as such for as long as you live."

"And all I had to sacrifice for this wonderful new life was my humanity."

Brogan shrugged. "A small enough price to pay for survival, I think."

"Do you? But then, you are still human."

Brogan had no response to this.

"How did you manage it?" Rheda asked.

"I procured a few bits of cast-off Nawat skin and used them to make a scent that I hoped would prove attractive to Asthyrian. I applied it to you while you were sleeping, and then we went to the palace . . ."

"And Asthyrian decided to take me as his newest bride," she finished.

"I'm not sure there was any decision involved. Smells have a powerful impact on Naga." Brogan's voice grew softer. "There are some things that we cannot resist . . . even when we know we should."

It had been torture to stand by and watch as the Pakwa guards came for Rheda. He could still hear her pleas ringing in his ears.

Don't let them take me! Please, Papa!

It was this last word, one that she hadn't used since she'd been a child, that had nearly broken him. But he had done nothing as the Pakwa removed his daughter from Asthyrian's throne room.

"Do you know what they did with me, Father? The Pakwa took me to the Chu'a's temple and there they began to . . . reshape me. The process was more painful on levels both physical and spiritual than I could ever possibly communicate to you. But it is over now, and here I am."

"So you are."

"You know what I have come for."

"Yes."

"That night when I was a young girl . . . the pounding on the door. It was Cinric, wasn't it?"

Brogan felt tears threatening, and he fought to hold them back. "Your brother had gone to the Chu'a's temple several days earlier to become Pakwa. What he didn't know was that after the transformation was finished, there was a task he had to perform in order to cast off his last shreds of humanity. If he failed to do it, the Chu'a would have him killed."

"He had to slay a loved one."

Rheda's voice was without emotion, and it sent a shiver down Brogan's spine.

"Yes."

"And you and Mother were aware of this?"

"I had planned on being the one, but your mother insisted . . ." Brogan couldn't keep the tears at bay any longer, and they streamed down his face. "When it was over, Cinric . . . cleaned up, and that was the last I ever saw of him. The Chu'a sent a message a few years later that he'd been killed in battle, fighting for 'the glory of our god.' I made up a story about your mother going to work at the palace. It didn't really matter if you believed it or not, just as long as it kept you from discovering the truth. Please forgive us . . . forgive *me*."

"You know that I have come for the same reason as Cinric. I must pass the same test if I am to become fully Nawat. And if I fail, Asthyrian himself will kill me."

"I know." Brogan wiped away his tears and did his best to get control of himself once more. "I've been waiting for you."

"And you are not afraid?"

"Of course I am. But I'm more afraid of failing to give you the kind of life you deserve. So, please . . . just do it quickly, and know that what I have done to you was done out of a father's love."

Rheda looked at him without expression for a long

moment before finally standing and walking over to him. Brogan closed his eyes and trembled as he waited for what was to come next. He felt Rheda's hands gently grip his shoulders, then her soft lips press against the flesh of his forehead.

Brogan opened his eyes and saw his daughter smiling sadly at him.

"While I do not completely understand, I have no doubt of your love for me. Or mine for you."

She started toward the door, her feet making no sound upon the dirt floor.

Brogan jumped up from the table. "Where are you going?"

She stopped but did not turn back around to face him. "Away. I will not slay you, Father. Not even to save my own life."

"But you must! It's the only way!"

He grabbed Rheda's shoulder and tried to spin her around, but he could not budge her. It was as if she were made of stone.

"Release me. Now."

The command was made in a cold-blooded voice that sounded nothing like Rheda. In fact, it didn't sound human at all.

Brogan withdrew his hand.

"Farewell, Father." She continued to the door and began to open it.

Brogan returned to the table and picked up the paring knife. "Do you remember what I said, Rheda? About how there are some things we cannot resist?" Before she could reply, he quickly drew the blade across the palm of his hand. Flesh peeled open and blood blossomed forth.

He held his hand out, letting his blood patter to the floor and its scent suffuse the air.

Rheda's shoulders stiffened, but she didn't immediately turn around, and Brogan feared that he had failed. But then his daughter slowly closed the door and let go of the handle.

As she turned to face him, fangs bared, eyes wild and hungry, Brogan's fear left him and he smiled.

His work—a father's work—was done.

FEW OF US

Jean Rabe

Jean Rabe is the author of more than a dozen fantasy novels, and three dozen fantasy, science fiction, and military short stories. Her latest novels include *The Finest Creation* and *Lake of Death*. She is an avid, but lousy, gardener; a goldfish fancier who loves to sit by her pond in the summer; and a movie-goer . . . if the movie in question "blows up real good!" Visit her website at www.sff.net/people/jeanr.

THE GUILLEMOT was perched on a narrow ledge on the highest eastern cliff. It was mostly an inky black, but it had white bands on its wings and a fog-white underbelly. On this summer afternoon its back was to the sea, protecting the single egg that rested between its red feet.

For more than an hour Grundal watched this bird and others from the safety of the cave. He could see dozens of guillemots on the lower ledges, a dozen flying overhead, some calling out with their shrill, hissing whistles, one of them an unusual mix of gray and brown. When he was a child, there were thousands of guillemots on this part of the island. They carpeted the cliff so densely that not a speck of rock could be seen. But through the decades the guillemots—like his kinsmen—had dwindled.

Now there were so few of his people left.

More than a hundred different species of birds came to the Faroe Island of Sudrey—a fair number to be certain, but half of what there had been in his long-ago youth. Only thirty or so species were natives, the rest were welcomed seasonal visitors. In the late spring through the early winter, there were large colonies of puffins, which were Grundal's favorite. They would fly above the crest of the waves and come to ground on the grasslands beyond the cliffs. There were a variety of gulls, and there were curlews, golden plovers, and gannets.

Grundal especially liked to watch the gannets, large white birds with pale yellow heads, with wingspans that stretched as wide as a human is tall. They made their nests out of seaweed, in breeding season so close to one another they could touch bills. And they would fly low past the shore in search of fish swimming near the surface. Grundal closed his eyes and listened to the cry of a lone gannet cutting above the chatter of the plovers.

The sun was setting, and so Grundal knew it would not be long now until the storm petrels took flight. In the light of the moon the petrels would look like a haze of insects rather than a flock of tiny birds. Smoky black with ivory tail bands and ungainly-looking webbed feet, they were his eldest son's favorite. Grundal and his son used to slip away from the castle at night, leaving the affairs of Sudrey behind and coming quietly to the cliff to watch the petrels swarm and drop to the sea, where they would feast on the small floating, crustaceans.

"Never again," he said sadly.

Grundal's eldest son—all his sons, his daughter, his

grandchildren—died when the barbarian invaders
came nearly two months past. His wife, Reidun, and
the surviving wives and children of Grundal's most
loyal followers escaped on the only boat the invaders
hadn't managed to sink. The women were to go to
Straumsey, the largest of the Faroe Islands. Grundal
thought they would be safe there, and that in time
Reidun would either send a boat back for him and
the rest or send a ship filled with warriors to help
repel the barbarians. More of their people lived on
Straumsey; the castle was bigger, the walls thicker and
taller and more defensible, the king perhaps wiser. But
perhaps not wise enough.

Grundal had overheard a pair of barbarian scouts
just yesterday. And though he couldn't understand
more than a few words of their language, he got the
impression from their gestures that all of the Faroes
had been conquered, and that the greatest number of
the barbarians had landed on Straumsey. Grundal slew
the scouts quickly and angrily tossed the bodies into
the sea.

Had Reidun's ship even reached Straumsey? Was
she alive? Had she, like Grundal and a handful of his
people, managed to survive the barbarian onslaught
and slip away to hide in the caves? Grundal prayed
to all the gods that she still breathed. And he prayed
that he and his small band had the strength and cunning to exact some measure of revenge and by some
miracle take his castle back. He would have ordered
his men to strike out for the castle many days
earlier . . . but of the dozen who lived and followed
him, four had been seriously injured and needed time
to heal. Too, he had hoped for a ship of warriors from
Straumsey . . . or a ship from Vagar, Austrey, Sandoy,
Nóólsoy, or even little Mykines . . . some added numbers to help with his planned attack.

But two months had passed since the invaders first crawled up the cliffs in the predawn light and took his men by surprise and then took his castle. He would have fought them to the very end while the women and children escaped, but there were too many invaders. His advisers Norbert and Kol finally talked him into running while there was still a chance. So they barricaded themselves in the dining hall and slipped out through the castle's lone secret passage—one his great-great-grandfather had the forethought to build a very long time ago.

One dozen of Grundal's people were all that were left on Sudrey Island. He'd scoured the caves often enough during the past two months to know that no one else had made it out. He'd watched the barbarians burn the bodies of his children and grandchildren and the others, tossing the bones in what passed for a mass grave. He stoked his hatred for them.

Two months. Help from the other islands would have come by now—if there were any warriors left to help. Perhaps he and his band were all that remained.

Grundal considered their downfall his own fault. He'd been lax, mellowed by the notion of two centuries of peace. There'd been no trouble since his grandfather's reign—two hundred years ago. Then men from the highlands swept across the sea from the southeast and warred for the sake of warring and for the sake of trying to take the eighteen Faroe Islands—lands they didn't need. Grundal's ancestors had driven those invaders away, though it had taken their best efforts and their best men. Sudrey's population never wholly recovered from that, the people becoming fewer just like the guillemots were becoming fewer.

But there'd been no more wars since his grandfather's time, and so there seemed to be no reason to post sentries or to expect further bloodshed. Grundal's father certainly hadn't expected trouble. And Grundal had not expected any either. Grundal damned himself for being too passive, too unsuspecting, and too thoroughly unprepared for the barbarian raid.

There'd been so much blood and death and friends' bodies shattered and burned by the barbarians that it hadn't seemed real to Grundal. *But it was all too real,* he whispered. And there were too few barbarians killed in exchange during the struggle. Grundal tried to chase the sight of his slaughtered kinsmen from his mind and focus entirely on the nesting guillemot.

His efforts were not successful.

"King Grundal, the light is fading." The blessed interruption came from Bodil, a warrior-maid who refused to flee to Straumsey with the other women. Her husky voice echoed softly against the cave walls. "We should head to Vigrid Keep now." She thumped the haft of her ax for effect. "It is our turn to draw blood and sever heads. I'll use my hands if I have to."

Grundal shook his head. "Not yet." The sun hadn't fully set. "Not until the storm petrels come out."

His stomach rumbled. He was hungry, had been eating little to make sure his men were being fed enough. It wasn't the fare they were used to in the castle. It was small seals they caught on the shore at night, fish they stole from the gannets, eggs they robbed from nests. Their vast gardens and their herds of sheep were in the hands of the enemy, the castle larder probably empty now. It was for food as much as anything that he and his men were going after the castle and its grounds. They couldn't continue to live indefinitely in these caves and on meager provisions. They had to take the herds and gardens back. They could die proudly in battle, or they could starve and freeze to death here when winter came. He didn't want to wait the latter event out.

"We'll go through the secret passage," he said when he saw the first petrel rise into the twilight sky. "Follow me. Be quiet and strong."

"Quiet and strong," Bodil repeated.

"We fight for Grundal," said another.

"For Grundal the Good."

"Aye, for King Grundal."

Grundal shook his head. "Fight for yourselves," he admonished. "My kingdom is in the hands of the barbarians. I'm a king no more."

He picked his way from the cave and along the high ledge, careful to climb away from the nesting guillemots. He didn't want to disturb them, and neither did he want flocks of squawking birds rising from the cliff and alerting any barbarian sentries.

He breathed deep, taking the sea air into his lungs, listening to the murmur of the ocean against the foot of the cliffs, the water rubbing against the rocks and sand. The darkness folded around them as they headed toward the high point where the castle sat on the western side of the narrow island. Though they had only five miles to travel, it took them the better part of the night to do so—to climb down one valley wall and up the next, crossing the green slope of pastureland that come morning would sparkle like gems from all the dew.

Grundal's castle was perched on the mountain just beyond, the stone blocks the color of the craggy protrusions they had started to climb. Bodil took the lead here, her long, thick fingers finding handholds and hauling herself up higher until she reached a slash of black in the rocks, another cave. She disappeared inside.

Grundal hung on the rocks as his fellows passed him and entered the cave. The wind had picked up considerably while they'd been traveling. The air whistled around his head, and he listened to the muted sound of the sea crashing into the western shore on the other side of this mountain. Though soft, it wasn't the gentle shushing he'd heard on the eastern side. It was crude and rumbling, sounding like the barbarians' voices. Beyond his castle was a sheer drop to the ocean, and he imagined swells hitting the rocky shoulders of the western cliffs. He happily imagined throwing the barbarians off those cliffs. He climbed into the cave.

It was blackest black inside, and not even his keen eyes could pick out the forms of his men. But he could smell their musty odors and feel their closeness. He stretched out his fingers and brushed Kol's muscular back. Then he stepped past his men and felt his way deep into the darkness.

Grundal accidentally discovered the secret passage when he was a child playing in the dining hall. He'd ducked into the massive fireplace to hide, so he wouldn't have to help clear the table. He bumped against a crooked stone as he went, and found that the side-wall swung back to reveal stairs that wound down into the bowels of the mountain. Later, he told his grandfather the king about his explorations.

"Grundal, when my own grandfather had this castle built, he had that passage made. He feared that invaders could come from the south and east or from more distant lands. He worried they would try to take this very castle and claim the island. And he wanted an escape route. He was right, in that the highlanders came during my father's watch. But we fought them off."

"Grandfather, why would anyone want to take this island from us? It's always been ours."

The old king shook his head. "Because the highlanders and others to the south and the east do not like trolls, young Grundal. In ages past humans fought

*against us because they thought us threatening and ugly
and considered us monsters. They wanted to wipe us
off this earth and make us only memories. And they
were successful throughout the world—save these Faroe
Islands. We're the only trolls left."*

*Grundal sadly shook his head. "We're not ugly,
grandfather."*

*"No," the old king agreed. "We're not ugly, and
we're not monsters, and no one will take this island
from us."*

But that conversation was long ago. And the island
had been taken.

"Taken two months past," Grundal said, rousing
himself from his musings. Grundal stretched a long
arm forward and felt where the cave wall turned
abruptly. His claws clicked against the stone and he
shuffled forward until he found the stairs. They were
smooth from the years and moisture in the cave, not
from use.

"Be quiet and strong," Grundal said. Then he
started to climb. His legs ached from the exertion and
his lungs burned. He was nearly ninety, not quite ancient for a troll, but certainly feeling the years.

The barbarians hadn't found this passage, or at least
hadn't been down the stairs. He could tell because the
air was still and heavy with stone dust, carrying not a
hint of the stench of humans. The stairway narrowed
toward the top, and Grundal scraped his broad shoulders on the stone. He felt blood run down his arm
where a shard had cut him. He didn't register the pain.

There was no worry that a fire was burning—trolls
feared fire and used it only for cooking . . . and then
very carefully. It was summer and too warm for the
barbarians to have a fire going. Too, it was well past
the humans' dinnertime, so nothing would be cooking
in the kettle. Still . . . he sniffed again and again to

be certain. No fire, but he picked up the unpleasant odor of men. He reached the landing and felt the stone of the fireplace wall in front of him. His claws ran over the bricks until he found the crooked one.

"Do you think any of them are in the dining room?" Bodil was right behind him.

He shook his head, even though he knew she couldn't see him. Then he tugged on the stone and the wall swung open. He stepped into the fireplace and crouched as he looked out into the room beyond. Here the stench of the humans was much stronger.

A single lantern was lit on the longest table, its wick turned down low. It wouldn't have been enough light for a human to see by properly. But it served well for Grundal, and he glanced into the far reaches of the immense room. He clenched his fists so tightly that his claws cut into his palms, and he stepped past the hearth, straightened, and motioned for Bodil.

The condition of the hall was repulsive. Plates with scraps of mutton cluttered one table. Here a bench was overturned. There, a high-backed chair was split. Norbert started toward the scraps, a string of drool spilling over his bottom lip and stretching to the floor. Grundal gestured to get his attention.

Eat later, Grundal mouthed.

Humans have no regard for things, he thought as he padded between the tables and toward the far door, the one that led to the kitchen. He looked over his shoulder to make sure that Norbert and the others were following. They were—but they were all hungrily eyeing the scraps. There was another way from this room, an open archway that led into an entry hall and a wide, winding front staircase. Grundal would normally take those stairs up, to the second floor where he suspected the barbarians were sleeping. But he decided on the back staircase instead.

· The kitchen was a mess. More dirty dishes and over-turned chairs. Two cooked sheep carcasses sat on a long counter, the legs removed and no doubt eaten. Grundal shook his head, realizing he shouldn't have led his fellows through here. As loyal as they were, as fixed on purpose as they were, they were trolls.

Norbert was the first to reach the carcasses. But Bodil was the first to eat. Grundal didn't bother to scold them or order them up the stairs. His voice would have to be raised above their chomping and swallowing, and he wanted to be as quiet as possible. He waited for a few moments, until the sheep bones gleamed in the starlight that spilled through a window. Then he motioned them up, his own stomach growling and scolding him for not taking part.

The stairway was narrow, but not so confining as the one that led from the fireplace and into the mountain. The steps here were worn from centuries of use, and he pictured himself and his brother sneaking down from their bedrooms to find a tasty tidbit late, late at night. His brother was on Mykines. Did he still live? Or was Grundal and his band all that remained?

Kol belched loudly just as they reached the landing, the baritone sound bouncing back from the wall.

"Sorry," he offered. "Didn't mean to. . . ."

Grundal waggled a claw to silence him and opened the door—to be met by an approaching human who was both startled and angry to see the troll.

The man was dressed like most of the other barbarians Grundal had seen. He was wearing leather boots tied around his ankles with twine, brown breeches and a tabard the color of the sea. Over that was a shirt made of small metal links that glimmered in the light of an oil lamp on the wall. And around the shirt was a thick belt from which dangled a sword. The man's head was topped with a helmet that looked to Grundal like a hammered silver soup cup. Long blond, braided hair hung from beneath the edges. A shield was strapped to the man's back, and he was reaching for it and his sword as he took a step away and sneered.

Grundal couldn't understand the words the man was loudly shouting, though he was certain they were some sort of alarm. The troll king took a step up to meet him, raised a clawed hand and swiped at his chest, severing some of the metal links. The man was bringing his sword up just as Grundal raked at him again and again, trying to shut out the man's angry, unintelligible words.

"His neck!" Bodil suggested. "There is no metal there."

Indeed, Grundal saw that this part of the man was not protected. The troll king's arms shot forward and his hands closed around the man's neck. He ignored the sword blow to his side and squeezed until the man's head came loose in his hands.

A cheer went up from Norbert, just as doors opened in the hallway and men came out, swords and axes ready. It struck Grundal that the humans were too small for this place, being at best less than half as high as the hallway, their fingers not made for the large door handles, so much space around their bodies. Grundal and his people filled the hall, as was proper, and their heads came within a hair's breadth of the ceiling. The space was not wasted on the large bodies of the trolls.

The men running into the hall obviously had been sleeping, as they were in various states of dress—none with the metal shirts and helmets the first man had worn. Their faces were smooth and ghastly looking, practically the color of eggshells, rather than the rich greens and mottled browns of Grundal's people. Some had beards. There were no attractive warts and moles and scars, and Grundal found himself pitying them for their hideousness. Maybe because they were so repulsive looking, they were naturally barbarous and warlike, he mused, as he pulled the head off another and slashed into the belly of one wielding a tiny ax.

The trolls had the advantage in this hallway. When the barbarians had invaded, the trolls had been in the open—in the fields and in the great rooms, where they could be swarmed and slain by the small humans. But here in this hall only so many of the little men could reach them. The trolls were slaughtering the ones who came at them, forcing the humans to climb up on the bodies of their fallen brothers to continue the fight.

Oh, if he had realized this when the barbarians came, Grundal would have ordered all his men into the hallways and let the humans come to them. What a fool he'd been! What a peaceful fool! If he'd only gave some thought to strategy that early morning, his people would have fared better. Perhaps they would have fought in all the hallways and been able to win. Perhaps his sons and daughter and his grandchildren would be alive.

His claws were slippery with the humans' cherry-red blood. It was warm and sticky on his fingers and made it difficult to grasp the necks and arms of the ones in front of him. Grundal redoubled his efforts, slashing at the face of one, while driving the claws of his other hand into the belly of another.

"They taste good!" Kol shouted. "Tender! We can eat them when we're through."

"If we survive this!" Bodil said.

Grundal glanced over his shoulder. Bodil was at the juncture where the staircase wound up to the next floor. She was swinging her ax at one of the more muscular humans he'd seen. The barbarian was fending off her blows with a large shield and jabbing at her with a spear. He was wearing a helmet, but this one had horns that curved upward from the front. And he had a commanding voice.

"Monsters!" the human shouted. Grundal registered the word, and had heard it spoken by the other barbarians on the day of the invasion. But Grundal didn't know what it meant. "Kill the monsters and keep this land for men! Send them to the pits of hell!" The words were a guttural buzz to the troll king.

"For King Grundal!" Bodil shouted as she pressed forward, driving the horned-man back up the stairs.

"For King Grundal!" cried Norbert and Kol in unison. The three words became a chant that was picked up by the rest of the trolls.

"Monsters!" a human returned. "Hear how the ugly creatures growl! Witless, incapable of speech. Mindless monsters!"

Kol howled long and loud when a spear found its way through the press of bodies and jabbed deep into his thigh. Black blood gushed from the wound and mingled with the red on the floor, all of it making the stone more slippery. Men and trolls had to concentrate to keep from falling. Norbert managed to edge in front of Kol, pulling the spear loose from his friend as he went. Norbert turned the spear on the human who'd wielded it, sinking the weapon through his stomach and into the stomach of the barbarian behind him. Kol shouted his approval.

Bodil had fought halfway up the stairs and could go no farther. The barbarian bodies were piled so deep in front of her that there wasn't room for her to squeeze beyond.

"Victory is ours!" she hooted, her throaty troll voice bouncing off the stairwell so loudly she felt the steps tremble beneath her callused feet. "Victory for King Grundal!"

"Kol?" Norbert paused in his slaughter when he heard a thud behind him. Kol was on his knees, clawed hands pressed over the wound in his leg. "Kol!" The blood continued to flow, fast like water splashing along in a stream. The spear must have struck an artery, for Kol could do nothing to stop the blood. His once bright-green face had taken on a drab olive hue. "Kol!"

Norbert took a step back toward his friend. In the instant of his distraction, one of the barbarians had clambered up on the pile of bodies and swung hard at the top of Norbert's head. The sword cut into the troll's skull and stuck there. Norbert hollered in pain and swung out blindly, ripping the face off the offender and sending him to the top of the pile.

"Barbarians!" Norbert screamed, as he tried futilely to pull the sword from his head. "Lunt! Ulf! Help me! Thurlow! Help!"

But the other trolls couldn't help him. They were following Grundal farther down the hall, tripping over barbarian corpses as they went. The troll king was heading toward doors that were still opening and still spilling barbarians out—these wearing the metal shirts and helmets, these more prepared.

Norbert fell to join his friend as Bodil found her way back down the stairs. She made quick work of the few barbarians that were near the stairwell. All were dead now at this end of the hall. She hurried to join the press at the other end.

"Ten of us left!" she shouted as she caught up. "Norbert and Kol are dead."

"Monsters!" one of the barbarians cried. "Slay the monsters. This is the time of men!"

Grundal was covered in blood by the time he neared the far end of the hall and could see the wide, winding staircase that led both down and up. He'd ripped so many heads and limbs off the humans that he'd lost count. Still there were more in this castle. He knew from the numbers he saw on the day of the invasion, and he could hear their footfalls from overhead and from coming up the winding stairwell from the entry below. Too many. And the ones from below were bringing torches—he could smell the fat-soaked burning wood.

"Fire," Grundal breathed. "In the name of my father, they mean to burn us here."

"Ten of us remain!" Bodil repeated, oblivious to the coming torches.

Grundal threw back his head and cried, a wild keening sound that stopped everything for a heartbeat. Then he gestured behind him with a bloody claw. "Back!" he called to Bodil. "Back down to the kitchen. We flee again!"

There were simply too many hateful, hurtful humans. The trolls had managed to kill dozens in this hall. So many human bodies lay scattered that the trolls had to kick them aside and climb over them to get to the back staircase that would lead to the kitchen. They paused only to reverently touch the still forms of Norbert and Kol.

"Take the fight downstairs!" Grundal ordered. He realized that while the hallway had worked to his advantage at the beginning, the sheer number of fallen bodies could block them in. All the barbarians had to do was set their fallen comrades on fire. The flames would spread to the trolls and swiftly consume them. The surviving barbarians would be able to pick away at them with spears, like they were caged animals waiting to be slaughtered or burned. It was time to find more space. "Hurry Bodil. Hurry Tyrkir! Hurry!"

Bodil led the way only to discover that barbarians had somehow swarmed into the kitchen—perhaps coming from the outbuildings or from the lower level, perhaps coming down one of the other stairways in the huge castle and working their way around.

"They have torches!" she hollered.

"Monsters!" the barbarians growled. "Burn the monsters!"

There was a back door off the kitchen, and Bodil took it, not bothering to open it, but slamming her scaly shoulder against the wood and breaking through. She flailed out with her ax as she rushed outside, trolls and barbarians following her. Without waiting for Grundal's orders, she headed to the western cliff and hurtled off it.

"Follow Bodil!" Grundal called. He clawed at the humans crowding him as his fellow trolls lumbered past. "Run!"

"For King Grundal we'll live another day!" Tyrkyr growled.

In the open under the starlight, the differences between the trolls and the barbarians were starker. The trolls were easily twice the height of men, their shoulders broad, their long arms thick and wrapped with ropelike veins. Their clawed feet and hands made the soft extremities of the barbarians seem infantile. And their red-rimmed eyes and elegantly twisted and bulbous noses, their warts and boils and scars put the features of the humans to shame.

Hideous rats, Grundal decided. The barbarians were little more than that to the troll king. But they had numbers! And they had fire. He watched as more spilled from the castle, these, too, with torches, all of them shouting things he couldn't understand.

"Drive the monsters to the cliffs!"

"Monsters!"

"Burn them!"

Grundal ran then, when he saw the last of his fellows dive from the cliff. His clawed feet churned up the rich loam, and his clawed hands batted away the barbarians who were stepping close and trying to stick him with their spears and swords.

Then he was free of them and free of the earth, falling through the salt-tinged air, the wind whipping around him and chasing the sweat from his great green body. He plunged into the water and sank. The barbarians threw their spears, none of the weapons reaching deep enough to hurt Grundal and his fellows.

"Hope that's the last of them." This came from the barbarian wearing the horned helm. "Hope we've cleansed this island of those wretched things. All the other islands are free of them."

"It's the last of their kind to be certain," someone answered.

The horned-helmed barbarian continued: "Don't know who originally built this castle, my friend Eric. Or who built the ones on the other islands. But I suspect their spirits are resting easier tonight now that we've driven those creatures from this place of men."

"Could those monsters have built them?" Eric posed.

A shake of the horned helm. "Not possible, my friend. Monsters can't build castles or anything else."

"For Norway!" one of the men shouted. It was a cry picked up by the rest. "For Norway and our king!"

"I thought I heard one of the monsters call the biggest one a king, too," Eric mused. "King Grendel, I think I heard."

The horned one sheathed his sword and headed back to the castle. "If the monster considered himself a king, he was the last. There'll be no more King Grendels."

*   *   *

Grundal watched a pair of guillemots that were perched on a ledge halfway down the eastern cliff. He wondered if they were mates, and he wondered again if his wife Reidun might still be alive. In his heart he doubted it. He suspected his small band were the last trolls in the world.

"And how many of us do you think are left?" Bodil posed, perhaps reading his thoughts.

"Few of us," Grundal replied.

The trolls would recover from this battle and wait a bit, climb back through the secret passage the humans still didn't know about. They'd raid the castle again and again and again, retreating when necessary and licking their wounds—and cutting down the humans' number in the process.

"Aye," Grundal said. His gaze followed one of the guillemots as it launched itself from the ledge and dove in search of fish. "Few of us. But it will have to be enough."

THE ANGEL CHAMBER

Russell Davis

Russell Davis lives with his family on a ranch in the Arizona/New Mexico borderlands. He has published numerous short stories and a handful of novels in various genres under a couple of different names. He divides his time between freelance editorial consulting, writing, and teaching.

OUR SKY is always gray.

Papa says it is because there is so much ash and smoke in the air. "From the . . . from the fires, Chaya," he tells me. When he talks, his voice sounds funny, as though the words are trying not to escape his mouth. "They burn all the time and turn the sky gray." Then he pats me on the head and tells me not to worry too much.

I don't tell him, but I do worry. I worry because we can't see the sun anymore, and the vegetable plants in our little garden space on the roof are dying. We need the food. Everyone here needs the food, and even though so many of us are gone, taken, there are still many mouths to feed. We try to share what food we have between everyone in the building.

I also worry because if you cannot see the sun, if

the sky is gray all day and dark all night, it is hard to feel alive, to feel close to G-d. I miss seeing the stars. Papa tells me they are still there, just as the sun is still there—but they are lost behind the clouds of smoke and ash. Overhead, I can hear the planes flying and sometimes I dream that one of them will land and take me way up high where I can see the stars and the sun and the moon. Where I can feel close to G-d again, maybe so high I could even see heaven.

The soldiers came for my Mama more than a month ago and they haven't brought her back. I don't know why they took her and not my Papa or me. Our neighbors mutter under their breath when they think I cannot hear them—usually the soldiers take whole families—and they wonder if Papa is working for them. I know he is not. He couldn't be. The soldiers are also gray, their uniforms gray, their eyes gray like the dead. He wouldn't work for them. He is a writer.

My Mama gave me this book. She called it a journal and told me to write down everything, that I could write about anything I wanted to, what I saw or thought. I asked her why and she told me that people who lived far away, in other countries where the sun still shined and the moon still glowed might not believe what they heard about what was happening in our country, to our people. "Write it down, Chaya," she said, her voice a stern whisper in my hair. "It may be all we have someday."

I didn't understand, but I always try to obey my Mama, so I write something every day. Some days, I write about the soldiers, about our neighbors, about the fighting in the streets over food and how the soldiers don't like the way we worship G-d. Some days, I write what I feel or think or about the garden. Sometimes, I write down little prayers, and I wonder if G-d hears these the same way he hears my prayers at night or at the temple.

I think maybe he does.

Today, I asked Papa when Mama was coming home. His eyes looked so sad and old and tired. He did not answer for a long time. He just sat and sipped his tea and his eyes were far away. Outside, there were planes flying overhead and I wondered if he was dreaming about them picking him up and taking him above the clouds, too. Then he said, "No, child. Mama is not coming home. Not ever."

"Why, Papa?" I asked. I thought I should cry, but I couldn't. The tears wouldn't come. "Is she dead?" I had heard that sometimes when people left forever it was because they were dead.

He took my hands in his. He does that when he wants to talk to me about something serious. I could see where ink had soaked into the skin of his fingertips, the lines and whorls visible in the dim light of our little kitchen. "She went into the . . ." His voice caught and though I have never seen my Papa cry, I thought he might then. He struggled for breath, then said, "She went to a place where the soldiers are making angels. A special chamber where the soldiers take our people and send them to G-d."

"The soldiers take our people away and send them to G-d?" I was confused. No one seemed happy when the soldiers came, yet if they were going to G-d, how could they not be?

"Yes, my child," he said. His voice was stronger now. "But they do not know it. The soldiers create an angel for each one of us they send into the chamber . . . G-d himself knows this and calls them to his side."

"Am I going to be an angel, Papa?" I asked him. "Will I get to be with Mama?"

Papa didn't answer me. I think he is afraid that I won't get to be an angel.

Last night, after I went to my cot to sleep—we used to have regular beds, and I even had my own room, but all of our things were left behind when we moved to this little apartment—I prayed as hard as I could that I could get to be an angel and see my Mama again. I miss her very much.

Then, when I was almost asleep, I heard her voice! "Kadosh, kadosh, kadosh." And I knew that she was with G-d and she was an angel and G-d was all around us. I could feel her arms around me and I thought . . . well, it's silly, but I think, no—I know I saw her.

I was kind of scared at first—she looked like a ghost, all pale and glowing, but then she smiled at me and I could see that G-d had given her wings. They were gray, but not gray like the sky and the smoke and the ash, but soft gray, like a kitten or how I imagine touching a dolphin must feel. I was about to call out to her, to yell for Papa to come, but before I could, I fell asleep. And I didn't even dream about the day the soldiers came and took her.

Something else happened, too. Very late, some of the soldiers came to our apartment and talked with my Papa. They woke me up. I couldn't hear everything they were saying, but Papa sounded scared and angry. He said, "I've done everything you've asked! I've given you the names! You took my wife, my Basya, now won't you leave me in peace?"

One of the soldiers laughed, then said, "You'll do more, and faster, or you and your daughter will be joining her!" His voice was ugly, like the time I accidentally broke one of my Mama's favorite glass vases.

His voice was a splintered sound, like his words would cut if they touched your skin.

I was afraid to move, afraid to breathe. I didn't understand why my Papa was so upset, why everyone was so angry, or what he meant about the names. Why did he want the soldiers to leave us alone? Didn't he want to go to where Mama was? She had been so pretty with her wings, and I know she's waiting for us.

Today, Papa said we are leaving. "We must leave, Chaya. We must leave tonight. The soldiers will be coming for us."

"Where will we go, Papa?" I asked. "Will we go to Mama?"

"Not if I can . . ." his voice trailed off. "No, child. We will run, far away from here. We will try to go to the New World. Your aunt and uncle are there, and they will let us stay with them."

This sounded almost magical to me. I had heard that in the New World, people could worship G-d anyway they wanted to—even on the street! That no one was allowed to go hungry, and that people weren't taken away to be angels and that people weren't always fighting in the streets or hiding from soldiers. I felt my heart expand with excitement, but then I remembered Mama.

"But, Papa," I said, "what about Mama? How will she find us? We can't leave without her!"

Papa took my hands in his and pulled me close. I could feel how frail and thin he was through his shirt, could feel his rapid heartbeat. "Oh, my little Chaya," he said. He stroked my hair. "You are so beautiful, like your Mama. Her hair was the same color as yours, like the wings of a little robin in the rain. And you have her eyes, too. Whenever I look at you, I see her." He was quiet for a moment, then said. "Chaya, we *must* run away from here. The soldiers will come back and they will take us both away. I . . . I promised your Mama that I would keep you safe."

I had heard him make that promise when the soldiers came and took her.

"We must go," he said. "Your Mama will watch over you from heaven and know where you are."

"But can't we go and be with her, Papa?" I asked. "Be angels?"

"Someday, Chaya," he said. "But not just yet." He stood and left me then to pack our few belongings.

I wonder what the New World is like. I wonder if Mama has gotten to meet G-d and see heaven and why the soldiers are so mean? We have done nothing to them, but still they come and take people away.

Everyday, more people are taken away, and the skies are all still gray.

Papa told me we would be leaving very late at night and I should try to sleep for a little while. He would wake me up when it was time to go. I was too excited to sleep, but I tried after saying my prayers and listening for Mama's voice and waiting to see her. I wanted to tell Papa about her, but he kept very busy during the day, and there was no chance. I had almost fallen asleep when the soldiers came back, and the one with the ugly voice was with them.

There was a lot of shouting and yelling and one of them hit Papa! After that, it got quiet and then Papa came to me and said, "I'm sorry, Chaya, but now we must go with the soldiers. We should have left sooner. They will take us away from here."

"To Mama?" I asked. I could see the red welt on his cheek where the soldier had hit him. It would be a big bruise.

He nodded, but said only to hurry. I was already

dressed, so I rose and followed him. The neighbors in our building did nothing to stop the soldiers as they escorted us from the building. There wasn't anything they could have done—the soldiers had guns and hate on their side. They didn't know about the angels.

Outside, there was rain falling, but it didn't cleanse the streets or make the air feel fresh and new. It felt like wet ash on my skin. We walked a long way and the soldiers led us to the back of a truck, shoving us and shouting for us to hurry up and get in. Then, it was like Papa woke up. "Let my Chaya go!" he cried. "She has done nothing! Please let her go home. The neighbors will care for her!"

"No, Papa!" I said. "I want to stay with you, to go see Mama!"

"Shut up, you worthless traitor!" the soldier said. "No more talking!" Then he shoved Papa into the mud on the side of the street. He raised his gun, and for a second I thought he was going to shoot him.

"No!" I screamed. "He's going to be with me and Mama, to be angels!" I couldn't imagine leaving him there, dead and shot on the side of the road, while I went to the special chamber to be made into an angel. To be with my Mama.

The soldier lowered his gun and stared at me. "An angel, is it?" he asked.

"Yes, sir," I said. I could hear Mama, could almost see her on the other side of the tall fence waving to me. "An angel."

The soldier laughed. "Angels," he said. I could hear in his voice that he didn't believe in angels. He turned back to my Papa. "Get up. You know where you're going. No use fighting it."

From the ground, Papa stared up at the soldier, and then he nodded. Slowly, he rose to his feet and I ran to him. "Are you all right, Papa?" I asked. His forehead had a cut on it and there was blood. I gave him my handkerchief and he wiped the blood away.

He pulled me close. "Yes, Chaya. Now, we must do as the soldiers say and you musn't speak to them at all. They are dangerous."

I nodded. The soldier with the gun and the ugly voice was obviously *very* dangerous. "Yes, Papa," I said.

We got into the truck and Papa didn't say anything more to them, and very little to me except to mutter for me to be quiet and do as they said.

I think maybe he had forgotten about the angels, too. But I didn't. I listened for them, for my Mama's voice, and even when the truck was going down the road and the engine was noisy and the holes in the road made us jump and bounce, I could hear her whispering, "Kadosh, kadosh, kadosh." She was with us, I knew it, so I did my best not to be scared.

It was early morning when the truck stopped and we were told to get out.

We were shoved through a large gate made of wood and barbed wire, and we held hands the whole way. Many of our people were there. I even recognized some of them. They looked sad and gray, like the sky. Some of them looked like they hadn't eaten. Most of them didn't speak or, when they did, it was a whisper. "What's wrong with them, Papa?" I asked, as we were ordered to stand in a long line of people.

"They are scared, Chaya," he said. "Very scared. No more talking now."

"Are you scared, Papa?"

I felt his fingers tighten on mine and I could barely hear his answer. "Yes, child. I am scared."

I squeezed his fingers back. I could hear Mama and if I looked sideways, right on the very edge of my vision, I could even see her. "It's all right, Papa. You don't have to be scared. If you listen, you'll be able to hear Mama say the prayer. She's watching over us right now."

He didn't answer and we stood in the line a long time. Overhead, the planes continued to fly and across the camp—on the other side of many small wooden buildings but still inside all the fences—was a huge smokestack. It bellowed ash and soot into the sky like the breath of a dragon.

If I squinted, I could see the tiny flakes flying into the air. Up close, they were a soft gray color, and floated into the sky with ease. They were feathers.

The soldiers, I realized, really didn't know about the thousands of angels they were making. I felt sad for them.

It is dark now and Papa is sleeping on the floor. He was very tired and sometimes he mumbles in his dreams. He seems scared and I want to wake him, but he needs to sleep. Outside there are bright lights everywhere, so I can see enough to write. I'm thankful that I still have my journal and my pencil.

When Papa and I finally got to the front of the line they made us . . . it was horrible, they made us undress and give them all of our clothes! Then Papa was taken aside and they shaved his head! All the soldiers were shoving people and shouting orders. I don't know why they didn't cut my hair, too. Maybe they forgot in all the confusion.

They didn't give us our clothes back, and they kept Papa's wedding ring and his watch. We were each given a gray pair of pants and a gray pullover shirt. They were going to take my journal, but Papa convinced them to let me keep it. "Where's the harm?" he asked. "It will keep her quiet."

By then it was late in the afternoon and we were

taken to one of the small wooden buildings. I wanted to ask about something to eat, but Papa shushed me before I could say anything.

The soldiers didn't bring us any food or water. We aren't the only ones here, but everyone has kept to themselves—mostly small groups of families. Before he went to sleep, Papa told me he was worried that they will separate us tomorrow. I think maybe he is right because when we were standing in line, I saw the soldiers separating some of the families. The men were taken to one place and the women and children to another. These were all people who had already been processed and were wearing the gray pajamas. A lot of the children were screaming and crying for their papas, but their mamas held them tight and wouldn't let them go.

Everyone is afraid. Afraid of the soldiers and their guns.

But I am not. I won't be afraid because I know I will get to be with my Mama soon. Right outside the bars on the window, I can hear her singing a prayer very softly. I know if I looked I could see her. I want to tell the others, tell them to look, to listen! There are angels all around.

I think maybe fear makes them blind and deaf to G-d's presence. Maybe they haven't seen the sun in so long they have forgotten how to pray.

Maybe they think G-d has forgotten them.

Papa was right. Today they separated us. Right after they finally gave us some thin gruel and water. I don't know where they took him, but he didn't fight them like some of the men have. He only knelt down by me and said, "Chaya, you must do what the soldiers tell you. Do not fight them or give them a reason to be angry. I love you."

"I don't want you to go, Papa," I said. I grabbed the leg of his pants, and could feel how thin he was. "I want to come with you. We can go together."

He shook his head. "No, child, my little robin. Soon enough, we will be together."

"Do you promise?" I asked him.

For a minute, maybe longer he didn't say anything, but then he nodded. "I promise you. We will be together soon." Then Papa stood up, kissed my forehead, and said, "G-d keep you safe, child." The soldiers shoved him away and he didn't look back.

Another one of them pushed me back toward where we had spent the night before. "Get going," he said. "You'll be seeing him tomorrow." Then he laughed.

I don't know why he thought that was funny. I ignored him and when I was back in the building, I returned to the corner where Papa and I were last night. No one looked at me or wanted to talk, so I'm writing some more in my journal.

I looked out the window and through the bars, I could see the smoke and ash rising into the sky, thicker than ever. I wondered if Papa was already with Mama. If he was, would he come with her tonight? Would I be able to see and hear him, too?

It will be night soon enough. I will have to try and wait patiently.

Something has happened, and I must write quickly. Morning will be here soon and I must not get caught.

Late last night, I said my prayers and lay down. I waited for Mama and hoped for Papa, and it wasn't long until I could hear them both. They were singing and praying right outside my window. I jumped to my feet, and pulled myself up on the bars enough so I could see out.

"Mama! Papa!" I said. They were so beautiful.

Papa's wings were larger than Mama's, but he didn't look as sad anymore. He looked . . . peaceful. They both looked peaceful.

"Chaya," he said. "Listen to me. Tomorrow the soldiers will take you into the chamber. The one I told you about. Before they do, you must dig a hole in the floor and bury your journal. Someday, someone will find it. Someday, our story will be known." Then he went back to singing and praying.

"Kadosh, kadosh, kadosh." It was so loud, I thought the soldiers would hear and come, but they didn't.

When they didn't, I wondered if he had really spoken at all. I even wondered if I was imagining things, because no one else seemed to hear them. Then I turned back to the room and I saw that the whole space was filled with angels. Tall angels, short angels, angels with hair, angels without. Every size and shape. They were all singing and praying—and only I could hear them. Everyone else was . . . it was like they were awake and asleep.

Just like that, I knew what I had to do. Papa said to bury my journal and I will, but first I have to write down something even more important than about the angels being real. In case someone finds this journal and I am already an angel and no one can hear me or see me.

Everything I wrote in here is true, but I didn't write enough. The soldiers were taking all of our people away. I don't know the details, but I heard that a lot of us were killed. I do know that very few ever came back when the soldiers took them. They took us because we were different; because we worshipped G-d differently than they did.

But the real reason they took us is the same reason no one here can hear or see the angels. They did it because they were afraid. And fear leads to hate and doing bad things.

I don't know much, but I know one thing. You can't walk in G-d's light and know fear.

I hope someday they feel better. If they could only see the angels, I know they would. Because I can see them, I am not scared a bit.

I've got to finish now. I've got to put this away and put the dirt over the hole I dug. Someone will find it someday. Outside, behind the clouds, the sun is coming up and I can hear the soldiers are talking and shouting orders to get us ready to go.

Today, I will go into the special angel chamber, just like Papa said.

I sure do miss my Mama and Papa. I can't wait to see them.

I wonder how big my wings will be?

INEFFABLE

Isaac Szpindel

Isaac Szpindel is an award winning screenwriter, author, producer, electrical engineer, and neurologist. His short fiction includes the Aurora-Award-finalist, "Porter's Progress" in the DAW anthology, *Space Inc.* and "Engines of Creation" in *Oceans of the Mind*. He is co-editor with Julie Czerneda of the historical SF anthology *ReVisions*, and author of the story "Morning Stars" found therein. The Aurora-finalist "By Its Cover" is being reprinted in *Hal's Worlds* and the story, "From Gehenna", will appear in DAW's upcoming *Slipstreams* anthology. Isaac's screenwriting has been translated into many languages and has aired worldwide. Credits include the Aurora-Award-winning episode, "Underwater Nightmare," for the Warner Bros. TV series *Rescue Heroes*, and he was head writer and story editor for the series *The Boy*, broadcast by Disney France, among others. Isaac is a frequent academic lecturer and an on-air guest on Canadian Talk Television. For more information, visit his website at http://www.geocities.com/canadian sf/szpindel/

S HE *SCREAMED.*
   The golem's blast engulfed her and the children. Stone and timber, notebooks and chalk, swastika and bits of bone and flesh danced in the maelstrom and settled.

The golem was naked now. Debris dropped from its clay skin: little bones from little hands, little teeth from little mouths, tufts of singed flesh and hair. Larger wounds in the golem's hide indulged the bones of their teacher. All wove together to form a tapestry of sulfuric striation.

The golem lifted a weighty leg, stepping through the rubble of what had once been Prague's Grand Priory. Twisted baroque decorations fashioned two centuries earlier in the workshop of Matthias Braun clawed through the wreckage, trying to impede the golem's muddy advance. The Nazi occupiers had made this once majestic edifice a schoolhouse for the children of those officers permanently stationed in the city, a city that was intended to become, in part, a museum to a slaughtered race. This Rabbi Menachem had told the golem while he had so lovingly strapped the explosives to his creation's earthen chest.

As it emerged from the ruins, the golem was aware that it had grown in size from the explosion. All else had been decimated. Nothing remained, nothing, but the *SCREAM* from the teacher who had noticed explosives, who had noticed the unholy damp clay of the golem's skin. She was gone now also, along with the unborn child in the fullness of her unsuspecting belly. All that remained was the sound of her last foreshortened cry on a still spring air redolent of rotten egg and burned flesh.

Only the *SCREAM*.

Its echo possessed the golem, and drowned the sound of the air-raid sirens that rose from the distance. Wounded and confused, the oppressors naturally looked to the skies for the source of such a blast. How could such an attack have come unseen from the ground? But it had, just as surely as the golem had been formed from that very same ground, animated through the mystic interventions of Rabbi Eliezer Menachem.

Once the golem reached an open street in the Maltese Square, Rabbi Menachem hurried out from his hiding place to join it.

"The power of the explosion humbled me to the ground and now rings through my ears," shouted Menachem in an attempt to overcome his own deafness. He was dressed in traditional black. A peppery and disheveled beard floated beneath Menachem's chin seemingly suspended from his ears by the dark ritual curls at his temples. His thin lips trembled, and his sunken black eyes glistened beneath the rim of his fedora. The hang of a long black coat accentuated his emaciated frame and his excitement. "They will see now, they will surely see now."

The golem hovered menacingly over the diminutive rabbi, awaiting Menachem's next command. A Goliath, the rabbi had called him, but the golem felt not at all like anything human as it stood before Menachem, pocked with the scars of explosive powder and stolen lives. Each mark on its skin, each impression of tooth and bone, a final epitaph to futures, worlds, lost forever. This one an artist, this one a judge, this one a killer, this one an emancipator, this one a mother, this one a father and on and on. Such little teeth, such little bones, thought the golem, and the bits of their teacher, and her *SCREAM*.

"Now, golem," Menachem commanded, "take me across to Josefov, along the banks of the river. And move quickly, so that we are not discovered."

The golem scooped Menachem into arms like trunks of oak, and bounded from the razed site that had moments earlier contained the innocent offspring of an evil oppressor.

The preternatural strides of the golem carried the two so swiftly that Menachem at first could not catch his breath. They became a blur that streaked up the left bank, past patrols on Cechuv Bridge, and beyond firing squads to the right bank of Smetana's precious Vltava and Prague's Jewish Quarter, Josefov.

There the golem lowered Menachem like a feather to the ground and once again waited for the commands of its master's voice. It could do nothing else, for it was bound to its creator's will, even above its own.

"Do you wonder, golem, why I have brought you back to this isolated place of your creation?" Menachem asked.

The golem was capable, but it did not wonder. The *SCREAM* echoed still through its clay skull and its soul, filling the golem's thoughts so that it wished only for its own destruction. But this the golem could not hope to communicate to its creator. It had been created without voice, without free will, yet it had a soul. And this soul felt the bite of children's teeth, the scratching of their tiny bones against its spirit. It felt the smoldering flesh of their diminutive frames press tight against its soul, it felt the *SCREAM*.

The golem longed also to scream, but it had not the ability. Why, then, create it with such a useless tongue? Its mouth served only as a receptacle for the parchment bearing the divine ineffable Name that rested inside. Menachem had inscribed and inserted the parchment in the final act of the golem's creation, and even now that same parchment burned the golem's tongue as the coals of the angels had burned the tongue of baby Moses.

"The council will see now the power and the justness of my methods," Menachem continued. "They will understand that to crush the evil of our oppres-

sors, a greater evil must be visited upon them." Menachem's eyes seemed to the golem to twinkle with the
fire of divine justice, or perhaps it was retribution.
"Soldiers and military targets are quickly replenished,
golem. They are targets for more conventional armies.
We must instead strike at what they hold most
precious."

The golem's life had measured the span of only this
day, but in that time it had learned of what Menachem
spoke. Menachem had watched his family burned alive
before him, even after he had debased himself in the
vain hope that they might be spared. The humiliation
of having been left alive, or perhaps it was the cruelty
of that final false hope, had robbed Menachem of his
humanity. This was the true holocaust, thought the
golem, not that so many were dying, but that they
were first dehumanized to die without dignity. This
was not the least of the oppressors' crimes, nor was it
the full measure of their evil.

"You have been effective, my dear creation, but to
fight an evil great in number, we must also increase
our numbers. And this is why I have returned with
you to these muddy banks, the very ground from
which I shaped your lifeless form." Menachem
crouched, plunging his hands into the wet earth. Dusk
was falling, and the setting sun painted the pale
patches of his skin in undulating shades of bloody
crimson.

In the distance, the incessant sound of air-raid sirens
wailed on. Menachem washed the dirt and debris of
the day's work from his hands in the running waters
of the river's edge. Then he rose and turned once
again to the golem. "The task of forming so many of
your brethren would require months of my time during which we would surely be discovered. But you
have been blessed with unnatural skill and speed.

Therefore, I command you now, golem, shape for me a host of thirty-five of your kind from the soil below and I will breathe into them life and will give them purpose."

The golem knew that without Rabbi Menachem's intervention the outlines would be no more than sculptured manikins. Only by uttering the many combinations of the ineffable Name of God could Menachem initiate the process that would instill within them life. The process would culminate with the insertion of a parchment bearing one form of the very same Name into each new golem's mouth. So had it been for the golem. All this the golem knew, for it had first awakened with the uttering of the Name, and had remained conscious through its full animation on the insertion of the parchment.

"Together, you and your brethren will go forth like a legion divine, clad in raiment of deathly fire. You will visit destruction upon all our enemy holds dear. You will instill terror in the heart of evil and you will destroy it utterly. You will deliver justice."

Was this justice, the golem wondered, as it stooped and plunged its death-pocked paws into the pristine sands of the right bank of the River Vltava. Its actions this day could not be made just through the simple invocation of divinity.

The wet sands of the Vltava filled the wounds created in the golem's hide by the innocent lives it had taken, and the golem was soothed momentarily. But mud escaped as it entered, refusing to stick to the wounds and to the bits of innocent lives embedded within.

Once again the *SCREAM* echoed within the golem's mind as if searching for escape from the golem's dumb frame. The golem longed for an end to this torture. Perhaps the rabbis that had opposed Menachem might come upon them, or perhaps the oppressors might, if the golem was able to tarry long enough. Then Menachem could command him no more.

"You are too slow, golem," barked Menachem, "increase your pace." The golem complied with inhuman speed as it continued to form the human shapes in the earth of the riverbank. Each completed form lay along the shore, like a muddy bather reclining at the Dead Sea.

Menachem produced a length of parchment of the same manufacture as the sacred *Torah* scroll. And with brush and ink in hand, he set forth inscribing the final variation of the ineffable NAME over and again across its surface. Menachem's movements were deliberate and precise. Any flaw in the form of the NAME upon the parchment and a golem would fail to vivify. Even so, Menachem's hand trembled. His body shook as he sobbed gentle tears along with his writing upon the parchment. Those tears, thought the golem, would not absolve either of them of their sins. No regret could compensate for what had been lost today, or for the horrors that were to come.

But the Name was too powerful, the golem knew, even in the imperfect hands of this man. The Name could imbue life, or destroy it, at its possessor's whim. What good then was a golem's soul, the golem lamented, if it must bend to the will of another. The golem cursed the Name and it cursed the Name's possessor all within its mind as it shaped yet another incendiary vessel of clay into the shape of a man.

As it worked, the golem's craft drew it closer to the Vltava's edge. Its waters lapped around the golem, but still refused to wash the crimes from its skin. Here, the finger of one who might have been a violinist, there the jawbone of one who had so adoringly kissed her porcelain doll. This one a poet, this one a murderer, this one a harlot, this one a saint. And again the *SCREAM* overtook the golem's thoughts, as the Vltava would not.

The golem exited the river and despaired, the *SCREAM* rattling its hide, the NAME burning its impotent tongue. Finished, the golem surveyed the work of its own hand. A line of preanimate clay idols stretched from its open palms, to its master who swayed now with feverish piety in completion of his unholy writing.

Menachem capped the bottle and attempted to wipe the ink from his hands with a tear of cloth. He then stood and called to the golem. "Return to me now, and do not disturb the perfection of our creations through the clumsiness of your clay feet."

The golem rose from the last of its thirty-five brethren, and stepped forth, taking great care to avoid its own handiwork by tracking the river's edge. And in this, the golem saw its opportunity. It had not been commanded to avoid the river, or to return by land. If it entered the river entirely, it might perhaps be swept away, or entangled, by the river's currents.

The golem plunged into the Vltava, but the river would not take it. Instead, the river's soft bed churned in the waters around the golem, heaping more mud and sand onto its growing frame. And throughout the golem remained obligated to return to its master. With each footfall, more riverbed unglued from its place of rest and gathered onto the golem, the wet earth feeding and increasing the golem's girth and height. The golem's skin cracked with the expansion and mud flowed in to fill the crevices, yet the debris of the innocents would not loosen, and those wounds would not fill.

When it reached Rabbi Menachem, the golem had grown to three times the measure of any man. Menachem grinned with pleasure at the golem's newly imposing appearance, obviously mistaking this to have been its intention in entering the river.

"Truly terrifying, thirty-six of your kind, with you among their number." Menachem mused. "Is it not written that by virtue of thirty-six righteous ones, the world is redeemed?"

The golem nodded silent assent. Its creation had endowed it with knowledge of the wisdom of the elders, of the books of Moses and of the works of the great sages. Such was the requirement of an animate soul. Such had become the golem's curse.

"Of course, of course, but you must always agree with your creator. If only I held similar sway over those two fools from the council, Rabbi Joseph and Rabbi Israel. They would prefer Prague become a mausoleum to a lost race. Even now I hear my family's pleadings join the chorus of the slaughtered; I sense the odor of their burned flesh borne on the wind."

You have added to that wind, thought the golem. The clouds seemed dark and dirty to the golem, unchanged since the moment of its birth. They were a herald of the evil that had prompted the golem's creation. It had thought it had been called upon to protect the People, as was its purpose, as its kind had done before during the pogroms in the times of Rabbi Judah Loew centuries earlier.

But Loew had been a different man fighting a different evil. And Rabbi Menachem was fighting a more modern and ruthlessly efficient malevolence that had entered and changed him.

Menachem had been a minor rabbi of a small Czech *shtetl*. With the Nazis' arrival he had watched his congregants herded into cattle cars, sealed inside and shipped to parts unknown. Menachem had not remained silent. As leader, as a human being, he raised stern objection to this treatment of his people. He had demanded to know what fate awaited them. The occupiers responded immediately. They removed Menachem and his family from the cars and commanded that he choose the order in which his two small daughters and his wife would be executed.

Menachem refused.

In response, he was made to watch his wife raped and tortured before him, and when finally his first daughter was also taken, he could stand no more.

He chose.

One by one Menachem enumerated the members of his family, and one by one, he watched, he heard, God help him, he smelled the sickly-sweet smell of them burning.

Broken and bereft of humanity, Menachem begged for death. Instead, he was sent to Prague, that he might suffer the memory of his family's fate the remainder of his life. That he might strike terror in others with the account of what had happened to him. Menachem would not. All this the golem knew, for all this Menachem had confessed to at the moment of its creation.

The makeshift Jewish Council that remained in Prague had immediately put Menachem to work, assigning him the task of cataloging the deluge of confiscated Jewish texts that flowed to Prague to be housed in the museum to an extinguished race that the city was to become. While sifting through these volumes, Menachem had come across credible accounts of Judah Loew's golem. The discovery inspired him. Dedicating many hours, he traced the accounts to further evidence, then finally to manuscripts that included Rabbi Loew's own memoirs containing a detailed recipe for creating a golem.

After much study and practice, Menachem had presented the Rabbinate with his plan: to create a new golem to carry out its prescribed task, to help their people in this moment of need. Some council members had reacted to Menachem with disbelief; others had mocked and ridiculed him for suggesting such mystical heresy. Only Rabbis Joseph and Israel had taken him seriously. Later, huddled in the decaying and blast cracked attic of Josefov's Old-New Synagogue amid broken artifacts, torn readers, and the dust of Loew's golem, they had confronted Menachem.

"Such matters are not for us to meddle with," Israel had whispered in grave tones.

"We must do something," Menachem had countered. "The Holy One, blessed be He, has bestowed this gift upon us, this power, for it to be used. Did not Rabbi Loew do the same?"

"What is a golem against these rockets and these airplanes and these boats that sail beneath the sea?" This from Joseph.

"We must employ the golem in new and unconventional manners that will strike terror into the very hearts of the enemy. We will paralyze them with terror as they do to us. If we can do this, they will dare not use their machines of war against us." Menachem had then described his plan of the golem as a "human bomb."

By Menachem's account, Israel's demeanor had become as that of a man who had taken deathly ill. "Such a deed is a crime, a crime against all humanity," he croaked.

"Such are our oppressors' crimes," Menachem had argued. "We die with no dignity, less than animals. My methods at least allows its victims some dignity."

"This is profanity, inhumanity!" Joseph's voice had shaken with rage. "It is a crime against the Holy One's commandments! It is a blasphemy against the Holy One, blessed be His Name!"

"Each life is a world. Is it not just to save many good worlds at the price of those born of evil? Is it no less than the judgment that the Holy One will impose upon them in the next world?"

Israel's voice had become a low breathless rumble and his skin had turned a tomblike white to match the streaks of his unkempt beard. "There is no justification for such actions in this world or in the next! Such evil begets only evil."

"You are meek and afraid. This is not what our people were *chosen* for," Menachem had responded.

"You are forbidden. No horror visited upon us, no tragedy justifies such greater suffering," Joseph had commanded. "Such actions would dehumanize us as surely as our oppressors do. You do not act in God's name, you defile it." Joseph's judgment had been final, binding, and uncontestable. And it had mattered not to Menachem.

Rejection had only fueled Menachem's hatred and had steeled his resolve. Menachem would proceed on his own and of his own accord.

The golem stood waiting, horrified by what had happened, terrified at what Menachem might next command. Still, the golem held to one final hope. It had taken Menachem the better part of a full day to speak the combinations of the ineffable Name that had animated its clay body. Surely now they would be discovered either by the oppressors or by the Rabbinate. This month of days the golem could not save Menachem, for the golem could not speak, he could not utter a single word.

"Golem, what do you think?" Menachem asked. The golem's inability to respond seemed to please

Menachem. "But you cannot answer, of course, as Rabbi Loew's golem could not."

The golem nodded without emotion, yet it longed to speak, to protest, to release the *SCREAM*.

"But then there is a Talmudic tradition of a golem that spoke a message from its master. And there is the more recent account of Judah the Pious."

The golem was unaware of these other golems, although it knew it was likely not the only soul to have been called down to inhabit such a creature. This soul, its own soul, the golem knew, would likely not be called upon again to inhabit any form of clay or flesh; not once it was judged for its actions.

"Judah the Pious animated a golem and endowed it with the ability to give spoken testimony in aid of an innocent man accused of murder. How then, did Judah the Pious accomplish such a wonder when the great Judah Loew could not?"

Fear welled within the golem. What was Menachem hinting at, in what further atrocities would he involve the golem?

"And then," continued Menachem, "a revelation. It is not that the great Loew could not create a golem that spoke, he simply would not. Too afraid, perhaps, of the power he might unleash. Think of it, a golem capable of speech, capable of repeating the incantations that created it, capable of birthing yet more golems."

The golem turned its weary head to regard the rank of clay offspring it had created. They lay along the shore of the Vltava, huddled side by side, like a murder of crows waiting for Menachem to bid them take flight.

"Now you see. By virtue of your tongue, these thirty-five and our world, might yet be redeemed."

Redeemed, questioned the golem silently, or revenged?

"But how?" Menachem asked. "How did the great Rabbi of the Talmud, how did Judah the Pious, accomplish such a feat? Nowhere in the account of his story is it described how such a miracle might be performed. Not in The Book of Creation, not in the Talmud."

The golem wished to run, but without the command to do so from Menachem, he remained rooted to the ground. All the while the *SCREAM* renewed its attack on the golem's soul, scratching broken nails against his earthen skull, clawing for escape.

The ashen Czech dusk gathered Menachem and the golem into its weightless shroud. Sirens continued to rise in the distance. Endless golems in Menachem's service might destroy countless worlds, not create them. Rabbis Israel and Joseph had objected to Menachem's method, but the golem knew that others would not once results were achieved. Some would fear Menachem's power and would support him. Those that considered themselves civilized, enlightened, those that ignorantly supported the seemingly downtrodden would do the same. The evil of the oppressors had created the golem as surely as Menachem had, and through the golem, that evil would grow to obliterate all good. The ineffable NAME that even now burned the golem's tongue had and would lead to unspeakable horror.

The golem knew now why Menachem had endowed it, a dumb creature, with such an unnecessary organ as a tongue.

"I searched for the answer," Menachem spoke again. "But it eluded me. And so, once more I returned to the account of the great Rabbi Loew. Loew had learned the secrets of the golem through a dream question, and so I did the same. At first, and for many nights, there came no response. And then, finally, a reply."

The golem could not believe the Holy One, the creator of all things, would answer such a man, would endow him with the knowledge and power to create such destruction and horror. But then the Blessed One had a habit of tempting humanity with knowledge at the price of innocence. Perhaps this was the toll exacted by free will.

" 'I will not tell you,' the Lord said to me." Menachem seemed elated, and the golem became confused. Why did such a refusal please this man? Perhaps Menachem did not yet possess the secret after all.

"At first I felt scorned," Menachem explained. "The Holy One had forsaken me as he had forsaken Abel." Menachem circled his waiting golem phalanx, examining them as he spoke, like a general inspecting his ranks. "I will not tell you, I will not tell you. The words chastised me over and over. Such a response was unthinkable. Surely there was a deeper meaning. So I dissected the letters of each word from the response, searched among them for anagrams, for riddles, for clues. I calculated their numeric *gematria*, summed their values, compared and tested the results for equivalency with the mystic codes I had uncovered, and still nothing."

Menachem's fervor rankled the golem, stirring the *SCREAM* that raged within, allowing it to regain force, to renew its attack. The golem could no longer remember the *SCREAM*'s source. Had it come from the teacher, from her unborn child, or was it the children? Or had it stirred into being by the golem itself?

Did it matter, after all?

"But in the darkest moment of my despair," Menachem was saying, his voice rising with the excitement, "the rightness, the justice, of my cause prevailed and I was enlightened." Menachem glowed with the heat of divine zealotry. "He will not tell me, I realized. He will not tell me . . . for I must do the telling! So simple, so elegant. To endow a golem with speech, it must be told to do so."

The golem's tortured mind shrieked with the revelation, trying to induce deafness. Tiny teeth gnawed at the golem's clay hide and chattered in protest. Tiny bones rattled their muddy purchases upon the golem's skin, attempting to raise a silent alarm upon the night. The stars blinked ignorantly down at the unholy congregation of the undead anticipating life. All around was darkness sliced by an occasional searchlight. The moon hung its head in shame and the light of man had been killed by curfew. The morbid clank of military machinery echoed through the darkness and drowned the cricket-clattered birdsong of the Czech spring. Why, wondered the golem, why does it feel so much now like winter?

"Judah the Pious had simply commanded his golem to speak," Menachem announced gleefully. "I need only do the same." Menachem raised snapping fingers to the heavens and bent forward as his heels began to dance out a *hora* of ecstatic prayer. "Then I need only instruct you in the correct combinations and pronunciations of the ineffable NAME, and through you my perfect creations will live. A feat requiring months of my days, you will complete in mere hours." Tears streamed down Menachem's face to fall upon and roll off the clay cheeks in the ground beneath him. Menachem seemed to watch the tears crack diminutive rivulets into their earthen facades with the rapturous pride of a parent. His gaze, that of a loving father awaiting the birth of a child.

And then Menachem halted, his expression turning quickly to puzzlement, then to shock, and finally, to anger. Lips trembling, he stooped suddenly to inspect the nearest of the thirty-five heads, then nervously poring over them, one by one, he froze in the dull starlight.

"Dumb fool, golem!" Menachem shouted with rage and recoiled from the golem's handiwork. "You have created them all without ears! How can I command an army that can not hear me? Useless ignorant lump, must I command you in every detail, or is this some strange treachery?"

The golem remained dumb, motionless. The *SCREAM* clawed within, the ineffable NAME burned, the little bones scratched, and the tiny teeth gnawed. But still, the golem could not answer. And if it could answer, what would it say? It did not recall forgetting the ears. Had it done so knowingly, or had it been the hand of God?

"Did you not think I would discover your blunder and form the ears myself, or did you think I would realize your stupidity too late? No, no, you are a mindless mound of mud, you could not betray me, your master, had you the desire. You are an imperfect creation and this is a sign of that imperfection. Or you were damaged in the explosion. In any case, I will have the answer from you in one simple stroke. I command you now, golem, speak!"

The golem felt its tongue burst into flame, kindled by the parchment that carried the ineffable NAME. Yet its tongue was not consumed. And the *SCREAM* withdrew from the golem's trembling lips, refusing to escape. Only a single, thin, dull word passed through. The word resurrected itself from deep within the golem's darkest recesses and rattled forth with a voice that hissed as if it had been suffocated and dragged across a crematorium floor:

"Murderer . . ."

"What?" shouted Menachem. "How dare you presume to accuse me, you treacherous, soulless stick? You are no longer fit to serve in God's name. You are no longer fit to carry the NAME."

Enraged, Menachem snatched at the golem's mouth and the parchment within. But the golem had grown too tall.

Menachem shook with furor, eyes wide and wild with what the golem realized was an all-consuming hatred. "Come to me, and lower your head so that I might remove the parchment from your mouth. And know now, that once I do so, you will be utterly destroyed."

In Rabbi Menachem's final command, the golem saw its opportunity. It stepped forward and bent over Menachem, its slick gray pate crumbling clay hairs onto the wide brim of Menachem's fedora. Had it been day, the golem's shadow would have engulfed Menachem completely in the same way that Menachem's evil had engulfed the golem.

Slowly, deliberately, the golem opened its mouth, exposing the fire that lay within. The parchment lay at the center of the conflagration, inflammable and soiled by mud.

"The divine flame will not burn the hand of the righteous, I need not fear," Menachem stated, then added, "You have served me poorly. And for this I condemn you now to once again return to the void from which I drew your disloyal soul."

With those words, Menachem reached up and plucked the parchment from the golem's mouth. One of the small teeth that had embedded itself within the golem, or perhaps a fragment of one of the bones, tore a gash into Menachem's hand as he withdrew it from the golem's mouth.

The golem began to convulse in violent waves. Bone and tooth released their hold from its crumbling clay and rained down upon Menachem.

Then a *SCREAM* whose horror bore with it only a modicum of the pain, terror, and loss of countless innocent victims resounded from within the golem. The *SCREAM* then gathered itself once more to peal through Menachem and escape onto the night in search of a new host. Menachem remained, trembling and petrified, at the crumbling clay feet of the shuddering behemoth that loomed precariously over him.

Then, a final explosive convulsion of clay and sand and the divine avalanche of dust that had once been the golem, swallowed Rabbi Menachem whole into the immense maw of its earthen jaws. Its settling dust suffocated the last impotent scream from Menachem's flattened lungs and prevented the last breath from passing his lips. In that moment the golem felt its own sinner's soul scream as little fingers, little wings, carried it away. And as the golem's soul descended, on fractured fingers and broken wings, ever deeper to the darkest void of *Gehenna*, it knew. It knew that it was not alone.

FLINT AND IRON

Rick Hautala

Rick Hautala has had more than thirty books published
under his own name and the pseudonym A. J. Ma-
thews, including the million copy, international best-
seller *Nightstone*, also *Bedbugs*, *Little Brothers*, *Cold
Whisper*, *The White Room*, *Looking Glass*, and *Follow*.
He also has had more than sixty short stories appear
in a variety of national and international anthologies
and magazines. A graduate of the University of Maine
in Orono, he lives in southern Maine with author
Holly Newstein.

THE VOICE, little more than a growl, came so suddenly from out of the darkness that it caught Arno
off guard.

"From flint and iron."

He flinched and, for a moment, forgot the response
his brother Johan had told him to use. He couldn't
actually see the person move toward him, but he felt
the distance close threateningly. The warm night air
fairly crackled with danger.

"Ahh . . . comes spark and . . . ahh, spark and
flame," Arno finally managed to say. In answer, the
person standing close to him exhaled softly, seeming
to relax as he took a step back.

Leaning forward, Arno strained to pierce the darkness that filled the alleyway. He wanted to see who he was dealing with, but, as always, the Shadow covered the night sky, blotting out the moon and stars. Arno was only eighteen years old, and throughout his life in Longthorn Valley, he had never caught even a glimpse of the moon, much less a star, at night. Like most people who had been born after the wars when the Shadow came, now almost forty years ago, he considered the stars just like the "Fair Folk" and all the other wondrous creatures the old people spoke of late into the dark nights—figments of peoples' imaginations. The times they spoke of—like fire itself—seemed no more real than life without the Shadow.

"You're late," the gruff voice said. It was low and ragged, a throaty growl that Arno found unsettling. He wondered how old this person was and what might have happened to make his voice sound so shattered.

"I . . . There were guards at all the crossroads," Arno said. "I had to cut across the fields."

A hand suddenly reached out and clamped down hard on his shoulder. The grip brought tears to Arno's eyes. He knew whoever this was, he could easily kill him, with or without a weapon. In a flash of panic, he wondered if he had been betrayed. The Overlord had spies everywhere—goblins and other servants of the Shadow—who might already have found out about what Arno was doing this late at night.

"Come with me, then," the rough voice said.

Arno almost lost his footing when the hand, still gripping his shoulder, jerked him forward into the dark throat of the alley.

The narrow dirt street was uneven, filled with ruts and holes and unseen rocks that Arno could have avoided easily during the day, when the sun was shining. At night, though, without even the faintest light to guide him, he stumbled and almost fell as he and

his unseen companion hurried along. He had to trust
that he hadn't already given himself up to one of the
goblin guards or some other creature that could see
in the darkness as easily as Arno could during the day.

"Where are you taking me?" he finally asked, hoping to sound demanding and keep the edge of fear
out of his voice.

"Do you have it with you?" the gruff voice asked,
coming to him out of the darkness ahead.

Arno hesitated, not sure if he should reveal what
he had found and managed to hide in his pocket earlier that day when he was working in the fields. If
what he had was, indeed, what he thought it was, there
would be no trial, no appeal. The goblin guard—if
that's who was leading him now—would simply slit his
throat and dump his body into the Andorn River
where it would float out of Longthorn Valley, under
the Shadow, all the way to the ice-bound rim of the
Eastern Sea.

"Well? . . . Do you?"

The voice was sharp with impatience. Arno wished
he had a weapon so he could defend himself if he had
to, but iron and steel, like flame, were against the law
for civilians. It would mean instant death if he were
to be caught with any of them. The strength of the
hand kept a firm grip on his shoulder, convincing him
that he couldn't overcome this person even with a
farm implement or wooden sword, the kind he and
his friends had played with as children.

"Yes," he said, his voice so low he could barely
hear it above the sounds their feet made on the street.
"I have it with me."

He cringed inwardly, waiting for the claws of a goblin guard to flash out of the darkness and slice open
his chest and belly, but no attack came.

"And we will see just how right you are when we

get there," his unseen guide muttered as though only half-convinced.

They walked for a long time in darkness, and all the while, the man maintained a firm grip on Arno's shoulder. It wasn't long before Arno became disoriented, and he suspected that his guide had taken several false turns, perhaps doubling back a few times in order to confuse him. Finally, though, the man jerked to a halt. Arno's eyes had adjusted to the pitchy darkness as much as they were going to. All he could see was the dark bulk of a building rising up in front of him. Looking up, he saw against the dull gray of the sky a single gable with a dark window at its pointed peak. Shivering in spite of the warm summer night, he jumped when his guide rapped once, lightly, on the wooden door. The sound seemed to be magnified in the darkness like the roll of a drum.

"Flint and iron," Arno's guide whispered softly, and from inside the house came the response, "spark and flame."

The night filled with the sound of a wooden bar scraping against the inside of the door. Then a dark gap—darker than the night itself—opened up before him. The hand on his shoulder tightened as the guide stepped forward into the darkness, dragging Arno along behind him. In an instant, the door creaked shut behind him. Arno caught only a fleeting glimpse of someone, nothing more than a black, dimensionless silhouette framed against the night. Then the darkness closed around him and squeezed.

"Let me have what you found," another voice said without preamble. This voice sounded lighter and much more friendly than the other, but Arno still mistrusted the situation. He tried not to keep reminding himself that, like all farm workers here in the valley, he should be asleep in bed at home, resting up for another day of drudgery and toil in the fields. Farm work started at the break of dawn, raising crops to feed the Overlord's slaves throughout the land.

Arno was shaking as he dug into the pocket of his tunic and clasped the rough object he had found earlier that day. Grit and rust came off onto his fingers. Just touching it the dark and not being able to see it, Arno was filled with doubt. Suddenly it seemed so small, so insignificant.

What if I'm wrong about this?

What if I'm wasting my own time and—worse—the time of these people?

What if this is all a setup?

An unseen hand reached out and gently prodded him, touching his chest. Reaching up, Arno fumbled to meet the hand as he handed over the object. Satisfied, he stepped back, wishing for nothing more than to be done with this and gone.

"Are all the windows covered?" the gruff-sounding voice asked.

"Yes, yes of course they are. Patience, Leino," the other, more pleasant-sounding voice replied. "It feels right, but now . . . now we shall see."

Arno cringed when he heard the rustling sound of cloth followed by a rough scraping sound. In an instant, a tiny shower of orange sparks exploded in the darkness. They were so bright and sudden they hurt Arno's eyes and left burning blue streaks across his vision. He felt like he had been staring at the sun too long.

"Yes, yes," whispered the pleasant voice, sounding more than satisfied. Once again the darkness filled with the scraping sound, and once again bright sparks flared in the darkness. Even when he was ready for it this time, the sudden brightness stung Arno's eyes. He imagined that he could hear a high sizzling sound as the sparks burned across his vision.

"You have done well, Arno," the pleasant voice said. This time, when a hand clapped him on the shoulder, Arno could feel that he was in no danger.

"How do you know my name?" he asked. The pleasant voice had used another name, Leino, but Arno didn't know anyone who went by that name. And he certainly didn't recognize either of these men's voices. What had his brother gotten him into?

"Do you want to be rid of the Shadow?" the pleasant voice asked. Before Arno could reply, soft laughter sounded from the darkness. "Yes, yes, of course you do. But you're too young to remember. You don't know what life was like before the Shadow came. Leino, here, he remembers. Don't you, Leino?"

"All too well," the man with the gruff-sounding voice replied.

The other man chuckled a bit louder. "A goblin sword laid open Leino's throat during the final battle on Bosdon Field," he said. "Leino's lucky to be alive, but—yes, he remembers. As do I."

"And I remember what it was like when we had fire to light the night," Leino said, his voice cracking with barely repressed anger. "We had *fire* to drive away the darkness and to keep us warm on winter nights. Now—" He made a sound in his throat like he was about to spit onto the floor. "Now, we cower in the darkness and burrow like frightened animals into our earthen hovels and shiver in the cold without fire and without iron to make weapons to fight back."

The other man's laughter came again, softly. He sounded like he had to muster the same type of patience with Leino that Arno's parents had to use whenever they were faced with his youthful impatience. But it had been more than three years since his parents died, and Arno and his older brother Johan were on their own.

"The time will come," the pleasant voice said. "It may not be in your lifetime, Leino. The burden may fall on the shoulders of young ones such as Arno or, for all we know, on the shoulders of his children or grandchildren. But the time *will* come. As long as we remember how to use *this*—"

Again, he struck the object Arno had given him against something else, and a brilliant cascade of sparks filled the room, flickering as they pushed back the darkness. In that brief flash of light, Arno caught a glimpse of an old man, his withered face etched with lines as dark as the tattoos that decorated goblins' faces. But he also caught a flash of eyes as blue and bright as the sky on a clear day in winter.

"You must take the boy back to his home now, Leino," the old man said softly, "and then we must return to the caves where we can prepare."

"Before I go," Arno said, surprising even himself when he found the courage to speak. "Tell me what it is that I have found. I was plowing the fields, turning over the topsoil, when the wooden blade of my plow fetched up on this object. I knew it was dangerous to possess it, and I would have left it where it lay. I should have let someone else find it and die at the hands of the goblins, or I should have buried it again and let it remain forever beneath the soil. But my brother, Johan, who was working beside me saw what I had uncovered. He was the one who put me in contact with you."

"Yes," Leino said, his growling voice filling the darkness with menace. Arno sensed that he would never want to make this man his enemy. "I know Johan, and I am glad that he brought you to us."

"So tell me—what is it?"

Before either man could speak, a faint sound reached into the darkness from outside. Arno and the two men tensed and listened as a soft, snuffing sound, like a dog, sniffing a lingering trail, grew gradually louder. .

"A patrol," Leino whispered harshly.

"Those goblins can smell iron," the old man said. There was a rustle of cloth. "Hush now."

The sounds outside the house grew steadily louder. Arno knew, if this was, indeed, a goblin patrol, the wooden bar across the door wouldn't hold them back for long. An iron bolt, perhaps, but that was one of the many reasons the Overlord had outlawed all metal in the valley. Holding his breath, his body tense, Arno waited for what would happen next.

The footsteps moved inexorably up the street, heading toward the house where the three of them cringed in the darkness.

"Oh, for a sword of steel," Leino whispered harshly.

"Hush!"

The sniffing sounds were right outside the front door now. Then a faint clawing sound came, sounding like a large cat sharpening its claws on the door. After a moment, voices speaking the Dark Tongue, which Arno did not understand, spoke.

There were at least two of them, and they spoke to each other as they sniffed and prodded the door, but then, after what seemed like a terribly long time, they moved away from the door, their footsteps and voices receding into the night. Arno and the two men breathed sighs of relief.

"If they caught the scent of iron, they will return," the old man said. "Quickly. Take the boy back to his home by the most direct route."

"Wait," Arno whispered. "You still haven't told me what it is I found."

"The remains of a weapon from the wars," the pleasant voice said. "This is an iron pike that was used in the final battle here on Bosdon Field."

Arno's breath caught in his throat.

"Bosdon Field?" he said in disbelief.

The old man sniffed again with laughter, but it sounded tight and dry, and there was no humor in his voice when he said, "Yes. You work in the fields every day, not even aware that the crops you sow and reap are nourished by the blood that was spilled that day when the last army of men fought against the Shadow and fell."

"That's not—"

"We never speak of it here in the valley," Leino said, "but it was the last, cruel gesture of revenge of the Overlord that the one area not always beneath his Shadow, the only place in the land where he allows the sun to shine is here so you can raise crops to feed his slaves."

"Goblins eat only flesh, and it is well-known that they prefer human flesh, but humans must eat, too. That is why the Shadow surrounds Longthorn Valley in a smoky ring. As much as the Overlord desires his Shadow and would have it embrace the entire land, the sun must shine here so crops can grow while the rest of the land . . . the rest of the land is in perpetual darkness."

"But we will fight him," Leino said, his voice a terrible growl. "We will take fire, and we will forge iron and steel, and we will defeat the Overlord."

"That may be, Leino," the old man said, "but not tonight. Tonight, you must take Arno back to his home, avoiding all goblin patrols. Then return here."

"Come with me then," Leino said, and he grabbed Arno by the arm and pulled him toward the door.

They were almost to Arno's house—he recognized the turns in the street and the dark silhouettes of the houses on either side—when the goblin patrol came upon them. There were three of them, and they were walking toward them from one end of the street. Arno knew it was goblins because he recognized the squeaking, chittering sounds they made when they scented them and closed in on them. They were the same sounds he had heard so often in the fields, when one of the plow animals or a worker would fall, and the goblin overseers would descend on the downed human or animal and feast.

"Run," Leino whispered, and he propelled Arno forward so violently he almost lost his footing and fell. "You can't help me now."

The goblin patrol hadn't yet rounded the corner of the narrow alleyway, but their horrible squealing grew steadily louder as they approached.

Arno knew that a storm drain ran off to the right, but he was reluctant to leave Leino behind. Clenching his fists, he prepared to take a stand and fight, but Leino turned to him and pushed him back again.

"Don't be a fool," he hissed. "Run! Now!"

The goblins' squeals rose louder, the shrill sounds echoing from the surrounding houses. As Arno ducked into the drainpipe, he wondered if they had already seen him. He hesitated, not wanting to leave Leino behind, and once he was inside the drainpipe, he peeked around the corner and watched as the huge bodies of the goblins came into view. Their wings were fully extended, so they touched both sides of the alley.

Their leathery skin made rough grating sounds as it swept against the earthen buildings.

Before Arno could act, Leino let fly a loud, bellowing shout and charged them. The frenzy of the battle was brief, and although he couldn't see it in the darkness, he knew that within seconds, Leino had been mercilessly slaughtered. The alleyway echoed with the goblins' howls and yelps as they tore the man to shreds.

Shivering with fright, Arno crouched in the drainpipe, frozen with terror. Then one of the beasts paused and, rising to its full height, turned and looked in his direction. With a shrill scream, it leaped toward Arno, who ducked back inside the drainpipe an instant before the goblin's claws raked across the front, removing huge chunks of dirt and cement.

Paralyzed with fear, Arno watched as the beast screamed and clawed furiously at the opening in an attempt to get at him. The air was chilled by the beast's horrible breath, and a dull, lambent light glowed in the monster's eyes.

Finally, once he realized that the goblin couldn't get at him, Arno shook off his fear, turned, and skittered down into the narrow pipe. He had played in places like this when, as a child, he had followed the drainage system all the way to where it dumped into the Andorn River. With the squeals of the goblin ringing in the confined space, he scrambled as fast as he could, praying that the goblins didn't know where the drainpipe emptied or couldn't cover the distance before he got there.

Morning came and found Arno lying on his bed of straw and shivering with terror. Tired as he was, he knew he had to arise at dawn—like always—and go to work in the fields. If he didn't show up for work, a detail of goblins would come to the house and take him away, never to be seen again. Field workers often disappeared, and replacements showed up regularly.

Arno was afraid that the goblin overseers had caught his scent last night and would be waiting to identify him when he showed up to work, but he passed by the guards and overseers without incident and set to work. The day was long and hard, and Arno was exhausted by noon, but he redoubled his efforts, knowing that any slacking in the pace of his work could mean instant death. By the time the sun was setting, and it was time to return home for a simple meal and sleep, Arno was beyond exhaustion. Work continued like that for a week, but in spite of the hard days, Arno realized what he must do.

Finding the old man's house would be difficult, Arno knew, but he was convinced that he had a good enough memory of the distinctive gable so he would recognize it if he ever saw it again. During the days, while going to and from work, he walked the streets, taking a different route each time and always looking up at the rooflines in hopes of recognizing the peaked gable. When he went out at night, dodging the goblin patrols was difficult but not impossible.

While growing up in Longthorn, Arno had learned to find his way around in the dark. After a week of fruitless searching, he was almost crushed by his need for sleep, but he was sure it was just a matter of time before the goblins found him. On the night he had escaped down the drainpipe, they had seen him, and they had smelled him. No doubt they had sent a smaller creature down the pipe after him to discover where he had gone. They must have his scent by now. Perhaps they were only biding their time before they came for him.

The night was hushed as most of the field workers either slept from the exhaustion of their workday or else cowered, trembling, in the night. Arno moved silently up and down the alleyways of the town, pausing every now and then to gaze up at the sky to see if he could discern the exact outline of the roof he remembered from the night a week ago. After several frustrating hours of searching, he was considering turning back to home and taking his chances in the morning when he drew to a sudden stop and looked skyward.

There it was.

He was positive.

The peaked gable looked like a single fang, black against the dull gray of the night sky. Arno was trembling as he approached the door, made a fist, and rapped lightly. Holding his breath, he waited, but no response came from inside the house. Casting a cautious glance over his shoulder, he counted to ten and then knocked again. Still, no answer came from inside the house.

"From flint and iron," he called out softly, keeping his face so close to the door he could smell the rot of it.

His ears prickled as he waited for the response "Come spark and flame," but the silence of the night remained unbroken. After casting a cautious glance over his shoulder, he reached out and felt around until he found the latch. It made a faint clicking sound when he lifted it. The leather hinges groaned as he pushed the door open.

The room was empty. He could sense that immediately. The air was stale and dry, and not a living thing moved within. He was turning to leave when he heard the sound of heavy footsteps coming up the street. Fear clenched his stomach like an icy fist when voices speaking the Dark Tongue filled the night.

He was convinced they had caught his scent and that he was trapped, but he shut the door and shot the wooden bolt, hoping against hope that the goblin patrol would pass by. His hands clenched into fists, aching to hold a weapon, even if it was something as simple as a farmer's hoe or a toy wooden sword. Pressing his weight back against the closed door, he waited for the footsteps to pass by the door, but they stopped right outside. The memory of hearing what the goblins had done to Leino the night he died filled Arno with terror and a deep sadness. He was too young to die, and he had never wanted to become involved with fighting against the Overlord or any of his minions.

A heavy fist came down on the door so hard it sounded like a crash of thunder. Gritting his teeth, Arno planted his feet in the dirt floor and leaned back against the rough wood of the door with all his might. He closed his eyes and tried not to imagine the sharp goblin claws shredding the old wood and tearing into him.

Desperate, he looked around, hoping to find something—anything he could use as a weapon, but he couldn't see a thing in the utter darkness. A horrible, sour taste filled his throat, and he let out a faint whimper when the fist came down on the outside of the door again, hitting it so hard his head bounced against the wood. A spray of light shot across his vision, and for an instant, he thought it was from the impact. But then another, larger shower of sparks lit up the room, and in the flickering light, Arno saw— or thought he imagined seeing—the old man. He was bent over, holding something in his hand—a long stick with a blunt, rounded end, and he was scraping the object Arno had given him against something else. On the third attempt, the sparks fell onto the blunt end of the stick, and flames burst forth. They wrapped around the rounded tip of stick in a flickering ball of oily orange and blue light.

"They've followed you here," the old man said, raising his eyes and looking earnestly at Arno. The wavering torchlight carved deep shadows into the lines on his face as he studied Arno for a moment and then smiled.

"Are you prepared to fight?" the old man asked.

Arno bit down on his lower lip to stop it from trembling as he stared in utter disbelief at the old man. He appeared to be wearing a heavy, black cloak that blended into the surrounding darkness so well his face seemed to be hovering, disembodied above the floor.

"They killed Leino," Arno said, his voice little more than a gasp.

"That's what I had feared when he didn't return," the old man said, "and that's why I have returned here, to wait for you to come back."

Outside, the goblins continued to hammer against the door. Each jolt splintered the wood a little more. Arno knew that the wooden crossbar wouldn't hold much longer.

"Do you know another way out of here?" he asked, fighting the desperation that was rising within him.

The old man cast his eyes downward and shook his head from side to side. "Sadly, I don't," he said. "There's just that one door."

Arno closed his eyes as the heavy blows from outside continued to rain down on the door. He was certain he was going to die soon, and he couldn't help but wonder if somehow—for reasons he couldn't fathom—this old man had lured him to this place to die.

"You asked me if I wanted to fight," Arno said, gasping with panic and pain as the pounding on the door rattled the teeth in his head. "I can't fight goblins with my bare hands."

The old man smiled and nodded sagely. The firelight underlit his features, casting his towering shadow against the rough-hewn ceiling and wall as he flung his cloak aside to reveal a sword in a scabbard strapped to his waist.

"Can you use this?" the old man asked with a twinkle in his eyes as he drew the sword. The blade rang loudly as it cleared the scabbard and caught the torchlight, scattering it into a thousand shards.

"My vows to my order forbid me from using weapons against any form of life—even those creatures outside," the old man said. "But if you were to wield this . . ."

"I've never touched a sword in my life," Arno said. "Not a real one, in any event."

Just then the door above his head burst inward, and a huge, black claw-tipped hand reached through the splintered wood. The claws just missed the top of Arno's head before he ducked to one side. He was unable to tear his gaze away from the old man who seemed to be in no particular hurry as he strode forward and handed the sword, hilt-first, to Arno.

"Do you know how to *use* a sword?" the old man asked.

Arno considered, but only for a moment. The door was splintering all around him as claws tore through the wood. He took the sword and, gripping the hilt with both hands, dashed forward a few steps and then spun around just as the door collapsed inward. The torchlight flared, illuminating the scene. The dark, winged creatures let out ear-piercing shrieks of rage and pain as they shied away from the garish glow, and Arno screamed and lunged forward with the sword, satisfied to hear an even louder howl of pain from one of the goblins as he struck. Black blood spurted like a fountain from the goblin's stomach and splashed across Arno's chest, but he ignored it as he braced both feet and swung a terrific uppercut that caught another one of the creatures under the jaw. The blade hummed in his hand as it carved through the goblin's neck, severing it to the spine. Gagging, the creature fell backward, screeching and twitching in the doorway when it hit the ground.

With the torchlight blazing behind him and blinding his enemies, Arno pressed forward. He cleared the doorframe, stepping over the two fallen goblins, and lunged out into the street. There was only one left, but it snarled like a caged wolf as it rose to its full height and then charged.

Arno crouched down low and, timing his swing, grunted loudly as he brought the blade up. The sword pierced the goblin's stomach and was almost wrenched from his hands as it cut upward. Something dark and ropy uncoiled as it spilled out onto the street, and dark, hot blood splashed Arno's face. The goblin flapped its wings and roared with rage and pain before collapsing backward. Its head bounced off the wall of the house on the opposite side of the street. Then it lay still.

When it was all over, in the sudden concussion of silence, Arno realized that he was trembling. He found it impossible to keep the sword raised, so he lowered his arms until the tip touched the hard-packed earth. The torchlight behind him suddenly went out. The old man stepped out into the street and snagged him by the hem of his tunic.

"It might be wise to step back inside for the moment," he said, his voice low and furtive. "Certainly, the sounds have raised the alarm, and other patrols will arrive."

Dazed and in shock following his sudden outburst,

Arno let himself be guided back into the house, stepping gingerly over the shattered door. He stood in the center of the room and listened as the old man scurried about, moving around the darkened room as if he could see everything clearly.

"We must leave now," the old man said. He paused in his activity and turned to Arno. "Are you satisfied with your sword?"

Momentarily stunned, Arno shook his head and wiped the goblin blood from his face.

"My sword? What do you mean, *my* sword?"

"The iron in the field. It called to you," the old man said. "You were meant to find it, and since the last time I saw you, I've been to the White Mountains where I used that iron to forge this sword for you."

Arno's breath came in ragged gulps, and the cool night air chilled his sweat-soaked skin.

"It appears to me that you have a choice to make," the old man said. "You can either stay here and take your chances that the goblins won't discover who's responsible for all of this, or you can come with me into the White Mountains."

"The White Mountains?" Arno said, his voice a faint echo as his last remaining strength drained away from him.

"Yes. I and others live in the White Mountains, under the Shadow like the rest of the world," the old man said. "If you choose to leave the valley and come with me, you may never see true daylight again. The Shadow has spread across most of the world, and once the goblins get your scent, you will be a hunted man."

"No, I . . . I can't go back to . . . to working in the fields," Arno said. "But I can't leave my brother."

The old man sighed. "Johan has his own path to follow, and he has helped us more than you realize.

We need fighters such as you. In the mountains, we can train you, and with the gift of fire, we will forge more weapons."

Arno considered the old man's words and tried to absorb the enormity of what he was about to decide. Like the old man had said, he could take his chances here in Longthorn Valley and hope the goblins didn't identify him, or he could go into the White Mountains and make a new life for himself, one that—perhaps—would include fighting against the Overlord and the Shadow.

"You have an intuitive skill with a blade," the old man said. "And given time . . . who knows? Perhaps you could lead men into battle against the goblins."

Arno closed his eyes, remembering the feeling of the sword in his hand. On some deep level, it had felt so good, so right. It wasn't just for Leino that he had enjoyed killing the goblins; the fight had given him a feeling of exhilaration. It felt good—for once—to strike back at the darkness and fear of living under the Overlord.

"But why?" he asked. "Why have you come to me?"

"Because you brought us iron, and iron when struck with flint makes sparks. And from sparks come flame, and in the light of that flame, perhaps . . . just perhaps we push the Shadow back."

The old man paused, and Arno saw his silhouette in the doorway as he cocked his head from side to side, listening for any sounds of approaching patrols.

"Someone is coming," he said. "If you're coming with me, we must leave now."

Arno braced his shoulders and nodded slowly even though he half-suspected the motion was wasted in the darkness. Or maybe it wasn't. He had the uncanny

feeling that this mysterious old man had ways that
Arno couldn't understand of seeing in the darkness
and into the inner hearts and minds of people.

Not yet, anyway, but perhaps with time.

"Yes. Let's go, then," he said, and he followed the
old man out into the night. Moving swiftly in the darkness, they headed out of town and into the forest to
secret paths that would lead them up into the White
Mountains.

PEEL

Julie E. Czerneda

Julie E. Czerneda, a former biologist, has been writing
and editing science texts for almost two decades. A
regular presenter on issues in science and science in
society, she's also an internationally best-selling and
award-winning science fiction author and editor, with
nine novels published by DAW Books Inc. (including
two series: the Trade Pact Universe and the Webshift-
ers) and her latest, the hard SF trilogy *Species Imperative.* Her editorial debut for DAW was *Space Inc.* Her
short fiction and novels have been nominated for several awards, including being a finalist for the John W.
Campbell Award for Best New Writer, the Philip K.
Dick Award for Distinguished Science Fiction, and winning three Prix Aurora Awards, as well as being on the
preliminary Nebula Ballot. A proponent of the use of
science fiction in classrooms, Julie is series editor for
Tales from the Wonder Zone (winner of the 2002
Golden Duck Special Award for Excellence in Science
and Technology), Realms of Wonder, and author of
such acclaimed teacher resources as *No Limits: Devel-
oping Scientific Literacy Using Science Fiction.* She currently serves as science fiction consultant to *Science
News.*

WATER SEEPS through the windowsill when the wind blows from the east. It finds a path through a crack in the plastic. It soaks the plaster within, lingers in hidden wood.

Best of all, it peels the paint.

Her fingers tremble over the imperfection, stroke the ripples like a lover's skin.

With a nail, she marks the edge of softness, then pulls ever so gently. The paint—its color of no importance—comes away willingly. She grasps the tiny beginning between fingertips, her tongue between her teeth.

She tries not to hope too much.

This is her lucky day. The paint peels with extravagant generosity, bringing with it strips of paper from the dampened wall. She shifts her fingers to the edges, careful to work with it, adjusting to the growing tension as the peel reaches the end of the invading moisture. It becomes stubborn and brittle and falls free at last.

She cradles the peel in her hand, watching it curl. Her fingers echo the shape.

She sits back to survey the result, the chill of tile unnoticed in the blush of triumph. Multiple grays mix with black specks of mold. Paper feathers the sodden plaster. She sees faces in textures; landscapes in whorls.

Change whispers in her ears. Enthralling. Enticing. Forbidden.

Footsteps.

She releases the curtain, tucks her hand—and the peel—in her pocket, stands. There is time for this, and no more, before . . .

"Oh, there you are, dear!" The woman's voice is soft and warm. Her face is smooth and lovely. Her

clothing is fitted, its color of no importance. There is
no flaw in form or gesture.

She touches the peel and remembers. There had
been lines beside her mother's eyes. Hard work and
sun had conspired. There had been lines beside her
mother's mouth. Laughter and worry had taken turns.

The woman's skin is perfect.

"Your ride's here, dear. Have a nice day at work.
Wear your coat."

She doesn't answer, simply walks to the door. The
rudeness brings no frown or puzzlement.

Nothing changes.

She touches the peel; her new talisman.

She walks with her eyes straight ahead. The sidewalks are clean and even, slicing obedient lawns. The
vehicle disturbs not a blade as it waits, silent and steel.
Its color is of no importance. A set of steps lead up
and in.

Faces smile from their rows. All are smooth and
lovely. She feels no warmth or welcome. She can't tell
them apart.

Her fingertip fondles the peel as she sits.

Murmurs, soft and melodious, thicken and twist the
air. "It's going to be a nice day." "Look at that sky.
Perfect!" "You know what Monday means." "We
never forget. Movie night at your place." She hums
without breath, a discordant, dangerous humming; rebellion in her bones.

She remembers. The peel left change in its wake.
A sign.

She knows to move as they do, without flaw, always
with purpose. Her hands reach. Her left picks up a
rod, her right the ring that slips over it. Make them

one, put them down. Her hands reach. Her left picks
up a rod, her right the ring that slips over it. Make
them one, put them down. The material is inanimate,
its color of no importance.

Murmurs gather around her feet, as if dust. Gentle,
warm murmurs. "What a nice day to be at work."
"Look how well this fits." "Here comes another one."
"It's so good to be here." "The movie will be fun, too."

Then, without warning, a shard falls, lifts a plume
of dismay.

"We could play cards tonight instead."

The murmurs choke themselves to silence.

Her hands reach, as all hands here do, in unceasing
synchrony. Her left picks up a rod, her right the ring
that slips over it. Make them one, put them down.

Her hands don't need her eyes. She lifts her gaze,
seeks the shard.

His face is smooth and lovely. He works in silence,
moving without flaw. But, for an instant, his lips mis-
place the peaceful smile painted on the rest. They peel
back, showing a glimpse of teeth. A rictus. It could be
fear. Or surprise.

Change.

Her groin burns. Her breath catches in her throat.
She cannot move.

Another sign.

His lips close, then open. "The movie will be fun,
too."

Her hands reach. Her left picks up a rod, her right
the ring that slips over it. Make them one, put them
down.

Inside, she hums something discordant, dangerous.

Different.

She sits, knees and feet together, back straight. On
either side, others sit, knees and feet together, backs

straight. Before them, scenes of carnage alternate with lust. Faces can't be seen. Voices have no words. Deeds have no context. It is the same movie they watch each Monday.

Her hand finds its pocket. Her fingers find the peel. It's smaller. It shrinks into itself. It will dry and fragment soon, becoming something new.

Finding the peel, she remembers. The man who sits to her left. There had been calluses on his palms. Thorns and gravel had etched them. There had been a broken nail and scars. Strength and tenderness had been in every touch.

The man's hands rest, flawless, on his lap.

"This movie is nice." "I always like this movie." "What a great day at work."

She simply stands and walks away. Her body blocks the image from their view. The rudeness brings no protest or complaint.

Nothing changes.

Almost.

Something changed today.

She almost smiles.

Leaving in the midst of the movie is . . . change.

Walking down the sidewalk, the ker-pat ker-pat of her small, quick steps the only sound is . . . change.

Alone, she dares revel in it, dares throw back her head and stretch out her arms, dares . . .

"Hello, dear." The woman's voice is soft and melodious. It comes from the dark beside her, a stranger's kiss. Shadows without substance tremble in the cold, east wind.

Dropping her arms, she savors her fear, in its way as novel as hope. "Hello."

"Why aren't you at the movie with your friends, dear?"

She says the expected. "It was nice." Then, with the peel in her pocket and the glimpse of teeth in her memory, adds: "The movie machine stopped working. It needs repair. I came home to see you. Mother."

The shadows stop moving. The world holds its breath. She clings to the moment, anticipation quickening her heart until she almost laughs. Then, smooth and warm and the same as always: "That's nice, dear. Let's walk home together." The figure steps out of the darkness, lovely and flawless. Perfect.

She simply walks on her way, ker-pat ker-pat, listening to the echo of following footsteps.

She smiles at the feel of storm in the air.

The next morning, the windowsill is dry and clean. Caulking leers from its corners. Below, the wall is pristine, pure, perfect. Its color has no importance.

Overcome with grief, she sits. The chill tile steals warmth from her bare legs and buttocks, robs her of sensation. She reaches a trembling hand to test for lies. The paint is solid; its finish immaculate.

Impenetrable.

Footsteps.

She's lost yesterday's peel. As every morning, a new garment waits on her bed, the old discarded. She grieves in silence.

"Oh, there you are, dear!" The woman's voice is soft and warm. Her face is smooth and lovely. Her clothing is fitted, its color of no importance. There is no flaw in form or gesture.

She touches the paint and sees nothing, remembers nothing.

"Your ride's here, dear. Time to get dressed. Have a nice day at work."

She doesn't answer, simply stands and goes to her

room to dress. The rudeness brings no frown or puzzlement.

Nothing changes.

Outside, she walks with her eyes straight ahead. The sidewalks are clean and even, slicing obedient lawns dusted with snow. The vehicle waiting disturbs not a flake as it hovers, silent and steel. Its color is of no importance. A set of steps lead up and in.

Faces smile. All are smooth and lovely. She feels no warmth or welcome. She can't tell them apart.

She joins the murmuring. "What a lovely day." "Work will be nice." "Don't forget it's my house for the movie tonight." "We never forget." She doesn't know which words come from her mouth.

She moves as they do, without flaw, always with purpose. Her hands reach. Her left picks up a rod, her right the ring that slips over it. Make them one, put them down. Her hands reach. Her left picks up a rod, her right the ring that slips over it. Make them one, put them down. The material is inanimate flesh, its color of no importance.

She reaches again, eyes blind by rote, and touches something warm.

His hand is out of place. Only by a breath, only for a heartbeat, but it is enough.

Her fingers, caught on skin, miss the next rod.

It's as if she's sleeping and only now awakes. She grasps the telltale rod and its abandoned ring, tucks both into her pocket with unfamiliar speed. Her hands reach, fingertips quivering. Her left picks up a rod, her right the ring that slips over it. Make them one, put them down.

Saved by rhythm, she looks up.

He's slower to recover. Before him a pair of connected rods and rings bounce aimlessly, unable to link themselves in the next step. His eyes catch on hers, a puzzling in their depths, then he looks back to his task, murmuring soft and warm: "This is nice."

Too late.

She remembers herself in his eyes.

And the scream comes from her soul.

There are worse things than remembering.

There is change.

She runs down the sidewalk, pat-ker-pat pat-ker-pat, dodging cracks and sprouts of frozen, ragged weeds, coughing as each breath brings more of the thick stench on the wind, shivering, eyes struggling to comprehend.

Reality is a peel, curled in the mind's hand, fragmenting as it dries, blowing away.

The buildings around her sag like a spinster's breasts. Every step takes her further into nightmare.

"Hello, dear." The woman's voice is hurried and harsh. "Why aren't you at work?" There is a sharp catch before each word, as though something is being reset.

She won't look. She won't answer.

She has seen beneath the paint.

Her ride waits for her the next morning. Nothing has changed.

Everything has changed.

She isn't home.

Paint hangs in long fingerlike curls from every wall. It lies in dry wisps, irregular and wild, like tangled hair or autumn leaves. Plaster has fallen, dusty clumps pulled free and thrown to the tiles. Wood stares out, like bones stripped of flesh.

Words stain her window, fighting the frost.

"I am real."
Their color is red.

She holds court with dusty shadow, watches others perform. Their skin is perfect. Her fingers, nails stained and broken, tickle dying shrubs, wander crumbling brick, seek . . . what? She has left the words behind.

Things have changed. It is not enough.

Her hand loosens a shard of brick—its color is of no importance—carries it into view. She brings it to her arm, cuts across softness, flinches with esctasy. The shard falls to the ground.

With a nail, she tests the new edge, then pulls ever so gently. The paint—its color of no importance—comes away willingly. She grasps the tiny beginning between fingertips, her tongue between her teeth.

She tries not to hope too much.

The paint peels with extravagant generosity. She shifts her fingers to the edges, careful to work with it, adjusting to the growing tension as the peel becomes stubborn. She pulls hardest of all, and the peel falls free at last.

She cradles the peel in her hand, watching it curl. Her fingers echo the shape.

She stares at what is exposed. The chill wind goes unnoticed. Multiple grays mix with black specks of mold. Paper feathers sodden plaster. She sees faces in textures; landscapes in whorls.

What does it mean?

"Oh, there you are, dear!" The woman's voice is soft and warm. Renewed.

She knows what she will see. A face smooth and lovely, no flaw in form or gesture. She stares at her arm.

Why is there a wall within herself?

"You've missed your ride."

Who put it there?

She stares at her arm and sees dark liquid welling up through the plaster. Suddenly, the torn edge of the paint becomes a line of fire. She looks up, eyes swimming with change.

The peel is in her hand. Power is in her hand. "You are not my mother." Her voice is discordant, dangerous. Her voice hums with power. "You are not real."

The woman's mouth melts as she speaks. "You need your coa . . ." Lips go. Chin follows. The wind whips the air with ice, tat-tat tat-tat, and the woman congeals into a lump of inanimate flesh.

Clutching the peel, she looks at the sagging buildings, the remnants of gardens. She looks at others, perfect in form and perfectly oblivious, waiting by the old bus. "You are not real." The words lift in the wind and fly back in her face, blinding and sure. "There's only me."

She doesn't need to watch. She feels it happen, a shifting of perspective, a clarity as cold as the coming night.

They are gone. All of them. All of it.

She's done it before. And before that. Uncounted befores and before thats. Each time victory traps her. She closes a fist over the peel, remembering.

She won once. Only once. Her power ravaged this world and all who lived on it.

Leaving her alone.

Alone—until she has to rebuild it or go mad.

Rebuild—until she becomes lost.

Lost—until she rediscovers her lie and destroys it. Leaving her . . .

Alone—until she has to lie to herself again.

She opens her hand and watches the tiny piece uncurl.

"No," she tells it. "Not this time." She tips her hand, and watches the peel fall.

The freezing wind at her back is her guide, the sleet driving into her flesh her companion. She runs with the storm, owns its screams, its fury, its destruction. Every step marks purpose. Every moment marks change.

Even the one where she finds herself on her knees, on her stomach, and then curls into a sigh.

Even the one where the snow paints her with peace.

COMES FORTH

Jane Lindskold

Jane Lindskold is the author of more sixteen novels, including the Firekeeper series, (which includes *Through Wolf's Eyes*, *Wolf's Head*, *Wolf's Heart*, *The Dragon of Despair*, *Wolf Captured*, and *Wolf Hunting*), *The Buried Pyramid*, *Changer*, and *Child of a Rainless Year*, along with fifty-some short stories. She lives in New Mexico, where she is always writing another book. For more information, check out www.janelindskold.com.

> *When from a hazelnut comes forth an oak,*
> *When from an oak comes forth a ram,*
> *When from a ram comes forth a flood,*
> *Only then will the people be freed.*
> —Ootoi prophesy

PROPHESY IS a strange and peculiar thing, for it can give comfort and assurance to those on opposite sides of a conflict.

Take the prophesy spoken by Kuntan, last of those who could claim clear blood ties to the chieftains of the conquered Ootoi. As it has been told and told again, Kuntan spoke those four cryptic lines as he lay dying. His voice, which had been faint and rasping from the pneumonia that had clogged and clotted his lungs, suddenly rose clear and strong, so that his prophesy was heard not only by those who crowded around his pallet, but by those who waited outside the tent. Among these was an overseer lingering somewhat nervously on the farthest edges of the crowd, so that he could bear news of Kuntan's passing to those who claimed to own the old priest's flesh.

Kuntan expired before anyone could beg him to interpret the precise meaning of those four lines, but no one doubted that his dying lips had shaped a true prophesy. Kuntan had lived faithful to the blood that ran in his veins, being priest where he could not be chief, giving wise counsel though he could not grant any reward or gift.

The Ootoi were a conquered people, their lands subsumed into the territory of the Gharebi who had defeated them in war. The Ootoi's ways and traditions had been preserved only because they were not too unlike the ways and traditions of the Gharebi who now called themselves "masters" and the conquered people "slaves." Indeed, the Ootoi and the Gharebi were not unalike in other ways, being similar in coloring and build—but slave and free are states so vastly different that it is easy to be blind to similarities.

So it was that no one who heard Kuntan's dying words denied that they expressed a true seeing, but how that true seeing was interpreted varied greatly depending on whether you were of the conquered or the conquerors.

The enslaved heard in these dying words of their last priest of the ruling line a reason for hope. They concentrated on the "when" that began each of the first three lines. If there were endless whispered debates as to how the various conditions were to be interpreted, this did not undermine the belief that someday, somehow, the Ootoi would once again ride beneath the wide open skies as a free people. It was a matter of "when" not "if," and this single word meant everything.

The overseer was trembling from his hair to his bootlaces when he repeated Kuntan's last words to his patrons. He remembered them perfectly, and recited them with care, with not a single deviation from the original. To the overseer's surprise, for he had seen the ripples of rebellion on many a slave's face before it was stilled to impassivity, those who heard his report did not find in it a reason for fear.

"We thought there would be worse," said a slim, immortal-seeming mage.

"I thought the old bastard would incite them to riot," said his even more powerful consort. "That would be one way for the self-aggrandizing fool to gain blood offerings for his grave."

"Fever-ranting rather than true prophesy," suggested a rich woman of considerable civil influence, but this statement was rebuked by her fellows.

"It was true enough prophesy," replied a high-ranking priest, "for Kuntan was a faithful servant of the gods. There is no possible reason that the slaves will find hope in those words. How can a hazelnut grow into an oak? How can an oak transform into a ram?"

"I suppose a ram could give forth a flood," said a powerful war leader with a coarse laugh, "if it peed enough."

The priest shook his head reprovingly. "It is not good to speak lightly of the words of the gods, especially as the gods have granted us such a blessing in this prophesy. They have assured us that the Ootoi will never be freed, for these are conditions impossible to meet."

The warlord, superstitious as are all who trust themselves to the battlefield, bent his head in apology and begged the priest's forgiveness. If he paid a large sum to the temple to erase his impiety from the ears of the gods, that is another story.

So events progressed for many years, until most who had heard Kuntan speak his prophesy were dead, and even the children who had heard the words taken so variously as reason for hope or reason for despair were old and bent and gray.

Although they had conquered cities, the Gharebi were still at heart a nomadic people. Their ways, rites, and customs were rooted in the days when they had driven their herds from grazing area to grazing area, using the accumulated wisdom of many generations to survive the changing temperaments of each season.

The coming of the great warlord and his years of conquest had changed this. Now there were slaves to tend the flocks and herds, to plant the seasonal crops, and to labor over the hundreds of repetitious, filthy, and demeaning chores that were the lot of any society, but perhaps were even more repetitious and filthy when a people chooses to always be on the move.

The Gharebi concentrated on the finer arts. Their children became warriors, priests, or artisans. They studied the intricacies of magic or commerce. The most honored knew the stud lines of hundreds of horses and how to detect in even the most knobby-kneed foal a warhorse of great promise. Horses remained central to the lives of the Gharebi, as they had been in the days when the Gharebi relied upon them not only for transport, but for meat and drink and shelter.

One of the great divides between the masters and the slaves was that the slaves were not permitted to ride. Slaves were permitted to tend the herds. Indeed, a job involved with the care of the horse herds was considered among the greatest of honors, almost as good as being free. However, if a slave was found astride a horse, no matter how valuable the slave and how swaybacked and inconsequential the horse, that slave would be instantly condemned to death—and though the condemnation was instant, the death itself was very slow, very public, and horribly painful.

The slaves were permitted dogs to drag their scant goods from place to place, and the punishments if one of those dogs should harm a master was such that the dogs all cringed at the very sound of horse hooves. So it was cringing and whining that heralded the coming of a small group of Gharebi into an isolated slave encampment one foul and rainy night when spring had but one pale hoof in the world and seemed about to pull back and permit winter a last good run.

"Hie there! Hie there!" came a commanding cry from a dark shadow upon the darker bulk of a dancing, nervous horse. "Service here and be quick about it!"

Not even stopping to grab her cloak against the rain, Narjin rushed out of the smoky snugness of the round-domed tent in which she had sat up nearly alone after a very long and trying day, followed by an even longer and more trying night. Almost everyone else in her extended family group was resting in other tents, the squat, round shapes gathered in a half-circle, their backs to the icy wind.

At the master's cry every adult and a few of the older children spilled forth. If one did not immediately rush forth from Narjin's tent, there was good reason.

"Hie there!" came the call again. The voice was male and deep. To Narjin's experienced ear, it also held a touch of apprehension. She wondered why.

Even the least of the masters could command any slave. The penalties if the slaves did not assist with eagerness and alacrity were so severe that only fools refused. None of Narjin's clan were fools.

Narjin's oldest son reached for the bridle of the speaker's horse, quieting the nervous animal with soft-voiced words. Others of the clan were bringing forth lit lamps. The children were chivvying back the dogs. However, notably, it was left to Narjin to speak.

"We are here, Master," she said. "How may we serve you best?"

"Shelter, clan-mother," the master said promptly, "and hot food. The storm came up on us unexpectedly, and we cannot make our destination this night."

One of Narjin's daughters brought a lantern near, and by its light Narjin could see the master better. He was well built, and balanced astride his dancing steed with a thoughtless ease that bespoke many hours in the saddle: warrior or priest, Narjin guessed, for he had not the slightly out-of-focus expression of the mage. His companions were three, two other men and a woman. One man managed a string of packhorses, the other rode protectively close to the woman, so close that it was evident that he was supporting her upon her horse.

It was hard to be sure, given the darkness and the sleeting rain that made the lantern flames flicker and hiss, but Narjin guessed that none of these masters were past their second decade. Indeed, they seemed to be on the younger edge of that divide.

"Shelter you shall have, masters," Narjin replied promptly. She spoke to the inhabitants of two of the larger tents. "Make your homes clear for the masters."

For the first time, the light caught the features of the daughter who held the lantern and Narjin must hold back surprise. It was Dmaalyn, the one she had thought unlikely to come forth, on this night of all nights, but there she stood.

"Dmaalyn," Narjin said to her daughter, "give me the lantern and go move the cook pot close to the fire. The masters must have hot food and drink. The rest of you get those tents cleared and swept. You, my older son, come help with the horses."

Her children and their families turned to obey. No one questioned why Narjin herself did not give over her tent, though it was among the largest. They knew she must have good reason—for she led them not only by reason of being their mother, but by being very wise.

Narjin hoped that the masters would not realize that they had not been given the clan leader's tent as they might expect. She also hoped that these were not among those who coddled their horses. If so, all her children might find themselves sleeping with no more shelter than the hides they stretched to give some cover to the biggest of the dogs. Were that the case, not all would live through the night—and one surely would die.

But the warlord on the lead horse did not make this request. Instead, he turned back and spoke to the man who still supported the woman.

"How is Telari?" the warlord said.

"Poorly," the man replied, trying hard for the pragmatic bluntness so favored by the Gharebi and failing to conceal his concern. "Her time is upon her."

Narjin stiffened, knowing she must pretend not to be eavesdropping. Happily, the warlord did not force her to maintain the charade.

"Clan-mother," he said, "my younger brother's wife is expecting her first. Have you any among you skilled in midwifery?"

"I have delivered many babies," Narjin replied

evenly, "and given birth to a good number myself—
many of whom stand here waiting to serve."

"Take charge, then," the warlord said.

Narjin resisted an urge to press her hands to her
face and keen in despair. She knew too well the penalties were she not to bring this child forth and preserve
the mother as well. Not just her life, but quite possibly
the lives of every slave here would be forfeit. Even the
dogs would die, for slaves paid a heavy toll were a
master to die when in their keeping.

"I will do my best," Narjin said, "but, master, this
is a woman's mystery. Is there another woman among
your number?"

"None," the warlord replied.

"Then give me my daughter, Dmaalyn, to assist me.
My other daughters and my sons will make you comfortable with the best of what we have to offer."

The warlord nodded, swinging himself down from
his saddle. Although the move was practiced, still
there was a stiffness to the motion that said without
words that these four might have been riding since the
previous dawn.

Narjin did not bother to wonder. Her place was with
the pregnant woman, and to her she now went. The
man with the pack string was giving orders to some
of her clan. Narjin was pleased to hear that he was
ordering the horses tied in the shelter of the trees. It
seemed that these were among the harder living of the
Gharebi—a good thing for her people, but probably a
bad thing for the pregnant mother and her unborn
child.

Dmaalyn came silently to help her mother. When
she took back the lantern so that Narjin might have
both hands free to assist the pregnant woman, Narjin
saw how drawn was her daughter's face. Dmaalyn
needed no explanation of what was at stake here.

The woman's husband had gotten her down from her horse, and was holding her cradled in his arms.

"Where, clan-mother?" he asked, his terseness more from worry than from rudeness.

"That tent," Narjin said. "Carry her in, then leave us."

The man looked as if he might protest, but again Narjin had reason to be grateful to the traditionalism of these particular Gharebi. Just as they did not coddle their horses, they did not coddle themselves. A woman was expected to bear her children with the minimum amount of fuss. The young man obeyed, carrying his wife to the tent and ducking through the door flap that Dmaalyn held open.

Don't let him look too deeply into the shadows! Narjin prayed silently. *Shadows, make no noise!*

The gods must have heard her, for the young husband put down his burden on Narjin's own pallet near the fire and with a curt nod that was an extreme politeness from master to slave promptly left the tent.

"I have water heating," Dmaalyn said, the first words she had spoken since the masters' arrival. "It had not all cooled from before."

"Good," Narjin replied, keeping her voice low. The pregnant woman seemed at best semiconscious, but caring about what was said around the masters was a ingrained habit. "Step out. Make excuse that you are fetching me some herbs, tell our kinfolk to make sure that no one speaks of the other events of this night. The masters are superstitious and might think we have brought on their disaster."

Dmaalyn nodded and padded away. She walked slowly and stiffly, but without undue sound. While waiting for Dmaalyn to return, Narjin began removing the nearly unconscious pregnant woman's wet outer things, so taking her first good look at her patient.

The mistress was young, but not too young to be woman rather than girl, as the swelling of her belly testified. Her golden-brown skin was unlined, except near the eyes where there were the beginnings of crow's feet.

Too much squinting into the sun, Narjin thought. *A warrior, then, maybe a sun's acolyte, but I think a warrior.*

Narjin checked and found calluses on hand and fingers, calluses that testified to hours spent pulling a bowstring. She tested and found muscles tight and strong along legs and thighs. At Narjin's touch, the pregnant woman opened her eyes to narrow slits, showing dilated pupils and irises almost as dark. She parted full lips, giving forth a gasp of pain as eloquent as the scream she clearly swallowed.

"I am Narjin, mistress," the slave said, ducking her head respectfully. "Your man and his companions brought you here. They are being tended to in other tents of my clan."

"Good," the young woman spoke with astonishing clarity given her evident pain and exhaustion. "Keep them there."

"This is a woman's mystery," Narjin assured her. "The men will keep away lest they anger the gods."

"Yes." The faintest of smiles lifted the corners of the woman's mouth. "We bleed, we scream. Out of pain we bring life into the world. Best these are mysteries to men or they might forget their own much vaunted courage."

The words were part of an old litany, twisted to irony. Narjin revised her estimate of the young woman. Acolyte, perhaps, dedicated to the Moon. It would explain the bow marks and the riding. Many of the Moon's acolytes began as warriors, then were ordained later.

"Mistress," Narjin said. "May I continue undressing you? Your clothes are damp and you might catch a chill."

"I place myself in your hands," the woman replied, her words both permission and veiled threat. Then she softened. "Mistress I am, but call me Telari. You're going to be looking up my crotch. It only seems fair that you have my name."

"Yes, mistress," Narjin said, then added in response to Telari's sternly in-drawn breath, "Telari."

"Good. Now as you undress me, distract me. Where am I?"

"You are in the tents of Clan Narjin," Narjin replied. "We are to prepare the grounds for planting."

Even before the days of the conquering warlord such had been done, by both the Gharebi and the then free Ootoi. Pockets of fast-growing crops were sown where the summer rains would run off and water them. As soon as late summer began to dry the lushness of the plains, all but a few of the people would resume wandering, so that the grasses were not overgrazed. A few would remain to make sure the fields did not become grazing for wild creatures.

Artisans often remained with them to work on projects that needed stability rather than the jouncing of carts. Any slave clan chosen to go ahead and sow a field had been given a position of great responsibility, and, as such, one of great risk, for the masters punished heavily any perceived infraction.

Narjin had enjoyed such duties in the past because for a few weeks—at least until the artisans arrived—her family could pretend to be free Ootoi and not merely slaves. Now she wished with all her heart for the safety of attachment to some master's train.

"Planting," Telari said, trying to hide her pain when a contraction rippled her belly and almost succeeding.

"We were going to meet the herds of my husband's father, so the horses and I could foal together. My brother-in-law swore he knew how to read the stars and find our way."

Narjin didn't need further explanation. The young warlord had neglected to calculate that spring and winter were still dueling for position. It is impossible to read the stars when the skies are cloudy. Doubtless, the young husband had wanted the lucky omen of having his first child born when the horses were dropping their foals. It was not unheard of for a generous clan leader to gift the newborn child with all the horses born on that same day, an inheritance well worth taking a risk for among a people who still counted horses above gold.

But it had all gone wrong for Telari and her husband—and for all Narjin's people as well.

Telari seemed to have dropped off, not so much to sleep as into a daze of pain. As Narjin removed the remainder of the mistress' clothing, she risked a glance into the very shadows she had been so grateful for earlier. A cradle rested there, near enough to the fire to gather heat, but away from the worst of the smoke. As if sensing the gaze upon it, there came the mewing noise of a baby on the verge of waking. Narjin rose, poised to go to the cradle, but the sound died to sleeping silence.

"What did you say?" Telari asked. Her tone was a touch querulous, but she was doing a marvelous job of pretending she wasn't in pain.

"I said nothing," Narjin replied honestly, sinking back down and tucking a heavy blanket over her now naked patient. "You must have heard the musicians tuning. Has your water broken?"

"Hours ago," Telari said, "but there was nowhere for us to stop. The men told me to hold on, that we couldn't be far from my father-in-law's camp, and so I did."

The baby's waiting so long after waters that guarded the womb had been breached wasn't good, but Narjin didn't say anything. Either Telari already knew, in which case the repetition would just intensify any fears she had for her unborn child, or she didn't, in which case there was no need to make her more afraid than she was already.

Narjin continued her physical inspection, and did not like what she was finding. "What have you taken for the pain?"

"Nothing," Telari said with fierce pride.

Narjin didn't see any wisdom in this, not when there were gentle herbs that could ease the edge of the pain without causing any harm to the child, but she said nothing. It was not her place to question what the masters did, only to repair the damage if they decided wrongly—and to pay the price of their anger if she failed.

"Could you keep down some broth? My daughter should be returning with some soon."

"I can try."

When Dmaalyn brought the broth, Narjin slipped in some herbs she already had prepared. If Telari suspected anything, she was too wise to comment. There is no cowardice involved in being tricked. Soon, as Narjin had hoped, Telari slipped off into sleep.

Motioning for Dmaalyn to step back to where they could watch and talk without wakening Telari, Narjin spoke softly, "How are you?"

"Frightened," Dmaalyn replied honestly. She bent and lifted her swaddled baby from the cradle and gave the softly fussing child her nipple. "Shall the infant and I go from here into another tent?"

"It might be wisest if you stay," Narjin answered.

"It is best if the masters do not know we have had a birth here tonight—and this is the one tent the men will not enter. From what I can tell, they are traditionals, and they may well be superstitious enough to believe that your labor cried out and awoke it in this other."

"And she? She looks so ill. Will she live through it?"

"I don't know . . ." Narjin admitted. "Her sinews are stitched tight from pain and too much riding. Her muscles have learned to bind, but not to loose. Still, there is something in this Telari that gives me hope."

"We must hope," Dmaalyn said, looking down at the red, wrinkled features of her sleeping baby. "If the mistress dies, so do we all."

And Narjin knew those words were a true prophesy—as true as that of Kuntan, for the truest prophesies always came from one who stood at the border over which life crosses. She squeezed her daughter's hand, then went back to her patient.

With Narjin's care and Telari's fierce determination, the baby came at dawn. Her mother's screams blended with the ritual songs the Ootoi had always sung at a birth. It was said that the songs kept the demons away. Narjin had never known what to believe. Certainly in all her confinements she had never so much as sensed a demon—but maybe that was because the songs had worked.

Maybe, though, the songs were to permit the birthing mother to feel free to scream, comforted in the knowledge no one would hear. Telari did scream, walking about, leaning on Narjin's arm, pulling hard on a rope suspended from the tent's most solid beam, fighting to learn how to loose—a thing that came easier for her when Narjin told her to remember that an arrow pulled back on the string is nothing until it is released.

After the infant came, the three Gharebi men all wanted to see Telari, but the young mother took advantage of her new eminence to refuse. She sent word to her husband that she needed to rest, and ordered Narjin to carry out the child for them to see. It was a girl child, sound in every limb, and Narjin was touched at the new father's delight.

When Narjin brought the child back inside, Telari gave her infant suck, then passed into deep and blessedly painless sleep. Narjin cleaned the baby, then wrapped it in swaddling intended for her own granddaughter's care. She set the newborn in the cradle rather than disturb Telari's sleep.

Telari would need that sleep. Already Narjin had heard from one of her sons that the storm had broken and the men planned to ride on later this day. The young warlord had ridden out with the first light and was now certain he could find his father's herds before dark. Telari would not refuse to go with them—not to remain with slaves. New mother though she was, there was too much warrior in her to give in. Narjin would wrap Telari's lower parts tightly, and warn her against pushing on if bleeding began. It was all she could do.

Narjin took a campstool and sat staring down at the infant's wrinkled nutmeat of a face, one hand gently rocking the cradle. Despite the difficulties of her mother's labor, Telari's baby was sound. Indeed, the newborn infant looked much as Dmaalyn's baby had at the conclusion of her mother's much gentler labor—head unsqueezed, features undistorted. Two girl children, born on the same night, to the same midwife. Two girl children, so much alike, but different in one crucial thing: one slave, one free.

A soft sound of cloth shaking down broke Narjin

from her reverie. Dmaalyn had emerged from the curtained alcove at the back of the tent wherein she had retreated with her child when Telari's labor had become intense. Her own baby was cradled in her arms. Her gait as she walked over to join her mother wordlessly showed the soreness she, like Telari, was too proud to admit to feeling

"Like little red nutmeats," Dmaalyn said softly, looking at the two wrinkled faces, "as alike as twin lambs."

Her voice was raw with love. It was a note that Narjin only heard in the voices of new mothers still half-crazed with the wonder of having brought forth new life, bonding heart to heart, soul to soul with the child they cradled in their arms as they had so recently in their wombs. It was strongest in first-time mothers, for they had no memories of long nights, illness, sorrows, and disappointments to blunt that wonder.

It was in this wonder voice still that Dmaalyn spoke, shocking Narjin with her words "So you know what we must do, don't you, Mother?"

Narjin studied her, knowing her own thoughts, but knowing this must come from Dmaalyn, alone and without coercion.

Eyes wet, Dmaalyn recited softly, " 'When from a hazelnut comes forth an oak.' I think we must plant that oak, Mother."

Without another word, though tears streamed down her face, Dmaalyn bent and changed her own daughter for the baby in the cradle. There was a frozen moment of time as if the gods themselves held their breaths, then it was broken by the jingling of harness from without.

Dmaalyn fled with Telari's child to the curtained alcove in the back of the tent as the door flap rose. The young warlord and Telari's husband strode in.

The husband spared a glance for the child that rested in the cradle, but his eyes were on Telari's face as he knelt by her side.

"Can you ride?" he asked.

"Of course," Telari said. "What time is it now? Two fingers past dawn? Wasn't I told I gave birth as the sun just peered above the horizon? Surely I can ride."

Narjin heard the sarcasm in Telari's voice, but the two men, caught in their eagerness to depart, seemed immune to any nuance.

"Good," was all the husband said. "Your horse is ready for you."

"Narjin," Telari said, propping herself up on her elbows, and from there rolling to her feet, "is my daughter ready for travel?"

"Clean and swaddled," Narjin said, lifting the child from the cradle. "So we might pray for her, may I ask, Mistress, what will you call her?"

Telari smiled. "She was born with the sunrise, so I thought to call her Andrasta—Dawn Rider in the old speech."

"A pretty name," Narjin agreed, pleased with the omens.

A far prettier name, she thought, watching the masters ride away, bearing her granddaughter with them, *than Hazelnut, but what a hazel she must be, if someday she is to grow into an oak tree.*

CLIMB, SAID THE CROW

Brooks Peck

Brooks Peck has been in love with the fantastic ever since he stole his sister's copy of Robert Heinlein's *Time for the Stars*. In 1995, he helped found Science Fiction Weekly, the first professional SF news and review Web site. He currently on the curatorial staff of the Science Fiction Museum and Hall of Fame in Seattle.

JON HAULED himself onto the summit of the mesa in the early afternoon. He rolled onto his back in the dust, his arm and leg muscles quivering, his heart thudding. It had been a harder climb than he'd expected. The black volcanic rock grew hot under the glaring sun, and heated air swept up the side of the mesa, making his eyes water and sting. It hadn't helped that he'd sliced open his water bag on a knife-sharp spine a quarter of the way up.

Still, here he was, and he could relax for a time in his favorite place—not this mesa in particular, but any high place. Away from the cults, the plagues, the floods of yellow muck, and the Wardens.

A crow landed on a nearby rock and gazed at him. Jon stared back, content to breathe and rest.

"You're a pretty good climber," said the crow. In

his exhausted state, this didn't seem strange to Jon. "But the best climber of all is the one who can scale the Avatnu cliffs."

"Never heard of them." Jon wasn't sure if he actually spoke aloud.

"They are the highest cliffs in the world," said the crow. "Climb them, if you dare." It took wing in a burst, fanning Jon's face with warm air.

Two months later, Jon clutched the side of the rowboat he'd stolen, puking up the last of his breakfast—also stolen. He rinsed his mouth with seawater, then staggered forward to tie the boat to a rock wedged in a tumble of boulders at the base of the cliff.

The Avatnu cliffs capped a narrow peninsula that poked like a crooked finger into a bay called Regret. The rock was blood-red at the base where the ocean wet it. Alternating bands of reddish brown and gray rose up until they blended into one color. Far taller than the mesa, the cliffs stood at least five hundred elbows high. Jon couldn't wait to get on it.

At first it had appeared that no such place as the Avatnu cliffs existed, that it was just nonsense bubbled up from his overheated brain. No one he knew had heard of them. Most people, though, didn't know the name of the town after next. There were no books or maps left in his town—they had all been destroyed years ago—so Jon walked three weeks to the provincial capital. He wandered the market until he noticed a chandler wrapping his wares in printed pages. That night Jon broke into the man's workshop. In a stack of musty volumes awaiting the knife, he found a copy of Twillard's *Cartographic Appendix to Motion*. One of the folios showed an Avatnu Point in the Northwest Province. Jon shipped out as a volunteer on a northbound slave transport the next day.

On the voyage he learned to cook for and clean up after 276 weeping, quarreling, complaining, and terrified children. He learned that some people—himself—never get their sea legs. He learned to eat fish, which he had never had before.

Last night, he had camped in a ravine out of sight of the Capital Road. A handful of vagabonds—outlaws and escapees—shared his fire. "Tomorrow I'm going to climb the Avatnu cliffs," Jon told them, because he thought he should inform someone first, before the event. The tramps laughed and scoffed.

"Even if you could climb the cliffs that no spider would dare," said a former schoolteacher, waving a smoldering blunt of sweetweed, "why would you?"

"A crow suggested it," Jon said.

The teacher shook his head. "Sweet talk."

Jon stood on a boulder and scanned the cliff. The lower face looked sheer, smooth and impossible to climb, but Jon let his gaze roam across the rock at random, waiting. Waves smacked and splooshed around the boulder. In time, the cliff began to reveal its secrets. He could start by resting his left foot *there,* on a slender ledge. That would enable him to reach a bump the size of a biscuit *there.* . . . Without deciding to start, he was climbing. He never hurried, settling into a routine of reading the cliff, reaching a hand or moving a foot, pulling up, and pausing again to study what lay ahead.

Soon he got stuck. Eroded at the base by the ocean, the cliff arched out over Jon's head, so he had to hold on tightly with his fingers and toes. He was right below an overhang, and from this angle he couldn't spot any fresh handholds. He thought he might have to climb down and try another route, but he decided to take a rest first, hanging free by one hand and letting his other limbs relax. The little stolen boat bobbed on the swells below him.

Jon swung onto the cliff again, reached up and groped above the lip of the overhang. He felt a crack that he could jam his hand into, and he heaved himself up hard. He scrabbled at the stone with his free hand, found a hold, and dragged his body halfway over the lip of the outcropping. Then he swung a knee up, squirmed higher, and finally planted both feet on the lip. The cliff slanted inward here, enough that he could lean against it and rest. He smiled, pleased with this small success.

A flutter of wings, and a crow swooped in to perch near him on the cliff. Jon smiled again—this was a positive omen.

"Hey, man," the crow said. "I see you made it."

Jon clutched the cliff harder. You need more air, he told himself. The crow's not talking.

The crow cocked its head, fixing him with its solid black eye. "Hello? Are you simple?" Its voice was rough and guttural.

"Ah, no," Jon answered.

"Good. How's it going?"

"What?"

The crow jumped from its perch, flapping madly, and landed on Jon's shoulder with a thud. *"How's it going?"* it screamed in his ear.

"Fine! Get off me!"

"Are you. Hard. Of hearing?" the crow screamed. *"No."*

"Good." The crow walked across his shoulders to the other side. "Good for you."

Jon briefly wondered if he should fight it off. Many unnatural evils stalked the world, after all. But this crow didn't seem malevolent. Besides, it had led him here, to the climb of a lifetime, and he was grateful.

"This your food?" the crow asked, pecking the satchel Jon had slung over his shoulder.

"Yes. Would you like some?"

"No. What have you got?"

"Some berries."

"Berries! Is that it? You're going to get hungry."

"I'll get to the top by this afternoon, find food then."

"This afternoon?" The crow hopped back to his other shoulder and looked up. "You think that's the top there?" It bobbed its head, pointing with its beak. "That's haze. The top's twice as high as that."

Jon looked up. "Oh. Well."

"You're not very well prepared, are you? You've got hardly any food or water, no rope—how will you sleep tonight? You're barefoot, by the gods. No, you're not the right man for the job. Better just climb down now while you still can. Look how scrawny you are. This isn't a game, you know. Stop climbing." The crow pecked Jon's shoulder. "Go home."

"No."

"No? Come on, you're not going to make it. Be realistic." The crow leaned close to his ear and whispered, "Are you planning to commit suicide?"

"What? No! I haven't got any money for food or rope, and if I try to steal any more I could get caught. Then I'll never make it back here. I'm here now, and I'm climbing this cliff *now*. I'm going to climb and keep climbing until I get to the top."

The crow stepped back to look Jon in the eye. "Glad to hear it," it said. "Your boat got loose anyway. I'm kidding—don't look down! All right, good luck, monkey."

"Wait, why did you bring me here?"

"You brought yourself here." The crow leaped off his shoulder and glided downward.

"What are you?" Jon yelled.

"I'm a crow!" it cawed, wheeling in the air. "A crow, a crow, a crow!"

Jon made steady progress during the morning, although for a while thoughts of the crow distracted him. He wondered how it could talk, and why it talked to him. But he soon dropped into the reverie of the climb. This was what he loved most about climbing, when the world narrowed to himself and the rock, and the boundary between the two became indistinct. He didn't think about how high he was; he didn't think about how far he had to go.

Until the crow returned, announcing its arrival with a shrill "Coming at you!" It landed on Jon's head, talons scratching his scalp as it flapped its wings to get balanced. "How's it going?"

"Ow. Fine. Could you not do that?"

"Sorry." The crow hopped onto his shoulder. There was a dusty smell in its feathers, and the tang of the ocean. "The rock looks kind of loose here," the crow observed.

"I know. This orange stuff is more crumbly. Easier to climb, though."

"Oh. Okay."

The crow didn't appear to be going anywhere, so Jon started upward again, aware of its slight weight. "Do you have a name?" he asked.

"Yes."

"Well, what—"

"I want to tell you a story. Help pass the time, okay?"

"Um, all right."

"Good. Okay, there was this guy. Wait, I should start earlier. A long time ago—well, not that long ago. Depends on how you look at it. Ha!" It cackled suddenly with laughter, raising its wings and puffing out its feathers. "Sorry, I just remembered something funny. Anyway, once there were these islands clustered in the ocean, and together they made up the whole world. The people on the islands never got along. They raided other islands, stole livestock and slaves, burned towns. Their victims would get angry and go attack the people who attacked them, or just attack someone weaker. Life in those days was chaotic and violent.

"In time, a leader arose on one of the islands. People called her the Navigator for two reasons: First, because she studied the stars, the winds, and the currents everywhere, and she wrote it all down in a book called *Motion,* a guide to sailing the whole world. Second, she built a huge fleet of ships, sailed out to the islands around hers, and convinced them to form a league of islands, all working together to their mutual prosperity. Some islands didn't want any part of it and, frankly, the Navigator conquered them by force, I won't deny it. The league grew. By the end of her lifetime, the whole world was like one island, and everyone lived together peacefully."

"I've heard this story," Jon said.

"Quiet. The Navigator's descendants ruled the world-kingdom after she died. There was no war or fighting for over two hundred years. But then a strange ship sailed over the horizon from the empty sea—"

A stone rolled out from under Jon's left foot. He dropped with a lurch, lost his left-hand grip and spun around with his back to the cliff. The crow leaped away. The sea below and the mountains across the

bay spun through Jon's vision. Pain stabbed his right
wrist, but he hung on. He scrabbled at the crumbling
gravel with one foot—the other found only air.

Grunting, Jon twisted back around to face the cliff.
More loose rock pattered over his feet. He fumbled
for a second handhold, lost the other, and skidded
down the cliff. His feet hit a ledge too hard, and he
teetered backward.

Wham. Something slammed him between the shoulder blades, and he smacked face first into the wall of
rock. Instinctively, he grabbed the cliff and held tight.
He heard a flurry of wings: the crow—it hit him again,
this time in the neck. "Okay!" Jon shouted. "I'm
okay—whoa!" He looked over his shoulder and almost got a face full of crow.

The crow flapped to a perch above him. It was pant-
ing as hard as he was. "Be more careful!" it cried.
"What's wrong with you? I thought you were good
at this."

"It was an accident."

"You should have tested that rock better."

"I *know.*" He was trembling.

"Then why didn't you? You only get one chance
at this."

"I was distracted by you talking so much."

"Now it's my fault? I see. Well, there's no need to
thank me for saving your life, I'm sure." It took off.

"No, wait!" Jon called, but the crow disappeared
around the curve of the cliff.

By midday Jon could see that the cliff did indeed
reach much higher than he'd realized. It also became
more fractured, broken into slabs like giant bricks.
Each block overhung the one below it by an elbow or
two, so Jon had to climb upside down to cross the
boundaries. At each one, he found himself dangling

farther out over the ocean. His shoulders started to
feel tight and sore, his stomach empty. He rested
more often.

During one rest, as he leaned with his arms along
a hand-wide ledge, he heard a familiar flapping. The
crow swooped onto the ledge, hopped a few times, and
flung down a silver fish. "Got that for you," it said.

"Oh. Thanks. You didn't have to do that."

"Sure I did. If you don't eat something more than
berries, you'll pass out and take the quick way down."

Balancing on one elbow, Jon picked up the fish,
sniffed it.

"It hasn't been dead very long," the crow said.

"You didn't catch it?"

"Do I look like a pelican?"

"Has this been in your mouth?"

"Crows are very clean animals."

"You eat carrion."

"Shut up!"

"Sorry, sorry. I do appreciate it."

Jon split the fish open with his thumbs, tried a small
bite, and found it tasted good. Maybe hunger made it
so, but he didn't care.

"Now I'll tell you the rest of the story," the crow
said.

"I know what happens," Jon said around a mouthful
of fish.

"Maybe, maybe not. Let's see. We talked about the
islands, the bad times, the Navigator, and the good
times. Okay, so one day not so very long ago, a
strange ship sailed over the horizon from the empty
sea. It was bigger than three of the largest ships ever
built, with red sails, and a pair of shut eyes painted
on the prow. Even though it was so big, there was no
crew on board. The ship's sails raised and lowered
themselves. The wheel turned with no hand on it. The

ship sailed through the outer islands to the capital city of the world. It came to a dock, and a single man disembarked."

"The Magus."

"Yes, the Magus. He hadn't taken two steps when his ship burst into flames and in minutes burned to the waterline. Now some say the Magus looked like an old man who walked with a stick and wore mourning clothes. Others tell it he was young, handsome, with golden robes and a white silk turban. He walked up the quay and through the harbor. The ground boiled where he walked, vomiting up insects and vermin. These creatures followed the Magus, hopping, writhing and scuttling. And as they scuttled, they grew. They grew as big as people, or bigger, with spikes, thorny shells and cutting blades on their limbs. The Magus walked through the capital at the head of an ever-growing army. When he reached the palace, the seneschal blocked his path. The Magus breathed on him, transformed him into a worm and crushed him underfoot. Then the Magus passed through every room of the palace. He turned cooks into rats, maids into cockroaches; he turned the footmen into voles, the honor guard into moths. At last, he found the royal family hiding in a secret room. He killed the king and queen and hung their heads by their hair from the gate. As for the prince and princess, no one knows what happened to them."

Jon sucked the last bits of moisture off a fishbone. "Then came the Edicts," he said. "And the massacre of Velm, and the compulsory child service, and the Wardens. Bird, this is my history, why are you telling it to me?"

"You know it all, do you?"

"Older people sometimes tell the stories, when there aren't any Wardens around."

"Did they tell you that in the southern islands it has started to snow acid?"

"No."

"Did they tell you that not all the children are put into service anymore? Sometimes one of the ships sails far from shore and the children are put to the knife during a midnight ritual. Did they tell you that the Magus is only an advance scout? He is the Opener of Doors for the smoke gods, the ones our blood gods banished after the creation of the world. He's bringing them back to feast on suffering."

Jon felt the familiar rising up of panic that came every time he thought about the future under the Magus. "I better get moving," he said. "Thanks again for the fish. Do you want this?" He put the fish's head on the ledge.

"Okay." The crow scrutinized the head, poked at it.

"Sorry I got mad at you before."

"Let's not talk about it."

"I was scared."

"Me too."

The crow pecked at the fish head, pushing it along until it pitched off the ledge. "Son of a bitch! What I wouldn't give for hands." It looked up at the sky, then back at Jon. "There's a storm coming, and it'll be dark in a few hours. Keep working a little left as you go and you'll come to a crevice where you can spend the night. "

"Can I ask you something?"

"No." The crow stepped off the ledge and dived away.

Jon pushed himself after that, worried about being caught on the cliff in the rain. Dark clouds boiled over the mountains and covered the sun. He couldn't get into his climbing rhythm and he fretted over each move, anxious, aware of how high he was. How long would it take to hit the ground from here? Three seconds? Four? Plenty of time to feel the wind rushing past and to scream and to cringe in anticipation of the terrible impact.

He shook his head, trying to concentrate. But he was having trouble making out the details of the stone. He closed his eyes, looked again. No better. It was getting dark.

He kept on, relying more and more on touch. Soon the last glow of evening vanished, and Jon was clinging to a cliff face in the dark. Cold raindrops pattered his back. *Next time,* he thought, *don't listen to the talking bird.*

"Crow!" he yelled. "Hey, you nosy crow, where are you?" Rising wind rattled along the cliff. *"Crow!"* he yelled again. Suddenly a blacker shadow rushed at his face. The crow landed on his shoulder and smacked his head with its wing.

"Shut up," it hissed. "Be quiet, already."

"Why?"

"You're disturbing the tranquillity of nature."

"There's nothing natural up here. Certainly not you."

"Be quiet or I'll give you such a pecking. Now what's the matter?"

"I'm stuck."

"Hmm. And why should I care?"

"Oh, come on, it's obvious you want me to get to the top of these cliffs for some reason. Help me."

"Ask nice."

"Please. How far am I from the crevice?"

"A ways. Reach up with your left hand . . . over a little . . . there, can you hold on to that bit?"

"Yes. Now my right foot."

"Ah, there's nothing really."

CLIMB, SAID THE CROW 137

"What if I stretch up on my toes, can I reach anything with my other hand?"

"Maybe. Try straight above your head."

It felt like the middle of the night when Jon finally pulled himself into a crack in the stone barely wide enough to wedge into sideways. He slumped with his cheek against the rock, soaked from the sheeting rain, his hands and feet aching with chill. His muscles burned, and he'd never been so tired. After a while, the crow returned—he hadn't noticed it leave—and put a small beach crab into his hand. Jon pulled off the legs and sucked out the meat. The crow climbed onto his shoulder, turned around twice and hunkered down, ruffling out its feathers. It was surprisingly warm against his cheek.

"Sleep," the crow whispered, "and in the morning I'll tell you the rest of the story."

"There's more?"

"Yes. At least I hope so."

Jon woke unwillingly, dragged from sleep by the crow tapping the side of his head. It was still dark. "Too early," Jon mumbled.

"Dawn soon," the crow said. "You've got a lot to do."

That brought Jon awake. "What? What do I have to do?"

"Well . . . Uh, okay, well."

"Tell me."

"I'm telling. Look, it's been thirty-eight years since the coming of the Magus—I know, you already know. But in the last few years he's been seen less and less. He keeps secluded at his summer retreat."

"How do you know that?"

"I have friends in high places. They're birds. Get it—birds? High places?"

"I get it already."

"Okay, fine. I'm just trying to break this to you easy."

"Break *what?*"

"Shush. What few seers are left say that the Magus is preparing for the real invasion, when he'll release the smoke gods into our world. And when that happens, it will make the current situation seem like a sunny day at the Festival of Free Beer and Sex. Agony and despair sustain the smoke gods, and they will sow vile horrors in order to reap the richest crop of suffering. Nature will become unbound and everyone will have eternal life—in eternal torment. This is why there are so few seers anymore. Most have committed suicide already.

"Now comes the important part," the crow said. "The Magus' summer retreat is here, built into the top of the Avatnu cliffs. The peninsula is blocked by a wall and troop garrisons line the road leading to the fortress. But no one guards the cliffs because they are considered the perfect natural protection. We know better, though. You can make it to the top. Actually, you don't even have to get that far—the Magus' chamber is close above us. You can climb right in his window."

Jon stared at the crow in the predawn light. "Bird, swear to me you're telling the truth. Swear to me I can strike against him."

"I am, and you can."

"Then tell me how to kill him."

Half an hour later, Jon leaned back and saw rows of windows dotting the cliff top. They marked the chambers and corridors of the fortress hewn from the rock. All was still. He reached over the windowsill of the Magus' room and felt a heavy curtain. As he pulled himself onto the ledge, the rasp of his trousers brushing the stone sounded very loud.

The crow rose past him, riding an updraft on outstretched wings. Jon gave it a nod, pushed one finger through the curtain and peeked inside. Blackness. A good sign. Hopefully, it meant that the Magus still lay in his bed—not asleep, the crow said, but in a strange torpor, perhaps communing with the powers he served. As long as Jon kept quiet, he should be able to catch the wizard by surprise. He took a few slow breaths, then swung his feet over the ledge and slipped inside.

He fell through darkness—farther than he'd expected, and pitched onto his hands and knees as he landed. His palms smacked the floor and he cringed, looking around, blind. But nothing stirred. There was a smell of decay, putrid and rank. It coated the inside of his mouth like paste.

Details materialized out of the darkness: curved walls blotched with color, the black rectangle of a door. In the center of the room, a dais, and on top of it, a tumble of cloth over the unmistakable shape of a man.

Jon heard the flutter of the crow's wings at the window. It poked its head through the curtains, admitting more light, and he saw—

Human hands.

They covered the walls. Hands of all sizes and colors, raggedly dismembered and nailed through the palm by iron spikes. Many were withered, skeletal, shrouded in the remnants of flesh. Others were bloated bags, ripe with putrefaction. And some looked perfectly normal—just hands, young and old, squeezed into fists, open in supplication, beckoning. A few clutched bits of rope.

The Magus lay twisted in the posture of a man

racked by nightmare. Embroidered velvet quilts covered him head to toe except for a gap around his face. As Jon began to make out the wizard's features, they shifted and somehow folded out of view, only to be replaced by another visage—then another—impossible to keep in focus.

Jon crept toward him, looking for something heavy to bash with. The heavier the better. But there was no furniture, no loose bricks, nothing. So he'd have to dart in and crush the evil thing's throat, then. Snap his neck. He'd have to move fast. The crow had said that the Magus exhaled a vapor that turned people into bugs and beasts. Jon must not let the wizard breathe on him.

His foot touched something—a wire—he knew it the instant he hit it. The wire stretched taut, and dozens of the dead fists opened. Each dropped a shining coin, and the coins rained onto the stone floor with a metallic clatter, bouncing, rolling, spinning. The Magus jerked and sat up with a groan that sounded like agony. The quilts fell away. Jon saw an old man, tired and bent. He saw a boy, wide-eyed with fear. He saw a man in his prime, spotted with fever. The Magus opened his mouth.

"Get away!" the crow screamed. But Jon hesitated, not wanting to lose this chance. Just as the Magus belched out a plume of white fog, the crow swooped in front of his face, blocking the blast. Jon staggered back, and his arm grazed one of the hands on the wall. He recoiled, then grabbed the shriveled lump and yanked it free, spike and all. The Magus inhaled with a wheeze. Jon rushed him, grabbed his head and jammed the dead hand into his open mouth. He gave it a shove and felt the spike pierce the back of the Magus' throat. He shoved again. The Magus gave a muffled squeal, thrashing his arms against Jon's chest and stomach.

Suddenly the Magus swept a quilt over Jon's head. By the time Jon struggled free, the Magus was standing. The floor at his feet fractured into a spray of cracks, and immediately insects squirmed from the cracks: red centipedes, black earwigs, worms and things Jon had never seen before. As they wriggled up, they grew. The Magus scurried behind the dais, more cracks splitting the floor with each step. The crow impaled a beetle the size of a walnut on its beak and flicked it away. "Leave these to me," it called.

Across the room, the Magus stood hunched over, tugging at the corpse hand in his mouth. Jon tried to leap over the dais, but his feet were still tangled in the quilt. He stumbled and fell onto the platform. The hand had come loose in the Magus' mouth as he worried it back and forth. Jon kicked free of the quilt, slid across the dais and reached for the Magus. But the wizard stepped back, pulling the hand free. His face coalesced into a jumbled mask, grinning in triumph. He inhaled. He breathed out.

And sprayed Jon with blood. Hot blood. It stung Jon's eyes and got into his mouth and nose, but that was all. He was not transformed. The Magus drew another breath, coughed, blood running down his chin. He gave a gurgling cry and ran for the door.

Jon charged after him and grabbed him just as he reached for the door handle. Talons erupted from the Magus' fingertips and he slashed cuts down Jon's arm. The pain was shocking. Jon kicked the Magus' legs out from under him, but the Magus clung to his shirt and they fell together. The Magus grunted, clawed at Jon's face. "Quit that," Jon shouted, beating the Magus' hands away. But not fast enough. The Magus grabbed the side of his head and the touch felt like a white-hot brand. Jon screamed and shoved him back. Spots flooded his vision. He reached up and felt his face, expecting charred skin, but his flesh was unharmed. Blinking, he saw the Magus trying to stand. Jon grabbed his ankle and pulled him back down. Bugs crunched and writhed under them. The Magus slashed at him again, and Jon jerked out of reach. Then he rolled forward and scooped the Magus up, throwing him over his shoulder. The Magus squealed and struggled and kicked. Jon stood, fought for balance, lost, lurched two steps and hit the wall. Nail heads scraped his shoulder and thigh. Dead hands clutched his clothes and hair. Jon bellowed in anger.

By the window, the crow danced with its wings outstretched, facing down a toothed worm twice its size. "Clear the way!" Jon shouted. He wrenched free of the hands, charged over the dais, skidding through bug parts and ichor, and flung the Magus out the window. The Magus' shriek followed him down as he fell, and fell. He hit the rocks, bounced off in a flapping tangle, and splashed into the water.

Jon fell to his knees, gasping. He could not get enough air. Hot blood seeped down his leg. Behind him, the room was silent. He turned. The insects were gone, even the mangled parts. The crow was gone, too.

Instead, a young woman with long black hair stood by the dais, smiling. "Well done," she said. "By destroying the Magus, you lifted the curse he set on me. And you have freed our world."

For a few seconds, Jon couldn't speak. "You're naked," he blurted.

"Oh, damn—don't look. Don't look!" She turned

away, covering herself with her arms. Jon pulled down a curtain and handed it to her. "Who are you?" he asked.

The woman wound the curtain around herself, leaving her shoulders bare. "I'm Princess Levore," she said, tugging her hair out from under the curtain. "I'd forgotten about this stuff." She shook her hair free. "After the Magus killed my parents, he turned me into a crow. I think he wanted to feed me to one of his creatures, but I escaped. And now I'm back." She grinned. "And the Magus and his *things* are gone. That just leaves the Wardens, and they have no leader. And guess what?" She hopped from foot to foot. "A small army of loyalists is set to attack this fortress if the insects go away—they're probably already engaged. They won't meet much resistance."

"How did they know they would get this chance?"

"Well, a little bird—"

"Don't say it."

"Sorry. Anyway, soon we'll control this fortress, and word will go out that the Magus is dead and the world belongs to us again." She stepped close to Jon. "And it's all thanks to you."

"How come—he breathed on you, but you didn't—?"

"I guess because I was already transformed, it couldn't happen again."

"But you didn't know that."

"No."

"That was brave."

"*You* are brave. And you killed the Magus!"

It was a lot to take in. Jon felt a mixture of elation, residual terror, and shyness in front of this beautiful princess. He was also starting to feel his numerous cuts and scratches. He wanted to lie down. Instead, he sat on the windowsill, leaned back and looked upward.

"What's wrong?" Levore asked.

"I was thinking, I haven't actually reached the top." He looked back at her. "But you know, I don't need to anymore."

"Good!" She darted close, kissed his cheek. "A queen needs her champion at her side."

RED STAR PROPHECY

Mickey Zucker Reichert

Mickey Zucker Reichert is the best-selling author of more than twenty novels and thirty-five short stories, including the *Renshai* trilogy, the *Renshai Chronicles*, the *Bifrost Guardians* series, *The Legend of Nightfall*, *The Return of Nightfall*, *The Unknown Soldier*, *Flightless Falcon*, the *Books of Barakhai*, and *Spirit Fox* (with Jennifer Wingert). A pediatrician, Reichert lives on a 40-acre farm and divides time between a zillion animals, family (including three kids who only seem like a zillion), and "real-life research" for the novels and stories. Claims to fame: Both parents are rocket scientists, and she has performed real brain surgery.

THE COTTAGE SHUDDERED in howling night winds; tendrils of air, cold as ice, breathed through gaps in the chinking. Rebah sat on the grimy pile of straw that served as her bed, unable to sleep for the rise and fall of men's voices from the only other room. She glanced across her parents' empty pallet to her brother, Katin. He was eleven, two years younger than she was. His shaggy mop of sandy hair fell around his face and onto his closed eyelids, making him appear childlike and frail. He slept with his mouth open, drooling a clear line of saliva.

Rebah smiled, glad her baby brother found the solace she could not. She did not know the purpose of the meeting her father had called, but it seemed important. The men's tones sounded urgent and, at times, angry. Everyone knew the law of the ruling *Arlethin* denied male slaves gathering in unsupervised groups of more than three, except in approved circumstances. Certain topics could earn imprisonment or execution, and her father had seemed distracted and nervous most of the day.

Unable to rest, Rebah threw back her threadbare blanket and pulled on her only set of clothing, a patched and itchy woolen dress that had become noticeably short at the wrists and hemline. She poked her head through the doorway into the other room. Her mother sat in the "working" corner, washing their claywear and diligently pretending not to notice the five men perched on the array of crates they used as furniture. Her father paced around his companions, his weather-baked cheeks creased with worry. He wore his dark hair short, streaked blond by the sun. His hands were huge, callused and scarred, the nails jagged with breaks.

Smaller and fairer than her husband, Yannoh crouched over the cleaning bucket. Raven hair cascaded down her back in a heavy braid. She looked up as Rebah entered and gestured the girl silently to her.

Rebah scurried to her mother's side and set to work, assisting in the cleaning without daring to speak. Her father seemed to take no notice of her entrance, addressing the other men in a weary voice that suggested he had already tried and failed to make his point.

"All I'm saying is that if we don't do something, we doom our children and grandchildren to the same slavery we've suffered."

A wasted-looking man with a gray-speckled beard

responded, "At least, Halor, it is a life. What you propose is war. Death for us and all our sons. Our wives and daughters, our elders and children, will suffer the punishment for what we have done."

A spark appeared in her father's gray eyes, ones Katin and Rebah had inherited. Both displayed their father's prominent features and their mother's skin tone. "That assumes we lose, my friend. There are many more of us than them."

A neighbor Rebah knew as Bear spoke next, a massive, hairy man far gentler than his namesake. "Much as I hate to agree with Largour . . ."

The others snickered.

". . . his point may be foregone. We have always been a peaceful people. What good are numbers without weapons or the training to use them?"

Halor used his stirring voice, the one he adopted whenever he encouraged his children through a difficult task. "Machetes and hoes, rocks and crooks. These will be our weapons. What training does it take to bash the heads of those who batter us with whips, slaughter our elders for sport, and boil our babies in stew pots?"

Rebah suppressed a gasp. It was not polite for women to eavesdrop on men, and her father would send her back to the sleeping quarters if he thought she deliberately listened. As her father had said, the slaves had come to outnumber their masters. Rebah knew every one of her mother's babies since Katin had been born had gone to the *Arlethin*, but she had assumed they found secure homes with childless folk. She had always relished the rare chunks of meat in her family's share of the watery gruel they ate for every meal. Now, her stomach lurched at the thought of what she might have eaten.

Rebah's mother seized her arm, a plea for silence.

The girl pretended to grow inordinately interested in a speck of dirt on her brother's bowl, picking at it with a fingernail.

The men showed no sign they had heard her. A man so slender he looked as if movement might break him rose, making a religious gesture. "You speak sacrilege as well as treason. Our gods sanction only good, never evil. They are gods of light, of life, and always, of peace." He quoted a favored line of scripture, "Forgive thine enemies; for only through love can you come to truly understand them. And only through such enlightenment can peace bloom through the world like a fragrant flower."

The only man who had not yet spoken snorted. Rebah knew him, too, a young man born with misshapen features that doomed him to bachelorhood. As a child, she had feared him as a monster. "Well, this flower stinks."

All eyes went to him.

"Look where the path of peace and understanding have brought us." He gestured broadly, clearly intending to indicate more than just the squalid, leaky hovel that served as Halor's home. "When the *Arlethin* took our land, we forgave them. When they took our belongings, we understood them. When they took our freedom, we responded with peace." He made a wordless noise of disgust. "The more we give them, the more they take. I agree with Halor. Sometimes violence really is the only solution."

"Never." The skinny man pounded his fist on his own knee, the force of the blow withered by its target. "Violence and war are never the answer. The gods will not allow it."

Bear stroked his hirsute face. "I doubt our grandfathers believed the gods would allow us to become slaves either. Yet here we are."

"And here we will stay," Halor added. "Until we do something to change it."

"Diplomacy," tried Largour, the man with the graying beard.

"Fifty years of diplomacy," said Monster-face, "has only worsened our condition."

Largour could not wholly deny the obvious. "I'm not saying violence is never necessary. There is the red star prophecy."

The skinny man who had quoted the gods nodded vigorous agreement. "We must wait for the chosen one of the prophecy."

Monster-face huffed out a sigh and rolled his eyes. He glanced at the women.

Caught studying him, Rebah glanced away swiftly. Now that she knew he was merely a human unluckily born, she no longer found his features hideous. They seemed more distinctive, in a strange sort of way, left eye larger than right, nostrils upturned, mouth and chin cleft and broad.

"Don't you get it?" he said. "The prophecy isn't real. It's a construct of our captors meant to keep us from revolting."

The skinny man looked at him as if he had gone suddenly mad. "What?"

Rebah listened intently. Prophecies and other religious matters fell to the men; women were rarely allowed in the listing lean-to that comprised the slave's temple. Yet even she had heard of the prophesied child who would one day be born to their people. He would carry a birthmark on his head, brilliant red and in the shape of a star. The gods destined this child to lead their worshippers in a war that would overthrow the *Arlethin* and usher in a new era of freedom, peace, and prosperity.

Monster-face explained his disdain, "So long as they

have us waiting for a boy who will never exist, we remain willing and easy slaves. They can do as they wish to us, and we will allow it while we bide our time waiting for this illusory savior."

The bearded elder leaped to his feet, his features a mask of outrage. "Enough of this blasphemy! I suggest we disperse before we're discovered and sent to the headsman." He glanced warningly around the group. "Say nothing of this meeting to anyone."

The men rose, some with clear reluctance and others obviously antsy for a swift leave-taking.

Rebah kept her head down, trying to appear so engrossed in her duties that she did not even notice the gathering. She heard the skim of their sandals at the door as they left in singles or pairs until only her father remained.

Halor clapped a tired hand to Rebah's shoulder, his calluses catching on the weave of her woolens. "Go to sleep, Sweet Petals. Your mother and I need to talk."

Rebah turned and gave her father a hug. His clothing reeked of grease and sweat, and the mingled dusts of mortar and grain brushed off onto her shift. He wrapped strong arms around her, rubbing her back with his familiar, comforting stroke. "Don't worry about anything, Rebah. We'll be all right."

Believing him, Rebah hurried back to the cottage's other room, where her brother still lay in blissful sleep.

A frenzied pounding at the door awakened Rebah with a start. Rolling, she glanced to her left. Moonlight trickled through gaps where the mortaring mud had dried and cracked, lessening the pitch darkness of the room enough for her to see that her parents' bed still lay empty. Katin lurched to a sitting position. "What?" he said tiredly.

Rebah silenced him with a gesture.

In the main room, a whispered exchange barely wafted to Rebah, too low to discern. Then, the door flew open with its usual groaning squeal. The high-pitched, musical voices of *Arlethin* followed, their footfalls solidified by fine leather boots and their movements softened by silks and linens. They always seemed so light and graceful to Rebah, their women so beautiful in gauzy dresses, fancy hairstyles, and dazzling, light-catching jewelry. In her childhood fantasies, she walked among them, her skirts swirling as she twirled in circles so airy she could almost fly.

Now, she dreaded their presences. The *Arlethin* did not deign to visit lowborns' homes, except on business of great significance. Her father and brother had no special skills. Halor labored among the other men building and repairing palaces, shops, and statues for the *Arlethin*. Katin would join him in a year, when he came of age. Her mother worked as a maid in several *Arlethin* homes, keeping their finery as pristine as their own simple hovel. Rebah held the most venerated position in her family, training as a healer; but many in the field showed more talent than she did. Though pregnant again, her mother was not yet halfway due; and this one, too, had already been promised to the *Arlethin*.

So Rebah sat silently in the dark, worried for the purpose of the masters in their cottage. Soon Katin joined her, wriggling over their parents' bed to clasp her hand in a silent plea for succor and understanding.

Having no answers herself, Rebah gripped his fingers tightly and waited.

Shortly, the booted feet retreated, and the door squealed shut. The silence that followed seemed terrifyingly deafening. Rebah strained her hearing for parental conversation, something to explain the strange visit in the night.

Though he did not suffer from the same restrictions she did, Katin chose to remain in place, clasping Rebah's hand, rather than step out and demand explanation.

Sobs shattered the silence, and Rebah felt tears spring to her own eyes, ignorant and unbidden. The grief inherent in her mother's crying reached to the depths of her spirit. She rose, Katin with her, and walked cautiously into the main room. Yannoh sat on the floor, weeping.

"Mama!" Rebah and Katin ran to her.

Their mother dabbed at her eyes, clearly struggling to control her grief long enough to supply comfort to her children. Failing, she lapsed into another round of furious, irrepressible tears.

Katin turned his sister a frightened look.

Rebah caught Katin's hand again and pulled him down so that they sat in a line, with her in the middle. She put an arm around each of them. "Mama, whatever it is, we'll be all right. Father said so."

Yannoh sniffled, making another attempt at composure. "Father . . . is gone, Rebah. They took him away . . . for treason."

Katin gasped.

Rebah's heart seemed to stop beating, and an imminent feeling of death stole over her. She knew what happened to men named traitors by the *Arlethin*. They disappeared for days, months, or years, only to reappear as broken, beaten skeletons of their former selves to confess to and denounce their crimes. They warned others of the slave class never to act against their masters, and the persuasiveness of their words determined whether they faced a swift death on the headsman's block or a slower one by stoning. "No," she whispered, studying her mother, tears blurring her vision. "Because of . . . tonight?"

"Someone told them."

Though plagued with a grief that precluded movement, Rebah still knew a flash of anger. "Monster-face?"

Despite her own distress, Yannoh still managed to reprimand her daughter. "Be nice, Rebah. His name is Ethorn, and he's a very nice man. Your father trusted him—"

Rebah could not forgive as easily. "Father trusted all the men here tonight, but one of them *did* betray him." She lapsed into sobs. "And us."

Katin looked up. "What are you talking about?"

Yannoh refused to abandon her lecture even to address her son's confusion. "Yes, Rebah. Someone apparently did. But you condemned Ethorn without any proof simply because of his appearance, and that is wrong. The *Arlethin* are beautiful and, yet, they do the greatest evil."

It was true; but, at the moment, Rebah found it impossible to care. Her chest ached, and she worried her heart might explode from the anguish. She searched for the goodness the gods demanded but found only despair and anger. "Well, whoever did it deserves to go in Father's place."

Katin glanced between his mother and sister. "What are you talking about?" he said louder.

Their mother continued to ignore him. "We don't know that, Rebah. It is wrong to condemn a man until you understand his mind, the details of his circumstances."

Katin stood up to confront his mother directly. "What men? What happened? Someone tell me!"

Rebah succumbed to a fresh round of sobs, and Yannoh explained while her daughter grieved. "Your father had a meeting here tonight. He took a dangerous risk, and he's paying for it."

"*We're* paying for it," Katin grumbled, his pale eyes blurring. "Why did he do something so stupid?"

Rebah would not allow anyone to disparage her father, not even her beloved little brother. She sprang to her feet, too. "It wasn't stupid! He was trying to help us. Trying to rescue us from this life of drudgery."

"He should have asked me first." Katin glared at his sister, his eyes narrowing. "I would have told him I'd rather live in slavery with a father than free without one."

Exactly why he didn't ask you. Rebah kept the thought to herself. It would only fuel his rage. "Those were not the only possible outcomes, Katin. What he wanted was to provide us with freedom *and* a father."

"And we got neither!"

Rebah started to respond, but Yannoh caught her arm. It was unseemly to argue with any man, including a younger brother.

Rebah then turned her mind to refuting the common assertion her mother made without words. Impropriety had never stopped Yannoh from vehemently disagreeing with Halor and making her position well understood by the family. Strong women were not only known to bicker with their husbands, they frequently won.

Before Rebah could object, Yannoh explained, "Everyone deals with grief in his own way. Katin gets angry; let him vent."

Rebah nodded, her own fire withering beneath an onslaught of overwhelming sorrow. Sobbing, the two women clung to each other while Katin raged around them.

Though constructed for the *Arlethin*, the town square seemed ugly and dank to Rebah. She noticed every crack and dull green moss splotch on the carved marble dolphins that graced the central fountain. As a young child, she had watched in fascination as sunlight gleamed from their slender snouts, and the movement of the water beneath them made their shadows seem to dance. Then, she had imagined their carven forms as living creatures, sluicing through the water while she rode them with a pure and delicate grace.

The weather appeared determined to vex her, bright and sunny in glaring contrast to the darkness of her mood. The *Arlethin* allowed the grieving families of condemned or dying slaves to come here and execute the traditional displays of grief: tossing stones carved with depictions or descriptions of their misfortunes into the water and watching them sink away, shaving heads, rending clothing. For one day after any tragedy, the *Arlethin* did not expect work from members of the victim's immediate family. Friends and more distant relations could visit on their breaks to join the solemnity or offer comforts and advice.

Bedridden with misery, Yannoh did not join her children at the fountain, insisting they perform the rituals without her. Stunned by the suggestion, Rebah had agreed without question, but the walk to the fountain with Katin left her feeling irritated and betrayed. At thirteen, she did not relish the burdens of explaining the situation to every man or woman who asked; that obligation belonged to her mother. Rebah's swollen eyes already stung from the tears she had thus far shed. The stones wrapped in a rag at her belt felt heavy as boulders. She and Katin would drop them into the fountain to watch them tumble to the bottom, and the gods were supposed to honor them by removing the agony from their hearts and souls. Rebah could not see how anyone, divine or otherwise, could lighten her burden. She was not even certain she wanted to lose the emotions she felt, however painful. To do so might lessen her love for Halor. She could not bear to forget him and all the joys they had shared, would despise herself for feeling any sort of pleasure so long as he remained absent.

At Rebah's side, Katin seemed to sense her need for silence and said nothing as they marched through the village and approached the central fountain. He, too, carried a pouch of small stones as well as a shaving knife, a vial of fatty soap, and a bowl for water. Soon, he would lose the handsome locks that had wound around his head like vines since infancy. They had come to define him: from the tow-headed toddler with bouncing curls running in crazy circles and laughing with wild abandon to the tangled snarl of his youth that Rebah combed with care lest she hurt him. She would miss his hair, more even than her own.

The *Arlethin* in the central square gathered their belongings as the children approached, leaving the fountain to the grieving slaves. The women's disdainful comments as they did so told Rebah their departure had nothing to do with concern for her privacy and everything to do with not wishing to contaminate themselves by consorting with slaves. For the time being, Rebah saw none of their own kind; but the first work breaks would start soon and, with them, the questions she felt ill-equipped to answer.

"What should we do first?" Katin asked, kneeling in front of the fountain to rest both pouches on the stonework.

Though she dreaded the task, Rebah chose the one that might keep her occupied enough to avoid conversation. "Shaving?"

Katin studied his reflection in the water. They rarely got to see themselves in anything large enough to accommodate an entire face; the muddy drinking hole provided to the slaves was inadequate for anything but boiling. "I wonder what I'll look like bald."

"Not as silly as I will, I'd warrant." Rebah opened the pouch of shaving tools, already spotting some of the first slave men coming to drink. She had never shaved a head before, but she had helped her father with his beard. She knew enough, she believed, to do a reasonable job without hurting Katin. He, on the other hand, had no experience at all. The image of the hack job he seemed destined to perform on her allowed her to smile through her tears. She doubted he would cut her; he had a gentle touch and tended toward caution. She would, however, need her mother to finish; or she might end up looking as if moths had mistaken her head for cloth.

"Sit," Rebah commanded.

Katin obeyed, facing inward so his shorn locks would not sully the fountain. He plunged his legs into the crisp, cool water.

Rebah began by chopping off great hanks of hair, watching the handsome tawny locks tumble to the ground fountainside. As a child they had glistened, yellow as the sun; and Rebah had wondered aloud if an *Arlethin* had sired him. Her mother explained that a child's hair started out light and gained color as he aged, that Rebah's own earth-colored locks had once matched Katin's. Time had proven her mother correct. The roots of Katin's hair grew a bit darker every season, though the sun bleached it now to the color of sand.

As Rebah worked, the slave men gathered to watch. A few addressed her; but she pretended not to notice them, focusing her full attention on Katin's head. Breezes skimmed the fountain, splashing her arms and face with cold pinpoints of water, and cut strands clung where the dampness touched her woolens.

At one point, she paused to mop her brow and cast a glance over the growing crowd. Ethorn stood beside her, quietly studying her technique. Startled to find his lopsided features so close, she stared just long enough to catch his gaze. Once she did so, she could not politely ignore him as she had the others.

"I'm sorry about your father," he said softly.

Rebah pursed her lips and nodded. *Was that a confession?* A lump formed in her throat, and her cheeks warmed. She did not know how to reply.

As if reading her mind, Ethorn added, "It wasn't me, Rebah. You know that."

Many of the slaves had difficulty reading Ethorn's emotions, given his strange, cockeyed appearance, but Rebah could tell he spoke the truth. In addition to the clear pain in his eyes, his tone held the perfect pitch of innocence.

"Who . . . ?" Rebah retreated from Katin, still clutching the shaving knife. "Who . . . betrayed my father?"

A murmur swept the nearest observers, and some took a cautious backward step.

"I don't know," Ethorn admitted. "But I'll find out for you and learn why."

Rebah managed a slight smile. She appreciated his efforts and the raw grief stamped across his homely face. He truly did care about the fate of her father and about the children he had left behind. "Thank you."

Ethorn shifted near enough for an embrace, though he did not touch Rebah. He seemed to worry that his ugliness might distress rather than comfort her, not knowing she would have appreciated his gentle, understanding hug. Instead, he whispered, "Don't give up. So long as Halor still lives, there is hope." With those words, he disappeared back into the crowd, as others came forward to ply her with questions.

Rebah turned back to Katin, indicating that her respite had ended and her work would, once again, occupy her entirely. She ignored the whispered speculations thrumming around her to focus upon the task at hand, as well as Ethorn's comforting. He meant well, she knew; but she also understood that her father's life would end the moment he surrendered to whatever torture the *Arlethin* applied to him. Once they found him ready to confess, repent, and warn, he would join the others they branded traitors. They would prominently display his head or battered corpse as a warning to others contemplating revolt. Anyone who attempted to honor his remains would risk similar punishment.

Once Rebah had Katin's hair shortened, she worked the fat and water onto his scalp to soften it for shaving. Starting at the crown, she shuffled the blade downward in a central stripe. A line of hair scraped off beneath her touch, revealing pallid scalp. At the base of the stroke, she discovered a hint of red. Rebah closed her eyes. *Gods damn me, I cut him.* "Katin, I'm sorry. Did I hurt you?"

Rebah's little brother twisted his head to look at her. "No, why? Are you trying to?"

Rebah's eyes flashed open. The red area remained but grew no larger. It was not welling blood. She studied it more closely, uncertain what she saw, then raised the blade and scraped carefully around it.

The crowd drew nearer. They seemed not to breathe.

Gradually, Rebah revealed the object hidden beneath the hair on Katin's scalp: a bright red mark in the unmistakable shape of a star.

Rebah burst into her family's cottage, nearly dragging Katin through the door. "Mama! Mama!"

The mass of men at Rebah's heels had the courtesy to stop at the entrance, and she made certain to slam the squeaky panel behind her. Released suddenly from his sister's hold, Katin staggered across the floor. "What is going on?" he demanded. "Have you gone wholly mad?"

"Mother!"

Yannoh appeared from the bedroom, disheveled, eyes swollen, face streaked with tears. "What is it, Rebah?"

"This!" Rebah indicated her brother's wildly patchy scalp with a frenzied gesture. "This! Katin . . . he's . . . he is . . ." She found herself incapable of finishing.

". . . the prophesied child," Yannoh said, patting at a hopeless snarl of her own hair. "I know."

Katin's eyes went round as coins, enormous. He twisted, as if trying to see the back of his own head.

"You knew?" Incredulity stole over Rebah, ready to ignite. "You knew? All this time, and . . . how could you . . . ?" It occurred to her suddenly. "If you had told us sooner, Father would not be—"

Yannoh lowered her head.

"You've known since he was a baby." Rebah's disbelief became accusation. She could scarcely believe her mother had hidden such a thing from all of them for so long.

Katin abandoned his gyrations to ask the important question, "Did Father . . . know?"

"No," Yannoh admitted.

Fire seemed to sear Rebah's veins. "Of course, he didn't know. If he had known, he would never have risked his life. He would have—"

"Risked Katin's," their mother cut in.

Rebah stared, seeing her mother in a new and unfavorable light. She had always thought of Yannoh as brave, enviably strong; yet she had performed a supreme act of cowardice. She had spared her son from war at the price of eleven more years of slavery and the loss of her husband's life. "How could you—?"

"You will understand."

"Didn't the midwife—?"

"It was not present right at birth. Later—"

It was Rebah's turn to interrupt. She pounded her fist against the wall of the cottage, unable to listen to more. There was no time or reason for questions. Outside, she could hear the men talking about the future in tones both grim and excited. Fists rapped timidly against the door. Rebah turned to open it, then glanced at Katin.

Her brother's legs had buckled beneath him. He clutched one of the crates that served as furniture, his face an odd shade of green.

Rebah could barely look at her mother, yet, as always, she turned to her for advice.

"Tell them to prepare for war," Yannoh said softly. "We need to finish the grieving process and will join them this evening, when the news has reached the ear of every one of our men."

Rebah lowered her head in thought, no longer instinctively trusting her mother. Nevertheless, the advice seemed sound. With a bold toss of her head, still covered with hair for the moment, she headed toward the door to inform the men outside.

Rebah huddled miserably in her makeshift healer's tent, amid dozens of others that had sprouted like mushrooms when the war began. The sounds of war had become familiar: shouts and battle cries mixed with screams of pain, the crash of steel, and the heavy thunk of wood. She had finally stopped cringing at every horrific noise, saving her dismay for the pounding footfalls that heralded another wounded man or boy headed her way.

She had seen stab wounds before. Impatient or irritated *Arlethin* occasionally skewered a slave whose speed or competence did not please them. Yet, those occasional events bore little relation to the masses of critically injured now carried to her in desperation. Nearly a third had taken their last breaths before they reached her. The others she patched and returned to the battlefield or sent to the open fields where training healers not yet of age and volunteers tended them until they recovered or died.

Between patients, Rebah huddled in wretched silence, worried for the warriors, especially her brother. Every patient, every carrier, brought a tale of the scarlet star, gleaming with the gods' light on the bald head of a child. Katin, Halor's son, chosen of the gods, shining beacon of freedom. Carried like a flag amid the strongest charges, he emboldened the men to feats of greatness. Untouchable, invincible Katin.

Rebah ran a hand over her own smooth pate, savagely concerned for her brother's safety despite the men's certainty of his invulnerability. The red star birthmark had come to Katin in infancy, yet she had tended his stubbed toes and crushed fingers, the gashes working stone had flayed into his arms. She dared not contradict the will of the gods, but it made little sense that they waited to bestow the red star's powers upon him until such time as Rebah had inadvertently revealed it to the world. No more sense than her mother hiding it.

Footfalls strafed toward her, their pattern heavy and frantic. Wincing, Rebah glanced through the flap she had left open to reveal her readiness for another patient. Four men carried a board upon which another lay, very still. Blood dripped from his ear, and crimson froth bubbled on his lips. Even from a distance, she could tell this one would not survive. With a sigh, she stepped forward to accept her charge, hoping she could at least ease his suffering and, more selfishly, that he would prove a stranger.

But she could not. And he did not. As the carriers rolled him gently to the ground, the ragged hole in his shirt blossomed into a violent red flower, and Rebah recognized one of the men from her father's meeting. Called Largour, he looked ancient, his skin nearly white and his dark eyes empty with shock.

The carriers said nothing, though two nodded and one shook his head sadly. They disappeared with the board they needed to carry others from the battlefield.

"Rebah," Largour whispered.

Surprised he could still talk, Rebah gave the man her complete attention. She knelt in front of him. Splattered with gore, his beard seemed to move rather than his mouth. She forestalled him with a raised hand. "Don't speak; save your strength."

Largour moved his head slightly, denying her request. "I . . ." he gasped, and bright red blood joined the brown on his teeth. ". . . must."

Rebah sat back on her heels but did not try to stop him again. He was going to die and had a right to do so on his own terms.

"I . . . gave up . . . Halor."

Rebah recoiled, and a stunning heat flashed briefly through her. To her surprise, no emotion accompanied it.

"They . . . they . . . caught me. Returning . . . home." Largour sucked in another large breath, extending the circles of blood. "Said . . . they would . . ." He grunted in pain.

Rebah closed her eyes, wanting to know the details

but hating the suffering that went with the revelation. Her mother's words streaked through her memory: *It is wrong to condemn a man until you understand his mind, the details of his circumstances.* She forced herself to study the wound. Deep into his chest, it had sliced ribs and penetrated a lung. No matter her ministrations, no matter those of the master healer, he would not live much longer.

". . . slaughter my family . . . torture me . . . if I didn't . . . give . . . a name." Tears filled Largour's eyes. "My wife . . . already . . . dead. My . . . children . . . all I have." Largour's breathing slowed and shallowed. His eyes slid closed.

Certain he had died, Rebah leaned across him to recite the final prayers.

Largour's lids squinted open suddenly. "Rebah, please. Forgive . . . me."

Caught by surprise, Rebah froze with her face a mere two hand's breadths from his. She could smell the raw, salty odor of blood, and she had to fight to keep from gagging. She tried to put herself in his place, seized by a mental image of herself caught in the grip of brutal *Arlethin*, their breath sweetened with herbs, their eyes steely and full of savage rage. She could hear her heart pounding in her ears, feel the terror shocking through her. Beneath the wild drumbeat of her own heart, she heard the musical sound of their voices threatening violence to her and her loved ones, demanding, beseeching, hostile.

"I forgive you, Largour," she said, her conscience clear. It was not just a kindness to a dying man. She meant it. *Forgive thine enemies; for only through love can you come to truly understand them.* For the first time, the trite scripture gained meaning, yet it seemed tattered and backward. Understanding had come first.

Without it, she could still have forgiven him in words but never in her heart.

Largour went still, eyes closed, features placid. He continued to breathe in ragged chaos, but for all intents and purposes he was dead. Rebah brushed a lock of sticky hair from his forehead, then kissed it lightly. "I forgive you, Largour. I forgive you."

With a sigh, she rose, poked her head out of the flap, and motioned for the carriers to take what remained of Largour to the field.

Gray evening descended over the healing grounds, and men returned in groups to share stories and meals. Rebah found herself tending smaller wounds, scratches and burns, superficial tears from mishandled weapons or near-misses that had not incapacitated. Her many failures had brought her to doubt her skills as a healer, and she appreciated the chance to buoy her spirits with small successes. The war was going well for the slaves. The men bragged of their prowess when they weren't mourning the fallen, and Katin held the primary position in their tales.

Though plagued by myriad concerns, Rebah managed to set aside her feelings of self-doubt. She chatted with the soldiers. Their excitement was contagious, and she soon settled amid the weeds, enjoying a meal of roasted coney and scavenged berries. Though scant, it tasted better than anything she had ever eaten, vastly more flavorful than her previous steady diet of gruel. The tangy, gamy taste of the meat contrasted sharply with the gray lumps soaked in water that occasionally came with the evening meal. Now, she licked every drop of grease from her fingers.

The battlegrounds grew quieter as the men on both sides ended their last skirmishes to retire to their camps. Gradually, the conversations around the fires grew more spirited than the war. Then, abruptly, a scream caught Rebah's attention, causing her to drop the bone from which she was sucking the final succulent bits of marrow. No one else seemed to notice it, but it chilled her to the core. It sounded like Katin.

Rebah leaped to her feet before she realized she had moved, sprinting toward the edge of the camp. She scanned the horizon, trying to see something, anything, through the dense shadows of trees. In the distance, the battlefield seemed to go as silent as a tomb.

Rebah pranced along the field, catching herself about to plunge into the trees at intervals. It would not do to run wildly into danger without any idea of destination. If the voice she had heard was Katin's, if her caring, innocent brother had become seriously injured, he would need her to remain calm and in control. He would take his cues from her; he always did. He would need her strong to stay strong himself.

Harried, running footfalls crushed leaves underfoot, and Rebah heard the distant rustle of swiftly navigated foliage. The sounds grew closer, more frantic. Still, a lifetime seemed to pass before a swarm of men crashed breathlessly from the woods, clutching a board on which lay a moaning figure. Though unable to see the victim, Rebah knew him without doubt. Surely, the soldiers would have rushed Katin to the most experienced healer had Rebah not grabbed one's arm and personally escorted them to the nearest, empty tent. Her manner and countenance brooked no defiance, and men accustomed to the superior position surrendered to this woman, their savior's sister, without question. They placed the board on the floor and tensed to roll him off of it as they had the others.

Rebah stayed them with a raised hand. "Leave him. He will do better if he isn't moved."

Again, they obeyed.

Rebah shooed them from the tent. Only as the last
one filed out to report the bad news to the soldiers
did Rebah look at her brother. His features contorted
in pain, and the hand clutched to his abdomen was
striped with blood. She glanced swiftly over the rest
of him, seeking other wounds that might need more
or as much attention. It was a common mistake of new
healers to become mesmerized by the most obvious or
horrific wound, usually a jutting bone, only to miss one
more life threatening. When Rebah found no other
bleeding, she gently pulled his fingers aside.

Katin grunted in pain.

Outside, Rebah could hear the gasps and moans of
the slaves-turned-warriors as the news of Katin's injury made the rounds. She could hear them fretting,
their stories of triumph melting into despair. "Without
the red star," a man said glumly, "we cannot fight."
Not one man contradicted the assessment, but several
muttered in bleak agreement.

Someone poked a head into the tent, and Rebah
hissed at him with the vehemence of a gander. "Stay
out! No one comes in here until I'm finished!"

The head withdrew with a swiftness that suggested
he worried for his neck.

"Rebah?" Katin said feebly. "Is that you?"

Rebah took a cloth and stuffed it into the wound.

Katin cried out.

"Quiet," Rebah commanded, her fury rekindled.
She hated her mother for not revealing the red star
sooner, in Katin's infancy, before Rebah had had a
chance to grow so attached to her younger brother.
She hated the *Arlethin* for all the evil they had in-
flicted on her people, for stealing her father, for injuring her brother, for making this war necessary. She
hated her own people for giving up so easily when,

moments before, victory seemed within their grasp. And she hated the gods for filling them all with hope, only to dash it with the thrust of an *Arlethin* sword. She wanted to run outside and scream her rage at the heavens, to curse the gods and men for all the world's injustices. Instead, she brought her face near her brother's. "Katin, open your eyes."

Miraculously, he obeyed, the gray orbs moist with pain. Nevertheless, he managed a smile. "Rebah." He coughed. "Am I going to . . . die?"

Rebah had not yet finished her assessment, but she dismissed his words as nonsensical. "What kind of damn fool question is that, Katin? Of course, you're not going to die."

"It . . . hurts, Rebah. It hurts bad."

Rebah suffered a flash of terrible sympathy but forced herself not to show it. "Roll over," she said, as much to test his mobility as to examine his back for more injuries.

Wincing and sucking in breath with every movement, Katin worked his way off the board and onto the floor in the proper position.

Rebah cut off his clothing to expose the dirt mottling his trunk, backside and limbs. It took the pattern of the coarse weave of his tunic. To her relief she saw nothing worse than scrapes and bruises. His life hinged on the wound in his belly, which she had not yet carefully assessed while she waited for the packing to stop his bleeding. Rebah turned her attention to his scalp. A head injury could also kill a man, without leaving much of an external mark.

She brought her face in close. The odors of stale sweat, rich earth, and the grease she had used to shave him filled her nostrils. Beneath it, she caught a whiff of something unexpectedly sour. She paused, trying to identify the familiar scent in an unfamiliar place, sucking air into her nose and attempting to sift the proper aroma from the others. She closed her eyes, allowing the scent to carry her to its proper location, the washing and dyeing vats. Her eyes flashed open of their own accord. *Red hibintus dye.*

Rebah's thoughts exploded in several different directions, then channeled into one. Grabbing another bandage, she wet it, then used it and her fingernails to scrub at the back of Katin's scalp.

"What . . . are you doing?" he asked, his voice more quizzical than anguished. He was still in pain, but it had nothing to do with her current ministrations.

A point of the red star chipped off onto the rag.

Rebah's heart pounded. *Mother, what did you do?* Suddenly, she understood. Yannoh had not revealed Katin in infancy, because he did not carry the birthmark; he never had. She had created it that very day, then sent Rebah to the fountain to reveal it to the other slaves in the guise of a grief shaving. *It is wrong to condemn a man until you understand his mind, the details of his circumstances.* Rebah thought about what her father had tried to do, how her mother had made his dream come true with a bit of red dye and careful painting. Ethorn had proclaimed the red star prophecy a hoax, an invention of the *Arlethin* to keep the slaves from revolting. Now, one clever woman had turned that tactic upside down. *I'm so sorry I doubted you, Mother. I didn't understand: your mind or the details of your circumstances.* Rebah frowned, knowing the future of the *Arlethin* and their slaves now depended on the cunning of another woman: herself.

"Katin," Rebah said, her demeanor softer, though she still hid all doubt and worry. "On your back."

Katin groaned, his brow spangled with sweat. "It hurts, Rebah."

"I know." Rebah ran a gentle hand across his head. "But it's necessary. Over, Katin."

Slowly, painfully, he worked his way back to his original position, no longer braced by the board.

Rebah edged the wadded cloth from the wound, trying to ignore her brother's whimpers. The blade had penetrated the layers of muscle and tendon but had not entered the abdominal cavity. *Gods be thanked.* She breathed a sigh of relief. Katin would live, so long as the wound did not fester. However, it would take a week, at least, for him to heal enough to rejoin the warriors. During that time, anything might happen. The men would lose faith in their invincible liberator. Without his presence, they might lose hope, and the tide of war would surely turn.

Rebah washed the wound with suckling sap. "Katin, it's not that bad."

"Truth?"

"Truth," Rebah promised. "You're going to recover fully."

Katin's balled muscles relaxed against the pain.

"Don't move. I need to let the others know." Without awaiting a response from Katin, Rebah stepped out of the tent to address the warriors and nearly crashed into a throng of hovering, anxious men. She found the tent surrounded, the entire horde waiting for her to speak. Several stood on deadfalls or perched in branches to see over the heads of the men in front of them. They all went silent at her appearance, and every eye focused directly on her.

Intimidated, Rebah cleared her throat before speaking. "Katin suffered a serious wound."

A collective noise traversed the crowd, a wordless sound that conveyed misery and concern.

"The gods were pleased with our progress but angered that we did not better protect their chosen one."

Rebah glared at the nearest men, who looked away as if she displayed the rage of the gods themselves. "They revoked his invulnerability to force us to rely more on ourselves and less on their graces."

Murmurs traversed the men, including some that suggested mistrust. Rebah realized she was treading a fine line. She would have to abandon her original plan for a more risky one.

Ethorn shoved to the front, his homely features so intent they seemed to hold the wrath hers could not fully display. "What do the gods wish of us, Rebah, sister of the chosen one?"

Rebah appreciated Ethorn's intervention and reminder of her status. "They say they will heal Katin fully tonight, provided no one disturbs us."

A cheer erupted from the gathered men.

"But we must promise to guard him more carefully in battle. To not allow an enemy sword to cut him down again."

Shouts and conversation shattered the previous hush. Rebah gestured at Ethorn, whispering, "I'm going to need your help."

Without hesitation, Ethorn followed Rebah into the healing tent.

Shouts awakened Yannoh from a sleep that had overtaken her while she paced the confines of the family cottage. She lay in a crumpled heap, legs aching and buzzing as blood flow returned to them in painful increments. She had spent the last week crying and worrying, hoping and praying. She could not recall eating or drinking, nor the last time she had deliberately lain down to rest. She had spent her days pacing mindlessly, beseeching the gods to forgive her boldness. Moment by moment, she sought some sign that they forgave her, that they blessed the war despite the sacrilege which had brought it to life, that she would not pay for inciting it with the life of her son.

Oddly, the closest she came to a reply was an *Arlethin* parable that ran repeatedly through her mind, refusing to be banished. In it, the savage leader of their pantheon intoned: "the gods give strength to those who master bravery, aid those with the courage to help themselves."

Now, Yannoh focused on the noise outside the cottage, reading triumph in the men's tone before she managed to sift out a single word. Her heart rate quickened to a savage pounding, and a smile broke her cracked and bitten lips. *Could it be? Could it be . . . we won?* She scarcely dared to hope.

The cries grew louder, stronger, whoops and hollers that clearly came from the people the *Arlethin* had once held as slaves. Two repetitive words rose over the others. The first she discerned gradually, "Freedom! Freedom! Freedom!" The second her heart discovered, "Katin!"

Katin! Yannoh scarcely dared to hope that the gods had spared her son. When she had held and kissed him in his sleep, then painted the star upon his scalp, she knew she had doomed him. No one belonged in battle, least of all a coddled eleven-year-old carried to the front. She had defied the gods; yet, even without their sanction or consent, she had known without need for understanding or logic that she had done the right thing. If Katin died, at least he died a hero, freed from slavery to stand tall among the gods. If he succeeded, his life would buy freedom for his people, and his name would live in history. She only wished she could have put her own life on the line instead of his.

The door banged open, and a raucous band of men entered, a half-grown, bald-headed child balanced on their shoulders.

Katin! Yannoh nearly fainted at the sight. *Alive. Unharmed.* She reached upward, and the men gently lowered their burden to her arms.

Yannoh clung, savoring the living warmth, tears streaming down her face. "Katin," she whispered. "Oh, Katin."

The men jabbered at Yannoh for several moments, but she heard none of it. Nothing existed but the embrace, the breathing, moving, heart-beating child in her arms.

At length, the men withdrew to bring the news home to their own families. Still, Yannoh held her baby and whispered, "Katin, Katin. I love you, Katin."

The door clicked closed, and the voices of triumph again grew distant. Only then, Yannoh received an answer, "Mother, I'm not Katin."

Yannoh jumped backward, nearly crawling out of her own skin. She stared at the child in front of her: filthy-faced, bald-headed, dressed in woven woolens in a style cut only for boys. Even then, it took her a moment to recognize Rebah. "R–Rebah." Realizing her daughter needed her affection every bit as much, she gave the girl another strangling hug. "Rebah, I'm so glad you're safe, but . . ."

"Where's Katin?" Rebah tried, her voice muffled. She gave her mother a gentle push. "Please, let me breathe."

Dread again clutched at Yannoh. Though thrilled to have her daughter back safely, she had never worried for Rebah, disengaged from the war in a healer's tent. Now, she realized, the girl had impersonated her brother, down to the painted red star on the back of her scalp. "How . . . ? Why . . . ?" Unable to finish, she shook her head and let Rebah explain.

Before Rebah could say anything, the door burst open a second time, the hinges shrieking like a wounded animal. Halor stood in the doorway, carrying a bundle draped in blankets. Rebah rushed over and shut the door behind her father, who set his burden down feet first. The figure beneath the blankets managed to remain standing, throwing back his wrappings to reveal a white-faced Katin.

Yannoh stood in shocked awe, frozen in place, uncertain whether to smile or squeal, who to gather first into her tired arms. Then, unbidden, tears burst from her eyes.

"Don't cry, Mama," Katin said. "I'm going to be all right."

Yannoh laughed through her tears. "I know, Katin. You're right. I'm just so very very happy."

With an arm draped around Katin's shoulders, Halor led his son into the bedroom to rest. He turned Yannoh a look that pledged a long and happy night.

As soon as they disappeared into the other room, Rebah promised more. "Mama, the *Arlethin* are gone. We're free. Free! Forever!"

Yannoh drew Rebah close again. "And it's all thanks to you, my beloved daughter."

Rebah laughed in her mother's arms. "Do you think our people will ever figure out that we tricked them?"

Yannoh considered the question several moments before speaking. The details did not matter. Many sons and fathers had died to make the world a better place for the survivors, their kin and their descendants, to bring freedom to a people of slavery. Those were the real heroes of a war that would never have happened but for the courage of a man to speak his mind and the deceit of the two brave women who brought his dream to fruition. "Someday, Rebah, the world will know our story. Such a thing cannot remain hidden forever. In the meantime, let the men enjoy their victory and celebrations, let them mourn the losses of peace and souls, and let them revel in the glory of the gods." She tightened her hold on Rebah. "We need neither fame nor recognition, for we already have everything that matters: our freedom, our family intact, and the bliss that comes of knowing that you acted with dignity and valor when the situation demanded it, risking your own life and love for those in need.

"Ethorn told me what you did, Rebah." Halor poked his head from the bedroom doorway, executing a gesture usually reserved for *Arlethin* kings. "You have my eternal respect. I couldn't possibly be prouder."

Rebah turned to face him, her smile enormous and her eyes alight. "I seem to have splashed a bit of red dye on the back of my head. Can you help me wash it off, Papa?"

Halor bowed. "Sweet Petals, I'd be delighted."

REKINDLING THE LIGHT

Jody Lynn Nye

Jody Lynn Nye lists her main career activity as "spoiling cats." She lives northwest of Chicago with two of the above and her husband, author and packager Bill Fawcett. She has published twenty-five books, including five contemporary fantasies; three SF novels; four novels in collaboration with Anne McCaffrey, including *The Ship Who Won*; a humorous anthology about mothers, *Don't Forget Your Spacesuit, Dear!*; and over sixty short stories. Her latest books are *The Lady and the Tiger*, third in her Taylor's Ark series, and *Myth-Taken Identity!* cowritten with Robert Asprin.

*T*HE INFANT was born on the day Shyma sang her last song aloud.

Gomlo held out his big, dark-skinned hands for his newborn son. The child had been bathed gently and wrapped in soft, warm brown blankets, his serene little round tan face peeking out from between the folds. The Miritu male admired the triangular sockets of the child's eyes, the tufts of black hair on his little round head, and loved him on sight.

"Let me feed him," Gomlo pleaded. He glanced at the bowls of ground meal and nuts that had been prepared by loving friends and family in celebration of the birth.

His mate, Shyma, shook her head. Her puffy, dark brown hair was matted and tousled from the difficulty of delivery, and her skin was as pale as the child's. "Time is short. Take him outside."

Gomlo bent his head in shame. "I can't. I can't do it."

Painfully, Shyma rose from the birthing bed, assisted by her mother and cousins, shrugged into a warm robe, and took the infant from him. She had feared he wasn't going to be able to take that last step. The task was left to her.

Gomlo wasn't to blame. He couldn't hear the music of the stars. Shyma could. She had been the singer for their village since the winged warriors fell upon them—had it only been three years? It seemed like the foot of the conqueror had been on their throats for centuries. The voices of the singers had been silenced, but she knew that this child would be able to hear the celestial songs. When the day came that they were free, he would sing them and lead the Miritus again to joy.

The cold, dry moss crunched under her bare feet. The spring rains were late. They had not been summoned, and didn't know when to come on their own. Shyma felt wild seedlings shifting uncomfortably under the surface of the earth. They would die soon without relief. If only she could give it. She turned her dark brown eyes to the sky.

Thank the cosmos, the night was clear. The bright, glistening stars greeted her joyfully, their high, thin peal like glass chiming and tinkling in her mind's ear. Shyma had always sorrowed for the rest of her folk, deaf to the wonder that she experienced. She did her best to repeat to them what she heard, but she always knew it was a poor reproduction. She stood for a moment, letting the song heal the pain in her torn belly, and the wrenching fear in her heart, then held up her son to the stars' light.

She heard a new song begin as the stars sang welcome to the baby. They named him Lomio. He squirmed and kicked, and she knew he heard—and understood—what they were saying, then, amazingly, she felt him answer back. He was the celestial songs made flesh. Even if he perished now, he would at least have come into his birthright first. Shyma was overjoyed. The news must now be proclaimed. Shyma threw back her head and burst out in song.

A whispering made the night wind feel colder. Bravely, Shyma continued with each verse, trying not to let her voice tremble, even when the black shadow blotted out the stars, and clawed hands snatched her baby from hers. She braced herself, waiting for the claws to rend her body as punishment for her song. Instead, with a tearing cry that was a mockery of the celestial melodies, the shadow and its companions rose into the sky, their shapes black rents in the firmament.

Gomlo and her family were there just inside the rough, bark-sided cottage as Shyma staggered back and closed the door against the night. Only then did she let herself weep.

"He is a singer, Gomlo," she whispered to her mate, as they nestled together in their sleeping place amid yards and yards of hand-wide woven gray wool bands that served their kind for blankets. She shivered. "I wonder where he will be raised."

"If he lives," Gomlo said, sadly. He arranged a heap of warm cloth over her back and shoulders to keep out the chill.

"He lives," Shyma assured him. "I can feel it. I can sense all the other singers."

And she could. They were almost the only spots of light left across the land. The celestial light that blessed the land was fading. Soon, people would begin to forget their birthright and starve and fade away. So much of their substance relied upon the light that was kindled in them when they heard the music of the stars that Shyma didn't like to think of what would be left when the last of it winked out.

The Miritus' religion said that all things were one. At the beginning of time all of existence had been a single substance, all singing the same eternal melody of pure and endless joy. Out of curiosity for what other sounds could be made, existence changed itself. It discovered darkness and brightness, heaviness and lightness, beginnings and endings. The combinations played upon themselves, evolving and growing until they became air and water and earth, plants and animals and stones, the wildness of storms, the searing of fire, the gleam of starlight and sunlight. Throughout all time the eternal song played as an undercurrent. It was still there; Shyma could hear it if she concentrated.

But it was hard to hear through the discord that threatened nature now. Almost three years before, silence had been imposed.

The Miritus had had plenty of warning. Word came from a few exhausted travelers arriving over the mountainous border of the land of terrifying warriors called *tikom* that descended from the sky on wings and tore their victims to pieces. These evil ones were twice the size of the Miritus, with wide, scallop-edged wings springing from their muscular backs. Their skin was shiny, a dark, almost black green the color of pond scum, but their eyes were a curious dead white. The people found it difficult to comprehend them when they spoke, and could never read what they were thinking, since the creased faces wore expressions so different from their own. They were the servants of a white-eyed sorcerer who followed his fearsome army into the ruined towns and took them over one by one. Mirit would be next.

At first the Miritus didn't believe the tidings. But a few more crippled and terrified refugees escaped to Mirit, all telling the same story. The Miritus thought that with the singers they had nothing to fear. They were wrong. Armies of conscripted, hypnotized slaves marched upon them, with the evil winged ones whipping them from above. The Star Lord mustered his own soldiers too late, inadequately armed, and marching behind untried commanders. They were decimated by a foe they could not reach and poisoned by deadly spells. The singers rose up, trying to drive back the darkness with the celestial songs, but they were overwhelmed. Hundreds of them died, cut in half in midair by the *tikom*. Unused to fighting, the Miritus fell. The Star Lord and his entire family were murdered, and *tikom* haunted the villages like hungry ghosts, carrying off townsfolk or farm beasts as they pleased.

The sorceror K'tot made his demands known very soon. Black-armored soldiers carried the word from village to village. The Miritus would work the fields for him. Failure of the farmers to appear was punishable by death. He gave orders for tributes of money, cattle, and crops to be collected monthly, with any failure to be punished by death. Anyone attempting to flee his or her village and who did not immediately surrender to the *tikom* would die on the spot. Singing was forbidden under pain of death. The Miritus were aghast. To try and live without the celestial songs *was* a sentence of death. Agriculture and healing required the power that came from the stars, not just water and sunlight and herbs.

The ill were the most vulnerable in the following interdict. A woman contracted marsh fever, always fatal unless treated. Her earthmate had begged Shyma's father, Grun, to heal her. Shyma remembered it as if it had only just happened. In their hearts they couldn't believe that K'tot would prevent one of his new subjects from being restored to health.

Without hesitation, Grun had gone to the woman's bedside and began his song. Within a few phrases, thin screaming filled the skies and the *tikom* descended, claws flashing. Shyma shivered at the memory. Grun's remains were not recognizable as a Miritu.

Atrocities like that were repeated all over the land. The *tikom* could hear music at any distance. The singers fell silent. The people talked revolution among themselves. Shyma refused to listen. She knew how futile resistance would be. How could they defend themselves against death from the skies?

For three years they had endured. Without the celestial songs the grain they grew did not satisfy them. Fruit and vegetables, what managed to ripen and be picked, tasted bland, and the yields were meager. Herd beasts never fattened up, no matter how much they ate, their fleece was thin and stringy, and a high number of lambs died. Knowing how vital the starsung grain was to survival, the storesmasters doled out tiny measures of what blessed corn was left over from previous years, before K'tot had come. Not much remained. Everyone knew it. Soon all the star-given blessing would be gone, maybe even this season. Many Miritu had killed themselves, unable to cope with living under the shadow, surrounded by silence.

Miserably, Shyma curled up against her earthmate's back, clutching her empty belly, and wished that the *tikom* had not spared her.

"I want my son back," Shyma said. She lay among their coverings staring at the ceiling. If she listened very carefully, she could hear the change in the stars' all-enveloping polyphony that now included Lomio's tiny phrase of song. Just a few notes. *Di-da-dee-dee, de-yu.* As he grew up it would mature with him, becoming more beautiful and complex.

"How?" Gomlo asked, sadly. "He is out of our reach."

"We must bring the music back," Shyma said. Gomlo let out a wordless protest, but she pressed on. "We will all die soon if someone does not."

Gomlo was not an imaginative man, but he frowned. "It's a long jump from bringing home our child to the liberation of the people, which is what must happen before the singers can sing again."

"That is just what I do mean," Shyma insisted. "Oh, it seemed so easy in my dream!" She closed her eyes, hearing the celestial harmonies in her mind. The music would set them free. But first the singers must free the music.

"What was in your dream?" Gomlo asked, crouching down beside her.

"I dreamed . . ." Shyma ground the heels of her hands into her eyes. "I dreamed that the music rose without K'tot hearing it. We rose up and overcame the *tikom*, and song filled the air! It was so beautiful." The very images in her mind gave her strength. She rose and went to the window. The pale colors of the morning sky were marred by the black mote of a *tikom* drifting this way and that in the distance. Listening. She shivered.

"Singing without being heard?" Gomlo mused. "Is it possible?"

Surprised, Shyma turned to see Gomlo's face wrinkled with thought. "Will you help me?"

"Of course," he assured her, coming to take her hands in his rough-skinned ones. "Lomio is my son, too."

"Have another child," her mother chided her harshly, when Shyma and Gomlo brought their idea to her. She was an older, thinner version of her daughter. "Don't sacrifice yourself so foolishly. Mourn and move on. I have." She wrapped both arms around herself, her lined face filled with pain. Shyma knew Narinik wasn't telling the truth. She still grieved for Grun every day.

"We'll avenge Father, I promise you," Shyma said, taking her mother in her arms and resting her cheek on her mother's puffy, graying hair, surprised at how much Narinik seemed to have shrunken over the last three years.

"You get your stubborn streak from him, you know," Narinik insisted, but she calmed down. She sat down on the edge of her bedbox. "Singing without being heard—how?"

"I don't know," Shyma admitted. "I only know that in my dream, I did it. Everything in the world is made of the music. I can hear the stars, and they sing without mouths. When we sing life into the plants, it stays. I can hear that. Before the world was formed, the songs existed, so they can't rely on our puny lungs and throats. So . . . is there a way I can bestow the energy of the stars without making a sound?"

"All substances are one," her mother said firmly. "So if your dreams tell you a thing is possible, it is. That is what your father would say."

*   *   *

Word spread quietly through the village that their singer wanted to revive the star songs. Many of the Miritus were afraid to become involved, fearing the *tikom* more than the slow death from starvation that awaited them without the celestial power. But more offered whatever help they could give.

"We, uh, we grieve for your loss, Singer," the town leader Cormlo said awkwardly.

Shyma was filled with love for her people. They all knew what they risked if her efforts failed. At the best, she wouldn't find the link to the primal music. At the worst, the *tikom* would hear her and tear her to pieces. Either way, the village would be no worse off if she didn't try. What good was a singer who didn't sing?

The thought of her own death didn't frighten Shyma as much as she thought it would. With Lomio's birth she had brought into the world a singer more powerful than she. She was expendable now and could try to free her people so her son could sing the songs again without fear, perhaps even someday engulf the evil ones in the stars' love and bring them to a state of peace.

"Listen," she told her friends and neighbors. "Feel. Tell me if you hear me."

Shyma sequestered herself in her cottage and set about her task as if it was a vital, physical job. The substance of existence sang without mouths or heard the music without ears. It was in the very stuff of their bodies. Everything around them was made of it, though it looked different. The stories didn't lie, Shyma knew. Or hoped. She had never had to put it to the test before. But . . . what if she could sing without words? Could it have the same effect? She'd never tried. In the years before fear there was no reason to find out because their voices had never been suppressed. And since then, no one had tried to find a different way. She must find a way. She wanted her child back.

In her mind she heard the celestial songs chiming and ringing. Their very joy made her impatient. Why could she not convey what was in them to her people in a way other than with her voice?

She began with her name-song. She sat or paced the floor in their tiny cottage, hearing the melody that she had first heard on the day of her birth. She knew the very core of it, the first few notes, and how it had changed. How did she, the person, connect with that phrase of music that sailed among the stars? How did she make it flesh? How did she change it? She felt the music like another pulse. More than anything, she wanted to open her mouth and release the song to the heavens.

Days of sweating work went by as Shyma listened to the vital, underlying music and tried to know how it reached her, and how it recognized and incorporated her into itself. At first nothing happened, but she persevered. For Lomio's sake, she repeated again and again. One day, in the middle of her endless repetitions, the song wasn't just in her memory, it was in *her*. She heard every syllable of her name song in her own voice. This time it was different from the days before. She *felt* it. She felt healthier and more whole than she had since the day of her son's birth, since before the *tikom* came.

The song was true.

"Shyma!" Gomlo appeared in the doorway, still holding his hoe, thick mud clinging to his boots and the knees of his trousers. He smiled. "I *felt* you."

"I know," Shyma beamed. She breathed in the star essence. How she had missed it! "Listen again."

Reluctantly at first, Gomlo's name-song was teased out of her memory, note by note. She had to think it through slowly, to make sure she got it right, after three long years of silence. Then, she sang it.

The melody was true in her mind. It filled her head so much she was surprised that it didn't leak out of her ears. Gomlo straightened his shoulders, and his eyes glowed with energy, as if it was early in the morning instead of the end of a hard work day.

"I feel it," he said. "I can't hear anything, but I know what you are doing. More. Do more. Can you?"

Shyma could. One by one she brought forth the name-songs of each of her fellow villagers, bestowing the blessings and joy of the stars upon them. With each melody she felt stronger herself, the vessel enriched by its contents. She was overwhelmed by the beauty of the music, like taking a drink of clean water after the longest, driest day.

"We have the celestial songs back," Shyma told Gomlo, tears running down her face. Heedless of his dirty clothes, Gomlo embraced her.

A few of the more sensitive Miritus ran to the hut, in the midst of whatever they had been doing.

Ru, the widowed herb woman who lived on the edge of the village came in with her eight-year-old daughter in tow. She patted her chest. "I felt so good just now. I don't know why I thought of you, but does it mean anything?"

"It does," Shyma said, pulling them into the embrace. "It means hope."

From that day she knew they could win. She worked to draw power from the stars, fount of energy, the simplest of their gifts, light. When she was tiny, Grun had made light in his hands to drive away her fear of the dark. Once she was grown and trained, she learned that a truly advanced singer could use light as a weapon. But such a use disrupted its song, so she tried to keep it to its purpose of filling the darkness. She stared at her hands, remembered her father and his song to bring light from the stars. With all her heart she concentrated, screwing her eyes shut, bringing his face and voice to mind.

A faint gasp interrupted her thoughts, and her mother's voice spoke.

"Shyma. Shyma, child. Open your eyes."

Shyma let her lids drift open. Her mother's brown cheeks and brown eyes were lit by a golden glow. Shyma looked down. In her palms lay a globe of soft, golden light. Grun's gift.

Shyma held the light, smiling at it with joy that she had not known in many years. She held out her hand to her mother, who squeezed her fingers. Shyma changed the song in her mind to one for healing. The grip became stronger. Some of the lines in her mother's face relaxed. She moved her shoulders, tentatively at first, and then more easily.

"The ache is gone," Narinik said, awed. "You can do it. You can do anything."

Too excited to speak, Shyma rose and hurried out into the fields. Gray-blue dusk was beginning to gather, but the dancing, half-filled heads of yellow-green grain seemed to whisper to her. She walked out among them, smelling their fresh, sharp scent and hearing in her mind the high, clear tones of the sowing melody.

"Bestow upon this land the blessing of the stars," Shyma thought-sang, holding her arms out as if she would embrace every stalk. "Fill yourselves with health and joy and light . . ." She ran through the song twice, until the whole field seemed to glow golden in her mind's eye like a quilt belonging to a king.

Gomlo came running, with Narinik hobbling behind

him, beaming. He picked her up and spun her in a circle. Shyma embraced him and her mother and the other villagers who crowded in to share the miracle.

"I can bless every field," Shyma told them triumphantly, finding her voice at last. "And, then, I can go."

Many days' travel over ill-kept, rutted dirt roads brought her at last to the heart of Mirit. Before the conquest, the people had stored grain in the Star Lord's citadel, the Moonlight Fortress. The gray stone citadel occupied a high, rounded hill that overlooked miles and miles of tilled fields and husbanded forests and orchards. For hundreds of peaceful years it had stood as a protection only against natural disasters. When the flood waters rose, as they did every few years, the Miritus and their animals took shelter there until the singers could sing the water back into place. It hadn't been used as a defensive structure for hundreds of years. The optimists said it would never be needed again. The pessimists felt that they had become too complacent. The pessimists got no satisfaction out of being right.

Shyma trembled on the enormous stone step, between the two black-clad guards of a race she had never seen before. She heard a discordant melody in their substance. They hated the Miritus, hated being in Mirit, and they stank of fear.

A scream sounded from high above. She looked up to see a *tikom* perched on the battlements above the gate like a horrible sculpture, the color of rotting moss on the clean gray stone. The *tikom*'s dead eyes glared down at her.

"What do you want?" one of the guards asked, hoarsely.

"My village is starving," she said. "I have come to beg permission of the lord to sing to the crops."

"A singer?" They took her arms and dragged her across the courtyard toward the high stone keep.

The vast space enclosed by the curtain walls was full of workers and machines. Shyma knew of war engines only through the old sagas. She had never seen any, but what else could these huge devices bristling with jagged metal spikes and blades be for but to besiege and to kill? K'tot was preparing again for war.

For a moment Shyma wondered why. The Miritus were too terrified to resist him, and the *tikom* killed anyone who even defied a rule. Then she realized these were not intended to be used in Mirit. K'tot meant to invade and conquer the next land.

Bent-backed Miritus in leather aprons worked alongside outlanders, hammering nails into the bodies of carts and siege engines. Word had come to Shyma's village of smiths, woodcrafters, and other skilled laborers who had disappeared, marched off into the night by K'tot's soldiers. Here they were. She was glad to know they lived.

By the stars, she vowed, *I will set you free, too*, she thought, before her sight of them was cut off by a stone wall.

Every child knew from lessons given by the village bard the rhyme about the citadel. "The star doors open upon the hall, the sunlight through the slit does fall, where gate would drop to trap in foe, but freely in a friend may go." It had a singsong chant, but she did not dare to voice the couplets. She felt eyes scrutinizing her as the guards half-carried her along the dark passage. Little light was visible. The fewest possible torches burned and sputtered on the walls, leaving whole sections of the way unlit. The guards hurried through the lightless sections as if it frightened them. A door here and there stood ajar upon a room lit by a single candle. Slaves of several races glanced up as Shyma passed, the terror in their eyes as plain as the reflection of the single flame.

At the end of the passage, two guards threw open tall doors to a vast chamber with a single chair on a dais in the center. Her escort thrust her forward at the foot of the dais, so she fell on her knees.

The song of the citadel described, "The throne of justice, seat of kings, a blessing on the folk who sing, cherished by the stars above, the Star Lord rules through strength and love." The being in the dark seat, made of Mirit's most precious red stone, its two arms carved in the likeness of shooting stars, held no love for her or any other Miritu.

For the first time in her life Shyma beheld a creature that made her doubt the teachings of her father, that all beings were made of the same substance and imbued with the celestial songs. The sorceror K'tot had skin of a malevolent blue, like dead flesh that had begun to rot. Hot, white eyes glared at her out of a narrow, inverse triangle of a face topped with a brush of wild white hair like dead straw. A slit close to the bottom point of the triangle opened. He pointed a long white fingernail at her.

"You dare," a voice boomed, filling her ears and her mind. The accent was foreign, and foul. "You dare to defy my edict? The songs are anathema."

"I beg you, lord sorcerer," Shyma pleaded, finding her voice, which sounded thin and lost in the echoing hall. "We'll die if the songs are suppressed forever. It won't take long. The grain will run out, the weak ones won't survive illness without the music to heal them."

"Then the strong will survive." The narrow face

leaned close, and the white eyes moved up and down, studying her. Shyma could feel a trail of heat where they passed. "You are strong enough to be a slave, but too much spirit. You would defy me."

"No, lord, I beg only for my people's sake!" she protested.

K'tot was finished addressing her. "Take her," he said.

Shyma froze as the guards seized her arms. Was he sending her to her death? "My lord, please! I only wish to serve."

K'tot reached for a solid gold cup held up to him by a black-clad guard. "That's what they all say," he grinned, as they dragged her away from the dais.

Her escort did not return to the courtyard. Instead, they steered her through a barred iron door and down a twisting, damp, stone staircase even more ill-lit than the corridor. Faint cries came from the depths, and the smells of old sweat, rusting metal, and rotting food welled up around her. Shyma concentrated on not tripping. The stone steps spoke to her, telling her where to place her foot next. The sorcerer might dominate her now, but the keep had been the home of the Star Lords for over a thousand years. There was no corruption in the strong fabric of the building. Shyma began to feel confident again. If she lived past the next hour, the citadel itself would aid her.

Her eyes grew used to the gloom, picking out a rusted sconce, a recessed doorway here and there.

At the bottom of the stairs Shyma's escort pulled her to a halt. An iron grille blocked the way.

"Open!" the soldier on her right shouted. A stout guard in black, his uniform greasy and disheveled, came forward and peered through the bars at them.

He fumbled at his belt for the huge keys that hung there, and unlocked the gate. It creaked as if it was not used to opening. "New prisoner."

"Name?" the jailer asked.

"Who cares?" said the soldier on Shyma's left. She shivered, but she was relieved. She would live.

The heavyset guard pulled a feebly burning torch off the wall and led them down a long, uneven passage that had to have been hewn out of natural underground caves. Pockets in the stone were filled in with mortar, leaving a square gap that held iron doors, featureless except for a small grille about chin-height to a male Miritu and a slot near the floor. Shyma lost count of the doors she was pushed past until the jailer stopped and unlocked a door. The guards shoved her in and slammed the door. The creak of the lock twisting closed and the receding footsteps were the last sounds she heard for hours except for her own breathing.

Shyma explored the small cell. The stone walls and floor were damp, but not unpleasantly cool. The legend said the citadel had been built over hot springs, which provided power and hot baths to the inhabitants above. She wouldn't die of sleeping on the cold stone, a relief, since there was no bed or blanket wraps. All she found was an earthenware water jug, empty, and a hole in the floor. The cell smelled only of stone. No one had been in here for a long time.

She pulled as much of the stuff of her robe under her bottom as possible for comfort, and sat in the center of the floor. She could sense dozens of pale golden lights nearby, living beings like herself. Some were faint, deprived too long of a sight of the stars. The guard's flame was a different color, reddish, as if the blood he had shed tainted his essence.

After an endless time, a faint jingle and a clank

came from the far end of the corridor, followed by another clank: the guard going off duty. The golden flames focused upon her.

"Who are you?" came a whisper from not too far away.

"I hear the stars," Shyma whispered back.

A sigh. Muttering as the word was passed back and forth between the other cells.

"We are all singers, too," the voice whispered. "I'm Banlo."

"Shyma," she replied.

"What happened, Shyma?" Banlo asked kindly.

"The *tikom* took my child," Shyma replied. "I have come to get him back."

A burst of bitter laughter came from slightly further away. "When you get him, will you please ask for my wife back? The *tikom* killed her three years ago!"

"He is not dead," Shyma exclaimed.

"Shh!" Banlo hissed. "The next guard will not come for some time, but loud noises carry here. We are punished, whenever the guards please. They enjoy our pain." He let out a low exhalation. "Not that the greatest pain is being deprived of our freedom."

"How did you come here?" she asked.

The others were eager to talk to a newcomer. There were thirty-seven of them alive. A dozen other prisoners had died for lack of light or star-blessed food, no one knew for certain. They were all singers from various small villages throughout Mirit, all but Banlo.

"I was the Star Lord's personal singer," Banlo said sadly. "I saw the sorcerer descend from the sky on scarlet fire. My colleagues and I sang all the power I could muster to fight him, but his spells seem a corruption of the substance of the universe. He burned me and my colleagues. I woke up here, missing one leg. They told me the Star Lord was dead, along with all of my friends, and the sorcerer now ruled. I have seen neither light nor a friendly face since then. All I know since then I learned from newcomers like you."

"I can give you light," Shyma offered.

Banlo's whisper was horrified. "No! The *tikom* can hear us sing, no matter where we are. You will die, and all of us will be punished. Not," Banlo finished, with an ache in his voice, "that death would not be preferable to this endless life in darkness."

"That is why I have come," Shyma informed him. "I can sing the songs without sound."

"If that were possible," the bitter voice in the distance said, "don't you think one of us would have learned how in all this time?"

"I don't know why I was able to do it," Shyma replied, "but I can."

"Prove it," a hoarse woman's voice said, trembling with emotion.

"I shall."

Shyma sat back on her folds of cloth and held out her cupped hands. She tried to hear her father's voice. Instead, the cackling, scoffing voice of the sorcerer interrupted her thoughts, mocking her. Angrily she pushed aside the memory, and reached deep into herself for Grun's gift.

By my father's memory, she begged the stars silently, *give me your light.*

A golden spark came to life, so bright in the blackness that it seared her eyes. But she cupped it gently and pushed it through the slot under the iron door.

"Do you see?" she asked.

"Light!" Banlo exclaimed, bursting into tears. "It is light! Oh, blessed stars, it has been so long! Oh, bless you, woman."

A murmur ran through the dungeon. It rose in excitement until the harsh voice hissed out.

"Silence!"

Shyma extinguished the globe and drew her hands back. Footsteps thumped down the stone stairs.

"Quiet tonight, eh?" the night jailor asked, his voice echoing in the stone corridor. "Good. No trouble, no punishment." He laughed cruelly. "Maybe."

Shyma and the others remained silent until the guard departed, hours later. The moment his steps were out of earshot, all the other captives began speaking at once.

"Do it again!" one pleaded.

"Show me how!"

"Show all of us!"

But Banlo was the most practical. "Can you sing any other songs?"

Shyma had been waiting for the moment herself. She had been feeling the substance of her cell door. It was honest metalwork, no claim to good or evil. The lock was a simple mechanism. It could use a little oil. It responded to a song of undoing that worked on knots, locks, and other fastenings. The door creaked open. One by one she unlocked her fellow captives' doors. They huddled together in the corridor smiling and crying for joy around a globe of light Shyma produced. Banlo had to be helped out of his cell, a tall Miritu whose left leg had been sliced off at the knee. He looked down at Shyma, gratitude in his warm brown eyes.

"A little key to open a big door," he said. "Teach us. Teach us all you know."   -

Every one of the singers was eager to learn from Shyma. In the two brief periods of silence that they had every day, she taught them to go inside themselves to hear their name-songs without making a sound.

"Hear it in your mind," she instructed them. "*Know* yourself singing. In your mind's ear, join in with your fullest voice."

As with her, it took a long time, but her pupils were more than willing to seize any thread of hope. As each succeeded in gaining the first toehold, the meager food they were given once a day became nutritious and strengthening, and long-unused muscles grew strong. The daily meetings when they could see and touch one another did as much for morale as the whispered lessons. In the company of others like her, Shyma made new discoveries. She learned how to alter substance. After some experimentation she pulled the stuff of her stone floor into fibers soft enough to sleep on.

Banlo scoffed at the mundane use of such a power. "We can use this knowledge," he said. "We can use it to change the *tikom*. They are our greatest threat. We will alter them so that they can no longer hear a singer's voice."

"But we're not in range of the *tikom*," the hoarse woman, Velama, argued.

"We are not near the stars, either," Banlo replied, "but we touch them. Concentrate. Save our fellow singers."

"Silence!" A whip cracked from the stairwell. They all scattered to their cells. "It's you, isn't it, Banlo? Need another whipping?" The day jailor stumped down into the dungeon. Shyma heard the sound of Banlo's cell door being unlocked, and the whistle and thud of the lash as it struck the singer's thin shoulders. "Hah. That'll teach you to make noise."

The singers huddled in darkness, but only outer silence. Their voices now flew freely from mind to mind.

"He will occupy this very cell when we overthrow

K'tot," Banlo's mind-voice sang in Shyma's ear, and she knew all of the others could hear him, too.

"How? K'tot is too powerful."

"No. His power is only strange to us," Banlo insisted. "He can be overthrown."

The old man's voice was filled with alarm. "There are too few of us! We need more help."

"We need to study the dark sorcerer's ways," Velama insisted. "To do that, we must make contact with more singers and teach them Shyma's ways."

"How?" the old man asked, scornfully. "We are in prison."

"Only our bodies," Banlo replied. "Thanks to Shyma," and she felt his energy envelop her like a warm blanket, "we can reach out to other singers without voices, without bodies, from *here*. We can learn how to defeat him, from under his very nose. All substance is one, no matter how corrupted it seems. We will find the key to his power, and render it harmless. From this very place, using the celestial songs, we will make Mirit strong and free again."

"Hear, hear," the old man said approvingly.

"Shyma?" Banlo asked, feeling for her.

She sat silent. His words had jarred her. From that place she could indeed reach out to other singers. Why had she not realized it? She let her mind drift out, looking for other points of light.

She found them. A cluster of infant singers lay in a dark nursery in a corner tower of the great keep. Nurses in black dresses passed among them, feeding them mashed grain or changing their swaddling. They were not uncomfortable or unhappy. They lay in cots playing with their toes and listening to the celestial music as it sang lullabies to them.

Shyma found Lomio, and let her mind caress him

with all the love in her being. Her child! He had grown so much! He cooed out his name-song in time with the eternal song. *Di-da-dee-dee, de-yu-du.* A new note! How she wished she could tell Gomlo! He could not hear her mind-voice. But, Shyma realized, he would feel the benefit if she mind-sang his name-song. She would, therefore, be able to reassure him they were alive.

She let her thoughts hover about her child. "One day, little one, I shall be able to sing you the song of how we won your freedom. Until then, sleep. Sleep well."

Shyma brought her thoughts back to her cell, no longer her prison, but a place from which to undermine the tyrant sorceror. And they would. Their freedom was not long ahead. She looked forward to singing her victory out loud.

From that moment on, the light began to return to Mirit.

IRAQI HEAT

Gregory Benford

Gregory Benford is a working scientist who has written 23 critically-acclaimed novels. He has received two Nebula Awards, principally in 1981 for *Timescape*, a novel that sold over a million copies and won the John W. Campbell Memorial Award, the Australian Ditmar Award, and the British Science Fiction Award. In 1992, Dr. Benford received the United Nations Medal in Literature. He has been a professor of physics at the University of California, Irvine, since 1971. He specializes in astrophysics and plasma physics theory and was presented with the Lord Prize in 1995 for achievements in the sciences. He is a Woodrow Wilson Fellow and Phi Beta Kappa. He has been an adviser to the National Aeronautics and Space Administration, the United States Department of Energy, and the White House Council on Space Policy, and has served as a visiting fellow at Cambridge University. His first book-length work of nonfiction, *Deep Time* (1999), examines his work in long duration messages from a broad humanistic and scientific perspective.

FAMILY:
    One of the perks of being a Major in Special Ops is that when you haul in back at HQ there's late

nite e-mail. Thought you'd all like to hear how it's going here in the post-war war.

We're up to our ass in alligators is how it is.

We were working the Sunni Triangle between Ramadi and Tikrit last week, looking for Ba'athist bastards. Hard not to shoot them in the back because running away is just about all they do.

We got some Ansar al Islam, an Al Qaeda knockoff bunch following their latest hot tactic—avoid us (don't want to die, never mind all the 72 virgins deal) and instead hit the Iraqis who're working with us. Police, utilities guys, engineers who actually know how to get things fixed.

It's been pretty hectic since the end of hostilities and the start of the real war. You know what they say about Iraq—dirty, hot, nasty, ugly—and that's just the people. To answer Uncle Max's question—yep. We expected some armed resistance from the Ba'ath Party and Fedayeen. We tried to get all of them we could in the campaign itself. Only now are the CNN commentators catching on that the slowdown S of Baghdad was to draw as many of their tank units out where we could get them easy. Intel predicted we'd get Fedayeen in those white pickups with machine guns mounted on the deck, and sure enough, we did. Saved a lot of trouble in Baghdad.

So if you're wondering, nope, the smalltime stuff isn't any worse than expected, and morale is A-1, except for the normal bitching and griping.

Gotta go. More maybe soon, when I get back to HQ. More fun in the field, believe me.

That night he dreamed of Fairhope and the bay.

Even in the fog of sleep he was sure of where he was, in a skiff gliding across the Chacaloochee spur north of the causeway. In among the cattails were alligators, one with three babies a foot and a half long. They scattered away from his skiff, nosing into the muddy fragrant water, the mother snuffing at him as she sank behind the young ones. The big legendary seventeen-footers he knew always lie back in the reeds, but as he coasted forward on a few oar-strokes he saw plenty of lesser lengths lounging in the noonday sun like metallic sculptures. A big one ignored the red-tailed hawk on a log nearby, know-ing it was too slow to ever snare the bird. By a cypress tree, deep in a thick tangle of matted saw grass, a possum was picking at something and sniffing like it couldn't decide whether to dine or not. The phosphorus-loving cattails had moved in farther up, stealing away the skiff's glide so he came to a stop. He didn't like the cattails and started swearing at them to get them to move on. He knew they were robbing sunlight from the paddies and fish below, making life harder for the water-feeding birds. But they wouldn't move at all. Then he woke up into the dry darkness.

Hey guys, been a while, I know.

I had beers with some press tonight. They were guys and one gal who have the cojones to be embedded with the troops during the fighting. I heard one today say that journalism is art. Hemingway complex, I guess.

I'm in Baghdad now, since SpOpComm 3 relo-cated here from Qatar. It looks, sounds, and smells about the same, but at least you can get California wine now at the local OC. We came to help set up operation Scorpion and Sidewinder—major (and long overdue) shifts in tactics. Instead of being sit-ting ducks for the ragheads, we now are going after the worthless pieces of aged fecal matter. I have a

combat mission coordinating a bunch of A teams.
Kinda modified *Star Trek* is what we do: to boldly
go (I know Mom, split infinitive) where no kick-ass
guys have gone before, seeking, finding and rooting
out the mostly non-Iraqis that are well-armed, well-
paid (in US dollars) and always waiting to shoot
some GI in the back in the midst of a crowd. To
seek out old civilizations and bring the news about
their old games being over.

New motto came down for us: NO BETTER
FRIEND, NO WORSE ENEMY. Hope so . . .

The GIs are pissed (not demoralized) because
they can't touch, must less waste, those taunting
bags of gas that scream in their faces and riot on
cue when they spot a cameraman. If they did, then
they know the next nightly news will be about how
chaotic things are and how much the Iraqi people
hate us.

And to answer Uncle Ernie, yes— Some do. But
the vast majority don't. More and more see that the
GIs don't start anything, are by-and-large friendly, if
a little jumpy, and compassionate, especially to kids
and old people. I saw a bunch of guys from the 82nd
Airborne not return fire until they got a group of elderly civilians out of harm's way. The Iraqis saw it,
too. A shop vendor brought them some dusty dates
to eat, after.

He went down to see the bodies a Marine unit had
reported. They were drifting downstream near Najaf
and he walked out on a damaged steel bridge to look
down as they drifted past. The bloated corpses wore
iraqi uniforms, but their wounds were not from combat. A lot of limbs were chewed and even torn off
and there were deep gouges in the legs and abdomen.
He looked upstream and in among the reeds were

lounging crocs like logs sleeping in the sun. They would roll over in the luxury of the warm mud and some gave off a moaning grunt, an *umph-umph-umph* with mouths closed but still achieving a throaty, bellowing roar. He had seen alligators like that before in Weeks Bay where the Fish River eased in, just below the old arced bridge. 'Gators seemed to like bridges. They would lie in the moist heat and sleep, top predators, unafraid. Crocs were lighter colored than gators, slimmer in the snout and with a big white fourth jaw tooth sticking out from the gum. But they were a lot like the 'gators he knew. Easy in their assurance that nothing could touch them, top predator arrogance. Until people came along, and rifles. He wondered if they had feasted on the Iraqi army bodies, acquiring a taste. Then one of the crocs turned and looked up at him for a long moment. It held the gaze, as if figuring him out. It snuffed and waddled a little in the mud to get more comfortable and closed its big eyes.

Last week I was tasked with putting together a special security detail at a hospital in Najaf. The Spanish patrol there, but seems we'd delivered a bunch of pharmaceuticals there (donated by big corporations) and they'd mysteriously vanished overnight. Saddam let go 30,000 prisoners just before the war, most common criminals, and a lot of them went back to the trade they knew. Those drugs were worth a fair amount, so I had another delivery made there. Then we posted a team around the hospital alley at night, IR surveillance only.

I went around to sit with them after midnight and sure enough, about 2 AM here comes a truck and out come guys carrying crowbars, AK-47s and manual jack-forklifts. We let them pop the bolt lock on the alley door and then give them an order to get hands in the air. Of course the AK-47s open up, but we're using silencers on our weapons and flash inhibitors, so they can't see our return fire. Clean, precise, silent, down go the AK-47 guys—and damned if the forklift guys don't pick up the AK-47s and start firing again. Spraying slugs in all directions, into pitch-black. Some people never learn. I picked up my piece—an M-16, 29 rounds in the clip—and got off a few.

So down they go, too. Only two guys out of the gang of eight survived, wounded. We called in a MedVac helicopter to take them out to the nearest field hospital.

They talked plenty. Turned out they were working for some of the dead ones, who were bad-ass Hamas fresh over from the Syrian border. The gang was boosting drugs and anything else not nailed down, hired by Hamas to finance their terror here. Living off the land, as it were.

The local teenagers watch the GIs and try to talk to them, asking questions about America and how to get wrap-around sunglasses like ours, and Gap T-shirts, Dockers, or—even better—Levis with the red tags, and Nikes (Egyptian knock-offs, but with the "swoosh"). They listen to AFN when the GIs play it on their radios. Mostly for the music, gawdawful though it is.

They don't participate in the demonstrations and tip us when a wannabe bad-ass with a Kalashnikov (an assault rifle, Mom, best thing the Soviets ever made) shows up in the neighborhood.

The younger kids are going back to school again, don't have to listen to some mullah rant about the Koran ten hours a day, and they get a hot meal. They see the same GIs who man the corner checkpoint, helping clear the playground, install new swing sets and create soccer fields. I watched a bunch of kids playing baseball in one dirty playground, supervised by a couple of GIs from Oklahoma. They weren't very good, of course, but were having fun, probably more than most Little Leaguers—for one thing, the parents weren't watching. (I always hated that—there, I finally said it. Sorry, Dad.)

He was back on the Fish River, at Grammaw McKenzie's farm. It was an unending hot summer day when his job just before lunch was go walk down under the cypress with the Spanish moss dripping onto the sandy soil and palmettos. He would pick up the net on a pole and take a fish head from the previous day's catch and put it firmly on the hook of an ordinary fishing line. He stood on the wooden wharf and had to be sure to cast no shadow onto the pale thin sandy beach that the tide had put under water. The fish head lay on the bottom and he swished it enticingly back and forth in the raw sunlight. Crabs came running from under the wharf quick as you please, eager for the old fish head. They would be good and fresh for lunch and Grammaw had the pot boiled all ready for them.

But this time as the three or four crabs gathered around the fish head, snatching for it on their way to the net that he had waiting on the end of the pole, something quick and long came out from under the wharf. It gulped down the crabs quick and sure, bobbing its head to roll one down the gullet before scooping up the next.

It was his old enemy, the 'gator that slept most of its days away in the reeds down at Nelson Point. It scared the occasional swimmer but never attacked. It went after any chickens that strayed too near the water, coming fast out of the palmettos on thick legs.

Many afternoons when Ol' Gator—that was what we finally named it—came out to the middle of the river, Grandpaw would try to shoot it with his big rifle, waving away the puny 0.22 that was offered. But even he could not hit the long narrow head with two bumps for eyes as it glided serenely away. Grandpaw would run out onto the old plank wharf for a better angle. Usually it had just swallowed a squawking chicken whole, and that's the way it happened in the dream, only really slow and with the smells of the mud flats swarming.

The chicken squawks had made Grandpaw mad, so that his teeth clamped down hard on his pipe. He stood straight as a rod on the wharf and fired five times and missed. His pipe stem broke off in his teeth with a click. Ol' Gator's two big eye-bumps never even turned to look back and the broad back just glided away, kind of contemptuous.

It was not the first time Grandpaw had tried for the 'gator and would not be the last. But in the end he never got it; that Ol' Gator was just too damn smart. Whenever Grandpaw lost a chicken, he tried, running out on the wharf while he jacked a round into his rifle—right up until he died. Nobody cared about losing a few crabs, but a chicken ate grain and could lay eggs.

This place is still a mess. But then, most of it has been for decades.

Hospitals are open and are being brought into the twenty-first century. The MOs and visiting surgeons from home are teaching their docs new techniques and one American pharmaceutical company (you know, the kind that everybody screams about as greedy) donated enough medicine to stock 45 hospital pharmacies for a year. A Marine caught two guys making off with a truck of that and nailed them both. Just think, no expensive trials!

Safe water is more available. Electricity is mostly back at prewar levels, but saboteurs keep cutting the lines. And the old Ba'ath big shots are upset because they can't get fuel for their private generators. One actually complained to General Mack, who told him it was sure a rough world.

The MPs are screening the 80,000 Iraqi police force and rehabbing the ones that weren't goons, shakedown artists, or torturers—just like they did in East Berlin, Kosovo, and Afghanistan.

There are dual patrols of Iraqi cops and US/UK/Polish MPs now in most of the larger cities. Basra's got 3.5 million inhabitants. Mosul has 2 million, Kirkuk has 1 million. How many hundreds of other small towns have not had riots or shootings? The vast majority.

Early on, six UK cops were killed in a small Shiite town by the ex-cops they were rehabbing. According to a Royal Marine colonel I talked to, the town now has about twenty permanent vacancies in its police force. He's a hulk from Belfast named Ruggins and knows how to handle terrorists after twenty years fighting with the IRA.

I heard one chatterbox on MSNBC the other night talk about how we're covering up our guys killed by accidents or other causes, but that's because we won't let them shoot footage. The numbers are small anyway. I got called in yesterday to look into two drowned while swimming in the Tigris and that was the coroner's report, but truth is they were both bit by crocs.

Yep, crocodiles! They're growing like crazy in the Tigris and Euphrates, maybe fed by all the bodies that have been floating downstream for years. Saddam's bullyboys had been dumping bodies in the Tigris and Euphrates and then telling the relatives to look downstream. I guess they figured it made the impression they were looking for.

So the crocs prospered. Big suckers, too. A college biology teacher here in a National Guard unit said he's studied the Tigris ones, and they're hunting in packs! I saw some crocs down Basra way when we went in to provide security cover for the Army engineers. Some locals were trying to stop the first steps at reclaiming that natural disaster. That's the best damn example I've seen of what Saddam did to his own people. Sure, they're digging up plenty of bodies, but the bigger damage you can see stretching east of Basra like a corpse on a slab. This is where he drained the means of life itself away from the swamp tribes.

See, in the Iran-Iraq massacre they called a war, the moron mullahs of Iran had executed over a thousand of the top army and air force officers. Thought they were still loyal to the Shah, y'see. (Remember him? How time flies when you're not havin' fun.) So Saddam sees this as a velvet opportunity to skate into southern Iran, grab territory and oil wells. Iran throws everything against him because they don't have an army worth a damn anymore. No air force, just plenty dumb infantry. It bogs down into trench warfare, WWI all over again. Even down to the gas warfare. Using battalions of kids fresh from school plus a week of training. Murder.

Iran tries to outflank the Iraqi lines by going through the southern swamp country. Over 400,000 people lived in this big flat country where the Tigris meets the Euphrates. A simple life in a country that is otherwise a big flat desert. They fished, crabbed, farmed estuary crops, the way some do N of Mobile Bay.

Past tense, though—because Saddam saw these Iranian troops circling around his lines, and decides he will just deprive them of that. Too hard to fight in mud flats and reeds. So he has his engineers carve deep canals down the main drift of the rivers, straight to the sea S of Basra.

Drains the swamps, destroys the livelihood of many people. Who protest. And get shot, or carted off. Saddam's Sunnis were glad to blow away a lot of ignorant Shiite farmers. And that was it for a huge tract of productive swampland and all the wildlife that lived there.

That put the war back into stalemate, which got settled when they ran out of men—over a million dead. Kissinger said, "The only bad thing about Iran vs. Iraq is that they can't both lose," kinda like Hitler vs. Stalin I guess—but he was wrong. Both countries lost big time.

So the Army engineers figure, let's block those cut canals, spread the water again like it was, and let the swamplands regrow. There are still patches left to start with. Good date farms; I tasted some at a roadside stand. The guy gave them to us; wouldn't take money.

The engineers move in with 'dozers, backhoes, get some mobile cranes from the port facilities to help. Working up from Basra, they find these side channels, and there are plenty of crocs in there. I guess the biologist would say there had been some pressure on them, because those crocs were real downass nasty.

Hey, gotta get off. I'll catch up later. This company computer has a signup list, even at 3 AM. Send this to the rest of the family around Baldwin County, okay?

He tossed in the sweaty night and realized that he had been dreaming again of the broad flat water in the Bay. And of Battleship Parkway, where he had visited as a boy, the start of his military career and fixation. Of climbing in awe through the battleship *Alabama* and its sidekick from WWII glory, the submarine *Drum*. Even then he had been surprised at how small the rooms were, and in the dream it was the same. An hour inside battleship iron and he longed to be out on the water, to smell the humid reek of the flats nearby.

Along the causeway were bait and tackle shops, boat ramps, and the Old Oyster House. Nowadays, and in the coasting arc of the dream, there were seafood joints designed to look beat-up and old and authentic, all separated by clumps of eight-foot sea oats. It was raining. The hard, heavy rain filled the bay to its brim, so he glided on the causeway like he was riding on water, the slick surface coming right up to the blacktop. In the distance an alligator lazed on the surface, barely moving.

Then he was eating. Big eating: deep-fried dill pickle slices, oysters in peppery batter, mounds of steamy shrimp. He was reaching for a beer when he woke up.

I'm down Basra way again, which is why you haven't heard. I was with a SpOp joint patrol unit that today sent five warriors of Allah to enjoy their 72 slave girls in Paradise. Hell of a way to get laid.

Way it happened was a mosque blew up this morning. Our Intel said the local Imam named Fahlil (who frequently appeared on CNN) was helping a Syrian Hamas member teach eight teenagers how to make belt bombs.

Oops! No more Fahlil, no more teenagers. Better living through chemistry. Right away the local Fedayeen propaganda group started wailing that we hit it with a TOW missile.

I got there with Col. Falcona and we shook our heads. If it had been a TOW, there'd be no mosque left. CNN and BBC show up and right away a slit-eyed guy was dragging around a piece of tin with blood on it, claiming it was part of the missile. The cameras rolled and he started repeating his story. One of my guys asked him in Arabic where he had left the rag he usually wore around his face that made him look like a girl, so he could slip through our checkpoints. Yep—was a local leader of the Fedayeen. We took the clown in custody and were asked rather indignantly by the twit from BBC if we were trying to shut up "the poor man who had seen his mosque and friends blown up." Our translator asked if he knew Arabic (which he obviously didn't) and pointed out that if so, he'd know the Fedayeen was a Palestinian. Guess what played on the BBC that evening? Did the Americans blow up a mosque? See (from three different camera angles) the poor man who is still in a state of shock over losing his mosque and relatives? Yep. Our friend the Palestinian.

The Army engineers are getting lots done. The swamps are coming back real quick with all that river water. Water buffalo lumbering by, ducks paddling through sheets of algae. I've even seen crocs migrating downriver to the old channels. Big swarms of them. I never saw 'gators moving in groups like that.

The Fedayeen don't like any of this. If we want it, it must be bad, right? We have about 400 nasties in custody now. We'll probably park them in the W desert behind a triple roll of razor wire, backed up by a couple of Bradleys pointed their way, if they decide to riot. Maybe a few will get to Gitmo, but most are human garbage that wouldn't take on your five-year-old grandson face-to-face. Snipers, mostly—hide and shoot and run.

Our first objective is to get the diehards off the street (or make them too scared to come out in them) and destroy their caches of weapons. We have collected more than 227,000 AK-47s and that's openers. Saddam bought a million of them from our pal Vladimir. The Syrians are pumping through arms and bodies, a lot old Hamas from Lebanon. (And formerly free Lebanon has been occupied by Syria for a quarter century; how come the U.N. doesn't care?)

I'm learning that it's gonna be a long haul (remember it took 10-15 years in Japan and W Germany). But if we don't stick with it, nobody else will, and we'll have some other loony running the place again.

Armageddon, here we come? (Remember, it's located on the outskirts of Jerusalem.)

He was back on the Bay again, twilight shading into fragrant night. Li'l Bateau was roaring at his back, an old skimmer he'd put together with high school buddies. Batty bucked and blared, and he loved every bit of its 500 cubic inch V-8 Cadillac engine. It was driving a madly whirring prop, all of them shielded by a wire screen from the blades. It was an airship of sorts. The prop drove them over foot-deep water far back into the bayous where no self-respecting wildlife ever expected to see a human.

Then they cut the prop and glided up into the fragrant, backwater paradise.

The birds didn't mind them. A coot skimmed low beside him, wings flapping madly, its feet comically dragging in the water. A kingfisher plunged beak-first into the muddy black water. A white ibis perched in a red cedar. From miles away the gaudy neon on Dauphin Street danced on the water in the thick humid night.

A 'gator snuffled at them. Showed teeth, defending its province. Then decided they were acceptable and rolled away into the black waters with a snort and a wheeze. Then gone. The lord of the realm, taking his leave of the commoners.

It's getting hot and humid hereabouts, but we got an hour before liftoff on a night attack. So I grabbed one of the staff computers and, maybe a week late, here I am.

The good news is that General Schoonmaker is going to be appointed Chief of Army and the old man is coming to Tampa to run the SpOps desk at CentComm. He's tops and will be getting his second star.

Whoopee! To me, it means that SpOps will be big time in future operations and after 18 years as a ground-hugger maybe I'll have a shot at a bird-level combat command. (The old man asked me to come to MacDill and be his ACS, but I told him no. I like the field, not a desk—not even one with a computer, woweee.)

As the movie quoted old General Patton, "God

help me, I love it." I do. Nothing more satisfying than working with the BEST damn soldiers in the world, flushing human refuse down the drain.

What the media folk don't seem to get is that this is the heart of the War on Terror. Just like our approach to Baghdad, we want to draw them out into the open, where we can shoot them. Now gangs of hotheads from Syria, Iran, Saudi Arabia are making it convenient for us. They come in, the Iraqi majority that hates them gives us intel, and we take them out. They self-deliver. Better to get them here than have to do it in the streets of Mobile.

Still, I'm up for rotation soon, and I'll be back there fishing and crabbing with the rest of you. I hope to see most of you and ask for some advice, not support. I know I've had that all along. I saw a card mounted above a desk here that pretty near says it all:

Work like you don't need the money.
Love like you've never been hurt.
Dance like nobody's watching.
Sing like nobody's listening.
Live like it's heaven on Earth.

He dreamed of an old misadventure, this time from before he had signed on and gotten his life straightened out. It was in a moldy motel joint called Las Brisas on the causeway. When he checked in, they offered an Elvis suite and showed it to him. In the dream he glided across the mushy carpets and saw at the suite entrance a black granite guitar embedded in white marble. He had a girlfriend with him and she was impressed that the suite came complete with hot tub and a four-poster bed. Elvis actually had stayed there; they had the sign-in ledger posted on the wall.

Then somehow he was hooting across the Bay and, with girlfriend still along, they were in Bienville Square. Smack in the middle of old Mobile. He felt more than heard the *sploop* of water in the tiered fountain, dripping beneath moss-draped oaks and ornate iron benches. The old birds were perched on the hard rusty iron, wearing their retirement clothes.

That's just how I don't want to end up, he thought very clearly in the fog of the dream. *Better dead first.* Then he woke up, soaked with sweat though he wore no pajamas.

Quick note, got to get ready for another twilight gig. We got word of a bunch of infiltrators from Iran, coming through the Hammar marshlands our engineers are opening up again with river water. They're using the old dodge Iran tried back there, two wars ago—slither in through the swampland. Only this time we know they're a bunch of Fedayeen with some heavy arms and crossing in squads. A Madan Arab tipped us off. If they get into Basra, they'll do real damage.

But that's an hour away. Let me catch up.

Last night's skirmish was okay, but I only got to see it from the air, looking out a chopper window. We boxed in a small band of infiltrators fresh over the line, was all. But I could see there was something else moving in the marshes, so I told the pilot to skim over the area.

There was plenty there, but it was crocs. They were bunched up on the sandbar and moving around, all agitated. Maybe our firefight had excited them? Only I'd expect it would drive them into the water, not out of it. More Iraq mystery. This place has a surplus.

The coordinated air-ground attack had gone well, encircling the village and pushing the enemy against the wetlands to the east. The choppers had caught a gang of them trying to bust out and they lay in clumps in the high saw grass they thought would hide them. They had tried to get away into the newly blossoming channels of the emerging swampland, but they did not make it all the way.

Walking by them, the first thing you heard were the flies. Swarms were crawling over the grimy, blood-soaked cloth.

They had tried to carry off a lot of gear; maybe they were running low. Calfskin haversacks were packed with rocket-propelled grenades, ammo for the AK-47s that lay all around, knives—some stuck in the dirt—and medical kits stolen from the Red Cross. A body with shrapnel wounds lay across an odd Soviet tripod machine gun with the breech jammed open. There were empty brass shells all around that as if the man had been shooting at the choppers. Or maybe at the Warthogs, which was plain dumb, giving away your position like that. Once the Warthogs left because it was getting dark, we went forward again, some using their IR viewers. We were searching for stragglers and holdouts.

A lot of papers fluttered in the dry breeze. Korans, pictures showing mullahs in turbans, bleaching out in the sun, an envelope with a photo inside of a woman lounging back naked with a wicked smile. The mixture of porn and Islam pendants and icons drew smiles from the troopers who checked the bodies for useful Intel, some of them already bloating from the heat.

Pictures of children and smiling brides and whole families, along with letters, letters, letters.

Their pockets were all turned out like little white flags of surrender, probably by locals who often swoop in after the attacking troops had moved on. The strew of bodies told the story of how they had been caught fleeing and tried to turn and offer some automatic weapons fire at both the sky and the Americans who had come on them suddenly in armored personnel carriers from their left flank.

A lot had been killed running, judging by the sprawl of them. One had made it just to the lip of a canal and had no head. There was deep muddy water in the canal and out of that numb curiosity two squads of SpOps searched for the head along the bank until someone shouted. The head was washed up on the shore opposite, twenty meters away at least and caught in some cattails. Nobody could figure out how it had gotten there unless it had floated. And it looked to be gnawed on. A couple of the corpses had shat themselves in fear and everybody stayed upwind of those.

I had a typical unit to take into the landing zone. There was your homey with attitude, a born-again skinhead loner sniper type, one motor-mouthed crazy Italian street kid, and the inevitable white-bread, big-jawed farm boy from Tuscaloosa. Him, I was partial to; fellow Alabaman and all.

But I wasn't ready for what came after the ground assault. We had the Warthog A-10s for cover, slinging its sheets of 30-mm cannon rounds at 4000 a minute. Where it hit there was a wall of blood. We caught them good and you could smell the fear in them as their units broke up. Some ran into some stucco apartment buildings near the marsh. A TOW hit it and started a fire. Some of them ran out, firing on automatic, just fanning the slugs around. Our sharpshooters dropped them pretty quick.

Things calmed down. The fire spread in the apartments and civilians appeared, carrying stuff out—junk, looked like to me, but precious to them I guess. The sun went down while we surveyed the marshy terrain, with a few cotton-ball clouds hanging low and catching the last of a ruby sunset. Our air cover went roaring away and we started rounding up. I looked over the dead. Most we caught before they could get back into the deep cover of the marsh.

Then one of my squads found some holdouts up in the saw grass, upwards of a hundred. They had been smart, hiding in the tall reeds below the bank. Looked to be Fedayeen, but some had on the old Iraqi Army uniforms. Maybe they'd been hiding in Iran all this time, waiting to sneak back in.

The sun was gone and the apartments were burning yellow—all we had for light. We took machine gun fire from them at such close range that I couldn't call in air support. It was like a deadly dance in the dark, rounds zinging by your head from directions you didn't know. Shouts. Orders in English, orders in Arabic. Shrill screams.

I had been standing talking to a captain about getting our wounded out—there were only two, and minor flesh wounds at that. The shooting started in twilight and I ran all crouched over toward a stand of spindly date palms. I was feeling stupid at being caught like that but even more so when I hit the ground beneath the palms and crawled over to the bank.

I was alone. Our guys were a hundred meters to the left.

A big marsh spread out in the dim light, with two

sandy banks below me. On the one nearest were bunches of Iraqis, dug in pretty good behind some dunes. But they weren't staying there. In the gray light they were shooting and running, but it wasn't toward our guys, who were to the left. They were running toward me.

It made sense—I was at the weak spot. But that didn't explain the screams. Loud ones.

I had only a sidearm, a 9mm NATO issue that I like. Out of the murk came a big Fedayeen wearing desert tribal headdress. Straight for me. The burning buildings behind must have back lit me. He saw me the same time I did him. He hammered out those loud AK-47 rounds on auto, and the dirt churned all around where I was kneeling. I fired once, got him in the chest and he flopped backward—helped by the AK, which was still slamming slugs at the sky. That was when I saw them.

The Fedayeen weren't running toward me, they were running away from . . . the crocs.

Their long bodies were running with surprising, darting bursts of speed. They came at the Fedayeen in coordinated bursts, from several directions. The Fedayeen could shoot one, maybe two, before another got to his leg. One quick whipsaw of that long head and the guy went down. Then the teeth went into the guy and the screaming started in for real.

I saw that happen to at least a dozen. There were more, judging from the shooting and horrifying cries. In the flickering firelight I saw the teams of crocs spreading out, taking on stragglers. Fedayeen came limping up the beach toward me, eyes stark white, lips drawn back in crazed fear.

They never reached me. I don't think their bulging eyes even saw me. They ran and hissed loudly. One by one the crocs caught up—so fast!—and bit into their legs. Once they went down, they were done for.

It didn't take long. I watched the last of them run madly into the date palms and the crocs catch up. It reminded me of Ol' 'Gator, but these were bigger, meaner, faster.

I didn't think. The last Fedayeen fell not ten meters down the beach from me and a huge croc bit deep into him. Behind it came two more. They saw me. Hissed.

And that's when it happened. I pointed my sidearm at them and they stopped. Not because of my pointing a puny 9mm at them. Something else.

I could see maybe twenty crocs. They had finished their work, the Fedayeen were all down. But the crocs weren't feeding on them at all. Not dragging the bodies back toward the swamp water.

Just then something blew in the apartments behind me, probably a propane tank going off. That lit up the area real well and I could see the shiny intensity in the croc eyes as their heads moved.

They were looking around. Looking at me. Not moving much, just heads swiveling in that evil way they have.

Some of our guys came into view then. They kept good fire discipline, didn't shoot unless they had a target. No Fedayeen left.

I got the feeling they were thinking things over. Remembering.

So we all stood there in the dim firelight as seconds ticked away. The crocs didn't come for me. I lowered my 9mm.

A lance corporal called over to me from fifty meters off, "What's this, Major?"

"I sure as hell don't know," I said and just then the crocs started to move.

All together, as if something had given a signal.

They turned their backs on us and walked—walked, not ran—back toward the swamp. Into the muddy brown water. Ignoring the Fedayeen bodies.

As if they knew we weren't the ones they wanted. Inside a minute, they were gone. Just ripples in the brown water.

Now this whole story sounds crazy and it's not going into my action report the way I told you all. You're family and won't turn me into the loony bin—at least not yet. Maybe you'll wait for me to get back to Fairhope.

But I keep thinking about Ol' 'Gator. Smart, quick, yes. I don't know the difference between crocs and 'gators, only the crocs I saw were bigger, stronger, meaner for sure than Ol' 'Gator.

I did some thinking and found that biologist. He allowed as how the crocs have been under "selection pressure" ever since the Iraqis drained their swamps. Some migrated upriver. Some held on. But they had to find new ways of making a living and maybe, just maybe, that made them evolve faster.

Now look, before you go shaking your heads, I know some of you back there think evolution is a tool of the devil, an idea Satan put into our heads. Or Darwin's anyway. But listen now, please.

We came out of a drought in Africa, 'way back millions of years ago. No way to shake your heads at those fossils. Data is data. It's a fact—we peeled off from the tree-swinging chimpanzees then. Dryness forced us down out of the trees to learn to hunt, and we got better at it. Better at talking, too, to coordinate hunting and finding food—so I'm told. We kept getting smarter. Not smart enough yet to avoid bloody messes like this one, but some of us are working on that, too.

So why couldn't that happen to the crocs? They learn how to work together. Hunt together.

And they remember back to who it was that drained their paradise, their Eden.

And they knew who didn't commit that huge crime. They knew the uniforms of the Iraqi Army. The Fedayeen, too.

They knew we weren't them.

Okay, I'm just a grunt with a few bars on his shoulders. But I saw what I saw. Evolution never rests.

What I hope is that we don't blow this chance. The crocs are on our side—or vice versa, I guess. And Ol' 'Gator would have been proud of them for damn sure.

We're all alone on this planet, we smart chimpanzees. And things seem to be getting worse. Lots worse. I'm thinking, we could use another point of view.

SLOW POISON

Tanya Huff

Tanya Huff lives and writes in rural Ontario with her partner, four cats, and an unintentional Chihuahua. After 16 fantasies, she's written two space operas, *Valor's Choice* and *The Better Part of Valor*, and is currently working on a series of novels spun off from her Henry Fitzroy vampire series. In her spare time she gardens and complains about the weather.

SHE LOOKED neither to the left nor right as they escorted her up to the small audience chamber. No need to look; she knew what she'd see. The tapestries that had bracketed the broad corridor for hundreds of years had been torn down, ripped apart for the gold thread they contained. The walls beneath bore the marks of hammers and pry bars as the invaders searched for the treasure they knew the Citadel contained. The air that had once carried the scent of perfumes and fine foods now stank of blood and fire and despair.

No guards in ceremonial armor, sunbursts gleaming on enameled breastplates, stood outside the double doors. The doors themselves had been reduced to thousand-year-old kindling, for this was where the Citadel's defenders had made their last stand. Her shoes stuck to the red-brown pattern on the marble floor— still too wet to be called stains. There were women in this room she recognized, their fate over the day and night since the fall evident on faces and bodies.

Some of them watched her as she crossed to the dais. Some of them had retreated too far into the deep corners of their own minds to even know she was in the room. She didn't blame them, but this was no time to retreat; not if they wanted to defeat the darkness. Strength of arms had failed. Other strengths were needed now.

The men on the dais wore looted silks and brocades as well as the stained linens and rough furs that had been under their crude but ultimately effective armor. The man they surrounded had slipped a wide-skirted, peacock-blue jacket embroidered with golden suns over a leather-covered torso. She had seen the jacket last on one of the younger princes. The cuffs were stained the same color as the floor.

He was that indeterminate age between young and old—those few years when skill and physical ability briefly matched. The flesh along his jaw was still firm and his clothing covered heavy, functional muscle.

She was at the edge of the dais before he noticed her, preoccupied as he was with the elderly man dangling from one scarred hand. Eyes the brown of sugar cakes just off the fire turned toward her, and widened slightly as she calmly met his gaze.

A heavy hand landed on her left shoulder. The deep voice of her escort commanded her to kneel as he shoved her toward the floor.

She turned her head enough to meet his gaze in turn and snapped, "You'll be there to help me back to my feet, will you?"

When he hesitated, visibly confused by both her response and her immobility, she shook her head. "Never mind, I expect I'll manage."

Gathering up her kirtle in both hands, she shifted her weight to one leg and lowered the other knee cautiously to the floor. Once she had her bulk settled more-or-less comfortably, she looked back to the dais. And waited.

The man with the sugar-cake eyes waited as well. His name was Arwed. If there was more to his name than Arwed, she hadn't heard. His men called him the warlord when they spoke of him and Warlord when they spoke to him—all things considered an unremarkable designation. He and his horsemen had ridden out of the west, conquering everything before them until they reached the Citadel and the sea and could go no farther. Turning north would take them up into the mountains, turning south to battles they could not win. Unless they learned to sail, this was where they would stay. She wondered how far back along the path of destruction they'd left their women and children or if these were the men without either and that was why they'd thrown themselves so entirely into war.

If Arwed expected her to fidget or show some other sign of fear, he was doomed to be disappointed. At her size fidgeting required too much energy, and at her age there were no fears remaining she hadn't faced. At this new angle, she recognized the man he held. The Duc of Arn—a man who had fresh brown bread and honey every morning with his coffee when the sun touched the edge of his office window—the king's chancellor. The *late* king's chancellor. The king, or parts of him, were hanging over the central gate.

After a long moment, the man who had removed

the king's head smiled. He had, she noted, good strong teeth. "They say you cook." His accent was thick but understandable.

She had been in charge of the Citadel kitchens. "I do."

"Did you cook for your useless dead king?"

"I did."

"They say you are the best."

"I am." The simple truth.

"Then you will cook for me." Arwed swept the arm not holding the chancellor around the room. "And these my conquering warriors!"

The men roared their approval. One of the women screamed, the sound cut short by the impact of flesh on flesh.

"Bring us food," he continued, "as the sun sets!"

Another roar. The sun had been the symbol of the defeated.

"I'll need to find those of my kitchen workers still alive," she pointed out once the roaring stopped.

"You need what I tell you you need."

Her voice could have dried apples. "I'm not as young as I once was. If you want food fit for eating for this number, I'll need help."

"You need a hand?" Almost too fast to follow he drew his sword and swung. A heartbeat later, the chancellor's pale hand lay twitching on the dais. He tossed the limp body aside—if not a body now, soon enough, she thought—and kicked the hand toward her. "How about this?"

It smacked against her hip. She looked down, looked up, and sighed. "Not particularly useful even had you left it attached."

Arwed frowned, looked at her as though he were seeing her for the first time, and laughed. It was a man's laugh. A "hail fellow well met, let's slaughter a few innocents" laugh. His men laughed with him, although only the few actually on the dais could have known why.

"I am pleased to see my men did you little harm."

There were bruises, dried blood crusted around a cut just above the steel-gray cap of her hair. "Perhaps I reminded them of their mothers."

He laughed again. "A terrifying thought! Find the people you need, Cook. When we eat, I'll decide if you can keep them."

When the Citadel fell, the conquerors were more interested in treasure rooms than the pantries. Armed men had come reluctantly to the kitchens and stayed only long enough to make sure the new order was understood. They'd searched for hidden warriors, had thrown some flour about—the greatest mess for the least amount of effort—had killed the head baker, and had taken away the three young girls who'd worked in the scullery.

She got one of the girls back—Brigatte, the youngest, wobbling on unsteady legs like a new-born calf, the purple imprint of large hands on both her arms. Three middle-aged women, two from the kitchens, one from the laundry, she found cowering and bloody in a corner. A little water showed the damage superficial—slit noses and notched ears. Cruelty for cruelty's sake. She could find none of the men. The odds were very good they had joined the baker in death. With time running out, these four would have to be enough.

"Get fires lit in both roasting ovens and in the larger stove." As her head emerged from behind the bib of a clean apron—the linens had been undisturbed—she noticed none of the four had moved from their huddle just inside the door. This wouldn't do. Food didn't cook itself. "Swords fail," she told them, her voice as matter-of-fact as it had ever been, her words chosen carefully to slide past the bored young man appointed her personal guard, "*that* fight is over, but people still have to eat."

The woman from the laundry moved first. She stepped forward, her eyes narrowed, searching. After a long moment, tight lines around her mouth and eyes relaxed. "My name is Anna," she said. "I'll get your fires lit."

"Thank you, Anna." She set Brigatte back in her familiar place with a pile of vegetables to deal with. Before she left, she cupped the child's chin with her hand and gently lifted her head. The girl sniffed once, then met her gaze. After a long moment, she nodded. "Good girl. You'll do." It was as close to comfort as she could afford to express. Her smile evoked a tremulous smile in return. "Exactly." A nod to the vegetables. "Now, we do what must be done because there is no one to do it but us."

As Anna, the laundress, tended the fires, she put the other two women—Rose and Molly—to seasoning joints of meat. A man designated the warlord would expect meat but this would be meat as he had never eaten it before. Seared dark and blood-red and each mouthful bursting with subtle flavor; he didn't have to notice the subtlety, but it was imperative he eat.

This would be the bait.

With the familiar sounds of the kitchens rising over the distant sounds of fire and pain, she set two large scoops of cornmeal to soak in milk from the one stone crock that had not been spilled. The Warlord's men had recognized bread, if nothing else, and there was no time to make more. It would have to be cornbread but, fortunately, there would be plenty of rendered fat from the joints.

When the cornbread, rich with dripping, was slid into the oven, she began the desserts. The cream had already sat in the cold room for two days, no point in wasting it.

And this would set the hook.

The smell of cooking food had brought another three of her people and one of the wine stewards to the kitchen. She tore linens into bandages, set the steward's broken arm and put them to work, hoping for more. The dumbwaiter had been destroyed in the fighting and actually getting the food from the kitchen to the warlord would require more hands than she had.

Then half a dozen noblewomen, too old to be used in more pleasurable ways, arrived prodded by the sword points of three young warriors. She didn't think for a moment that the warlord had anticipated her need, only that he had found another way to humiliate the conquered. His reasons didn't concern her, only that there were now hands enough to carry the food.

She gave them tea and slices of an apple cake she'd found protected by an upturned bowl. When their guards protested, she pointed out that they needed strength enough to carry the food.

"They drop; we kill!"

"Suit yourself, but your warlord will object to his supper bouncing down the hall. If I feed them," she added slowly and deliberately when they looked confused, "they'll carry the food, your warlord will eat, you will eat, everyone will be happy. If I don't feed them, they'll drop the food and they'll be killed, but no one will get any supper. You want your supper, don't you?"

They did. The smell of cooking food was very nearly overwhelming. They salivated, but the warlord's dogs were too well trained to pull meat from his table.

In the end, she gave them apple cake as well.

Three of the women were sunk deep in shock, but she thought they would emerge in time. Two of them were frightened but angry. One had nothing but anger remaining.

Arwed frowned as only five of the women returned to the small audience chamber with his meal.

"Where is the other, Cook?"

"The Lady Adelade objected to serving you." She reached out and with the edge of her apron swept an assortment of nasty bric-a-brac to the floor, then stepped aside to allow Molly and Rose to place the first joint on the table. "One of your warriors killed her."

"And what did you do, Cook?"

She beckoned Anna forward and showed her where to place the dish of new onions and peas glistening with butter. "I objected to the mess."

The smell of the food was almost enough to mask the scent of death in the room.

The warlord pulled at a braided cord around his neck and from behind the peacock-blue and linen came a gleaming ivory spiral about as long as his thumb. "Do you know what this is?" His smile suggested he was about to win whatever contest of wills they had been involved in.

"Yes." So this was why, in spite of the guard, he hadn't been worried she would poison him. "It's the point of a unicorn horn."

Leaning forward he touched the tip of the horn to the nearest joint. "If there is poison in my food, I will make these women eat it."

Of course he would. She wasn't stupid.

There was no poison.

Still smiling, he indicated she should approach him and when she was near enough, he placed the point of the horn between her eyes. It was warm and sticky with juices. "Don't you want me dead, Cook?"

She'd never heard that a lie was a type of poison to a unicorn, but her days of attracting unicorns were far behind her. Not that it mattered, she had no intention of lying to him—particularly not a lie he would never believe. "Of course I do."

Of course she did.

"Your food is getting cold," she added. "It's a lot better tasting if you eat it hot."

Tucking the bit of horn back against his skin, he shook his head watching her through narrowed eyes. "What makes you so fearless, Cook?"

She shrugged. "People have to eat."

Later, as he devoured a large bowl of crème brulee, crunching his way through the caramelized crust, he graciously allowed her to keep the people she had.

The next morning she brought him eggs and sausage—her own recipe—and fresh-baked biscuits and two kinds of jam and coffee thick and dark and sweet. Two hours later, a bowl of sugared almonds and a fresh pot of coffee. Two hours after that, a whole golden-brown chicken filled with truffles and chestnut stuffing and more coffee.

As people died and history burned and chaos moved out from the Citadel, it was business as usual in the kitchens, an island of calm amidst the spreading destruction.

"Damn that unicorn horn," Anna growled as she yanked the last feathers from a goose and threw it down on the table. "You could have killed him a dozen times by now!"

The kitchen guard stopped chewing long enough to laugh derisively.

The goose had been fattening for the king. Oblivious to the battle passing by its crate, it had merely gone on eating.

She reached into the cavity and carefully freed the swollen liver. She would season it with paprika and ginger and sugar, then sauté it in hot goose fat before serving it to the warlord with sautéed onions and apples and a bottle of the king's best dry sherry.

"The food has changed, Cook." The warlord stared at her suspiciously, tapping the unicorn horn against his palm. "I did not say you could change the food."

She shrugged. "I can only cook what I have. I have no milk. I have no cream. I have no butter."

"Then get milk and cream and butter," he snarled, threat implicit in his tone.

She waited. To ask *and if I don't?* aloud would challenge his authority and force him to respond. She wasn't so foolish.

"Where did you get these things when you cooked for your useless dead king?" he demanded at last.

"The Citadel had a dairy, but the cows have either been slaughtered or driven off, and the dairy maids . . . well, they also have either been slaughtered or driven off."

"Get cows. Get dairy maids. Get out and cook!"

The dairy was under the warlord's protection. The calm spread from the kitchen.

At first Arwed rode out every day to terrorize what was left of the town. With the thick walls of the Citadel to retreat to, he feared no reprisal. The Citadel had stood, dressed-stone anchored deep in high rock, for over six hundred years. It had only ever been taken once.

"This food stinks of rot!"

Wiping the contents of the thrown apricot dumpling off her face with a corner of her apron, she rolled her eyes. "It's not the food, it's the room." Flies hung over the darker corners.

"So fix it."

"In order for the food to smell and taste as it did, this room will have to be cleaned. Daily."

"My men . . ."

"Do not need to piss where you eat."

He thought it was funny to see those who had been ladies scrubbing up the filth of their conquerors, so he kept them at it. His men taunted them; deliberately made more mess for them until they were so overwhelmed and exhausted they had no time to clean the small audience chamber where he took his meals.

"I killed the sniveling one, but the rest work no harder or faster." Arwed wiped his blade on the skirt of the peacock-blue coat.

She set a tray of lemon-ginger tarts on the table, the sweet glaze glistening golden in the afternoon sunlight. "Then they're working as hard and as fast as they can. If you want them to finish, have your men leave them alone."

"My men do as they please, Cook."

"My mistake. I thought they did as you pleased."

The taunting continued, but the women were left to clean in peace.

She cooked him pork ribs—huge racks glistening with fat, basted with sugar and tomato sauce and dried chilies—and got permission to rebuild the pigpens and find some stock.

"I'll need swineherds."

"For what?"

"Swine also have to eat, or they'll come skinny and tough to the table."

"You can have two." He wiped grease from his mouth and pointed. "Those two."

One of them had been a Lady of the Chamber, one a duchess whose lands were to the west and had been overrun. She had come to the Citadel for safety. Now they were swineherds.

Another ripple of calm.

The few chickens she had been able to round up were being kept in a room that had been used for the cutting and arranging of flowers; a small door that had once led to a cutting garden now led to a chicken yard.

She threw the mangled chicken down in front of him. "That was to have been your supper, but one of your men thought it would be funny to let the dogs in with them."

The warlord laughed. "It is funny. Kill another chicken for my supper."

"Very well. Then there will not be enough chickens to supply you with eggs for your breakfast." Eggs scrambled with sautéed garlic and mushrooms. Eggs poached and perched on thick slices of last year's ham, covered in a white sauce fragrant with rosemary. Thick slices of fine white bread dipped in egg and fried in butter then dusted with sugar or drowned in sweet syrup.

"Fine. Who let the dogs in?"

"He did." His name was Chouin, a scarred and grizzled veteran of the warlord's ride to the coast. He had followed her to the audience chamber, laughing, secure in the knowledge that he was one of the conquerors and she merely a cook.

Arwed's hand flicked out and a knife buried itself in the man's throat. He looked astounded, gurgled and pitched forward, hitting the floor with a wet thud. "The rest of you, stay away from the birds." And to her. "Happy, Cook?"

One less chicken. One less warrior. "Yes."

A small vegetable garden, small because the warlord had begun with little use for vegetables and desired them even less as time went on and she tempted his palate. The pigpen. The chicken run. The dairy. The kitchen. All to provide food for the warlord and his men. Food and as much of the sweet rich coffee as she could get them to drink.

Seven cleaners kept the marble halls gleaming so that filth did not overwhelm the food.

The laundry reopened when the peacock-blue coat began to carry a scent more pungent than the roasted garlic and apple that accompanied the roast goose. Anna moved from the kitchen and found three women to help her.

More workers were needed in the kitchen to feed those who worked to keep the warlord and his men fed.

There were those who said she betrayed her people

by serving the conquerors, but her people were safe under her eye. They ate scraps and leavings and food that once would have gone to the Citadel's pigpens while the warlord ate braised liver cockaigne with wine, crown roast of pork stuffed with sausage and chestnuts and parsley and cream, potato chunks pan-fried in lard and dusted with dried chili, fried potato cakes with sour cream and paprika, buttermilk rolls and honey biscuits served thickly spread with butter, jelly rolls, seven-egg puddings with a chocolate-maple glaze, and cornstarch custards with sweet cheese crumble toppings.

The king's wine cellars were emptying.

A man who came to be called the warlord was not in the habit of denying himself.

She cooked.

He ate.

"I'm almost out of flour."

"So?"

"No flour, no baking."

"Get more."

"The nearest market town still standing is four days' ride, north up the coast road."

"Then I'll send some men; they can use the exercise. All this good food is making them weak." Flesh moved with the back of his hand as he swiped at the grease dribbling down his chin.

"If your men ride up to the town, the people will disappear. They won't get any flour."

He snorted. "So what did your useless dead king do?"

"There were carters who went to the market towns and came back with food but they're gone. Your men killed them, took the horses, and burned the carts."

Caramel bubbled up thick and sweet as he shoved a spoon down into an apple raisin cobbler. "One of the rats scrabbling in the ruins around this drafty hunk of stone can drive a horse and cart. Find that rat," he told the room at large. "And a horse and a cart. And someone they care about to make sure they come back. Two of you," he added grinning, "accompany the cart. There are dangerous men about."

"They'll need money to buy the flour," she reminded him when the laughter died.

"So take what you need!"

"I'm a cook." A nod toward an elderly woman on her hands and knees scrubbing the marble floor. "She used to work for the chancellor. She knows money."

"You!"

The woman started and lifted her head. Her own left ear hung on a cord around her neck.

"Deal with this!"

Then the kitchen needed fuel. And then sugar. And then as the days turned, strawberries for pies, new potatoes to be fried with spring onions, and peaches for cobblers.

The carters started rebuilding, protected because they brought supplies for the warlord's table. Those of the warlord's men who rode out with them wore the colors of the Citadel so that the people in the market towns wouldn't run from them.

Word spread. A thin girl with bruised eyes brought a basket of oysters to the kitchen door. After feeding the girl and giving her loaves of heavy brown bread to take home to her family, she prepared deep-fried oysters with seasoned bread crumbs and andalouse sauce.

The warlord wanted more.

And the oyster harvesters came under the warlord's protection.

The woman who used to work for the chancellor came so many times to the warlord for coin, he gave her access to the treasure he had taken with the Citadel.

"And you will die if you cannot account for every copper," he snarled through a mouthful of thick sliced beef.

Clean hair dressed neatly over the ruin of her ear, she bowed her head.

Arwed continued to test everything she served him with the unicorn horn certain he would, at some point, be poisoned. He tested the meat through thick rinds of crispy golden-brown fat. He tested the potatoes roasted in their skins and then drenched in sour cream and sprinkled with chopped chives. He plunged the horn into the gleaming white heart of the bread, then in turn into the jams and flavored honeys he spread thickly over it. He tested each nut in its crunchy sugared coating. He dipped it into the coffee and the cream. She was commanded to stand by at every meal until the test was done.

He no longer rode out and his leathers had been replaced by loose silks and velvets plundered from the wardrobes of the Citadel. But he was still the warlord and warlords needed armor that fit. Armor needed blacksmiths and leather workers. Drawn by the gold from the Citadel, some of those who had fled before the destruction returned to the town.

Those of his men who still preferred to wear their armor guarded the carters and the oyster harvesters lest the bounty for the warlord's table be taken from them. They guarded the gates of the Citadel and every day a different warrior stood guard in the kitchen. The warlord had no wish for his men to have closer access to his food than he did. As she chopped and rendered and sautéed, she noted which ones of her guard asked what and noted especially the fewer who asked why.

"I am out of coffee and nearly out of chocolate."

He rolled his eyes, nearly hidden now in pouches of flesh and spat, "Get more."

"These things come from the south, on ships. The trade is complicated."

"Then I will make it simple for you, Cook." The point of his blade buried in the tabletop, he leaned toward her, breathing heavily, his face flushed. "I rule here. If I say get more, get more!"

There were women in the Citadel who understood trade, who had sat silent beside fathers and husbands. Some now worked cleaning the halls, some in the kitchens, one in the dairy. She was just as glad to set them to work they understood because every single one of them had at one time or another let the meat overcook and the potatoes boil dry. The less said about their experiences with eggs and cream, the better. The women from the town, who replaced them, rolled up their sleeves and did as they were told.

She finally put the aconite—carefully distilled from tincture of monkshood—in a crème brulee. It had been, since that very first meal, his favorite desert and he demanded she prepare it two or three times a week.

Arwed stared at the piece of unicorn horn as the

black climbed slowly up the spiral. His eyes widened, his jaw dropped, and, after a long moment, he leaped from his chair.

"You thought you were safe!" he roared. "A hundred of these I have eaten! A thousand!" He jabbed the now ebony horn toward her. "You dared to think I would not check because of that? Ha!" Dark circles of red appeared on each cheek and began to spread. "Am I a fool? Am I?" he roared at the watching men and women. "No! I have conquered and I have killed and I taken what I please!" The red of his face had begun to purple and his eyes bulge alarmingly. "You have made a fatal mistake, Cook! I will have you roasted in your own ovens! Turned on your own spit! Salted and boiled and . . ."

His mouth opened. Closed. Opened again, but no sound emerged.

The fingers of his left hand curled and as he clutched at the peacock-blue fabric over his breast with his right, the horn fell and cracked through the praline crust of the brulee to protrude over the side of the custard dish like a stick of fluted licorice.

He stumbled back and just before he fell, she caught his gaze and held it.

Swords had failed.

Gasping for breath that wouldn't come, he crumbled to the floor.

The small assembly room was silent for a long moment and she began to worry she would have to do this as well. Then the woman who had worked for the chancellor of the old king, who now commanded the treasury of the captured Citadel, rose to her feet and snapped, "Don't just sit there! You and you, carry him carefully to his bedchamber! You! Find a healer! Cook!"

She waited.

"Return to the kitchen."

Arwed was dead by nightfall, but the structure held. She wasn't surprised; she had never had a soufflé fall.

The new warlord was one of the men who asked why. By his side was a woman of the Citadel, her belly round with new life. When that child came in time to rule, he would not be a warlord but a king. Perhaps there would even be sunbursts on the breastplates of his guard.

She busied herself preparing the funeral feast.

After all, people had to eat.

THE WEAPON

Michelle West

Michelle West is the author of several novels, including *The Sacred Hunter* duology and *The Broken Crown*, both published by DAW Books. She reviews books for the on-line column *First Contacts*, and less frequently for *The Magazine of Fantasy & Science Fiction*. Other short fiction by her has appeared in dozens of anthologies, including *Black Cats and Broken Mirrors*, *Alien Abductions*, *Little Red Riding Hood in the Big Bad City*, and *Faerie Tales*.

I.

IN THE QUIET of isolation and a long-nursed pain, a woman knelt, praying to her god to give her a child. Because she was golden-eyed, she could be certain that her pleas were heard, for she was Daughter to the Mother—and because she was certain she was heard, she was also certain that Mother rejected her supplication. As a child, growing up in the certainty of knowing that the Mother *could* hear her, she had often pitied those who would live their lives in uncertainty. Time had eroded pity, or worse, begun to turn it inward.

The gift of god-born children was rare indeed in the

small and fractious Baronies, for the Barons rooted them out without mercy, often destroying whole family lines in an attempt to destroy those who could willingly, inexplicably, consort with gods whose offspring might challenge their rule.

Only in the temple of the Mother, where healing was offered—and controlled—were such slaughters avoided. But even in these temples, the god-born were rare.

A miracle, denied those who lived in the shadow of the Baron's rule. After all, what parent willingly offered a babe to death?

Mother, she thought, rising. *Grant us your child. I am no longer young, and I must raise my successor. Grant us a child.*

But the Mother was silent.

The Mother's Daughter seldom summoned her Priests and Priestesses to this room, this hall. But when she did, she did so for a reason: blood did not cling easily to marble.

"Amalyn," the Mother's Daughter said, to the youngest of her attendants, "I want you to go to the Novitiates."

"But—"

"Now. The Novitiates will know, when the Baronial carriage empties into the Courtyard, which member of the family our visitor is. I *do not* want them to panic."

"But—"

"Amalyn. You are barely out of their ranks; they know you, and will trust your reassurances."

"And if I have none to give?"

"Find them."

Amalyn's eyes closed. It was a type of surrender. She backed her way out of the nave, toward the door that led to the rooms that housed the novices who served the Mother. They were crowded now. Every person that the temple could save, they had—and proof of it could be found in the cramped quarters the Priests and the Novitiates shared.

"You aren't the only Daughter of the Mother that the Blood Baron has killed—"

"You *will not use that title*," she said, her voice as cold and severe as any autocratic noble's. "If it is my time, it is my time."

"We can't afford to lose you—" Her words died as Amalyn struggled not to say what they all knew: There was no other god-born child in the temple.

"Yes," The Mother's Daughter replied quietly. "We can. But we cannot afford to lose the Cathedral; we cannot afford to have the name of the Mother silenced across the lands." She hesitated and then added, in a more gentle voice, "We serve those who have no other hope. And because we have obeyed the rule of our Baron, Lord Halloran Breton, we are the *only* church that has not been destroyed or driven underground. Our responsibilities are to those who have no value to the Baron. And because we can heal, child, we have value."

"Our oaths," Amalyn whispered.

"Oh, yes. If the Baron kills any of those who serve the Mother at my command, I will close the Healerie to his entire clan. But if that happens," she added, with just a hint of fear, "you must be ready to flee; if we serve no purpose, we will become as the others."

"But you could flee *now*—"

"Hush, child. The Baron sent word that he wished an audience; it is not his way to be so tactful when he desires a death. I am content to wait upon his command."

Amalyn left. Only when the door swung shut behind her did the oldest of the Priests bow.

"Iain," the Mother's Daughter said, granting permission to speak.

"Why has your agreement with the Baron never extended to your own life?" He said this with quiet respect—and managed to imply several decades' worth of reproach in the almost uninflected statement. He was good at that.

She shrugged. "It's enough to protect those who serve." And then she exhaled. "Not even the Baron can be offered affront without exacting a public price, and what better victim as balm to his pride than the Mother's Daughter herself?

"Let the temple stand," she added softly.

No one was certain whether or not it was a prayer.

Baron Halloran Breton was, in these times, a man to be respected. Of the Barons, he alone had managed to subdue his neighbours, binding them in ways that she did not care to imagine to his cause. And his cause?

He had not yet named himself King. But even casual analysis of the geography of his campaigns made clear that he desired a Kingdom; he was first among equals, if he held any man to *be* his equal.

He was not a handsome man. This much was a known fact. But he might have been, had the cast of his expression been less forbidding. He was tall, and he wore his height as if it were a mantle. Age had not lessened him; it had broadened his shoulders and crafted lines across his face that made clear he was a man of little humor.

He traveled with four guards.

It was one third of even the most minimal number

that she had seen him use before, and this gave the
Mother's Daughter pause. But not so much pause that
she did not bow. The Priests and Priestesses who
served her chose the more expedient gesture of obeisance; it was certainly the one with which he was most
familiar. They adorned the floor, the robes across their
supine backs a spill of thick cloth. A cloth not so fine
as his, and not so stained by travel.

"Is this hall secure?" he asked as she rose.

"We have not the soldiery you have at your disposal," she replied quietly. "Nor the wizards. But inasmuch as it can be, Lord Breton, it is."

His eyes were already roving the vaulted ceilings;
torchlight flickered a moment across the dark of his
eyes, reflected there. *Caught there*, she thought, *as if
he had swallowed it in his youth.* She knew the Mother's pity then, but was wise enough to hide it; his
father, the previous—and very dead—Lord Breton,
had been a famously cruel man.

And Lord Breton had decided, in the end, to abide
by the life his father had chosen for him. He had
learned, first, fear, and when he had passed beyond it,
he had never forgotten the price fear exacted. Fear
was the tribute he desired; fear gave him a measure
of power.

But no peace, no security.

He turned to the guards at his back; they were
perfect in every way. Silent, grim, obedient, they responded to this slight gesture, and turned from the
hall. He met her gaze, and his own flickered across
the exposed backs of the most trusted of her
servants.

She understood the command in his glance.

"Leave us," she said quietly.

They rose, not as perfect in their discipline as the
soldiers of the Baron. But they offered no argument.

When they were gone, he turned to her. "Mother's Daughter," he said coldly. "I have granted you willingly what few Barons have chosen to grant even lesser temples than yours. I have seen the worship of your goddess spread across my cities and my towns, and I have done little indeed to stop it, although I, as the rest of the Barons, have little use for the gods."

She said nothing.

His smile was thin. "You are in the prime of your power. I have seen it before. I have also seen the decline of such power. Age, in the end, will leave you bereft; will you pass willingly from the halls that you rule?" Before she could answer, he lifted a hand. "They are words," he said, "no more." He stepped toward her, and she saw the mud leave the soles of his boots. "I do not understand you. I believe that you feel you understand me. And perhaps you do. I have let you spend your life upon my people in return for services that the mages cannot render me, and I am satisfied with our bargain. I have given you those who have chosen to break my edict; I have killed them, in your stead, so that your hands might remain bloodless. I have seen your servants," he added, "and they do not all bear the blood of your Mother; there are those who would raise hand against killers; those who would rise up to the status of executioner.

"But you keep them contained, and they are protected while they serve in your name."

"In the name of the Mother," she said at last.

"Oh, indeed." He paused; his hands slid behind his back and he stood there, staring at her, the harsh lines of his face tightening. "I am not certain that you will be a suitable guardian," he said at last.

It was not what she expected to hear. It was, in fact, probably the last thing she expected to hear.

*   *   *

When he had first taken power over the corpse of his father—a phrase that was not exactly literal, as there wasn't *enough* left of his father to technically be called a corpse—he had come to the temple, bleeding, burned. Twenty years ago, and she remembered it still. She had been a simple novice, albeit golden-eyed.

The Mother's Daughter of that time had offered him the respect of obeisance in front of the congregation that had gathered—that still gathered, huddling now in their pews—before the Mother's altar.

Skin dark with ash and sweat that he had not bothered to remove, he had gazed at them all, hawk to their rabbit; she had watched, from the doors that led to the nave, thinking that he might destroy the service to demand the healing that was his by right of power. Thinking, if he were not granted it, that he might destroy more. He certainly looked, to her practiced eye, as if he were in need of healing.

But he had confounded that expectation. Into the spreading, the uncertain silence, he had walked as if he owned the temple. "I am the Baron Breton," he said, and the exultation in his smile did not quite penetrate the quiet dignity of those words.

The Mother's Daughter bowed. She rose, but not quickly, and moved to stand by the altar, placing her palms against its surface.

"You have not flourished in the reign of my father, but you held your own. I respect that, Mother's Daughter. I desire your company; I will tour my city before the waning of the day." He paused for a moment, and then his gaze crested the bowed heads of the men, women, and children who were wise enough not to meet it. But Emily Dontal, golden-eyed novice, was not so wise, and she met those dark eyes beneath those singed, bleeding brows, and almost forgot to move.

"Who is the novice who attends you, Mother's Daughter?"

The Mother's Daughter said nothing; he had expected that, but his lips thinned.

No, she thought. Seeing him, understanding now that he desired a death to mark the beginning of his reign, to mark his prominence. She had stepped forward, ignoring the gaze of the Mother's Daughter to whom she owed both service and obedience. The latter she forsook for the former.

"I am Novice Emily Dontal," she said, bowing. Bowing low. She might have knelt, but she thought if she did she would never rise.

"You are golden-eyed," he replied.

"I am the Mother's."

"Good. You are the first of your kind—with the exception of the Mother's Daughter—that I have seen in the temple, and I have had occasion to visit during my youth. You will accompany us as well."

"Novice."

"Mother's Daughter."

"You will stay by my side, and you *will not* speak."

"Mother's Daughter."

She had learned much, in traversing those streets.

The new Baron Breton had come to the temple with a small army. He led the men, the Mother's Daughter by his side, through the streets, proclaiming his rule. He led them to the heart of the high city, and there, he set them free, for in the high city were the men who had gained great fortune in the service of his father.

There, she knew, his sole living brother resided. And he, too, was not without his men.

She had read of war. It was something that was
fought over distant plains, and distant patches of land.
This sudden terrible knowledge: this was the Baron's
gift. To her.

It was a scar she bore still. The soldiers clashed,
and this, at least, she could bear in silence. When the
first volley of quarrels flew from the distance of buildings, when they pierced armor and men fell with
grunts or screams, she flinched, and the Mother's
Daughter gripped her shoulder like a vise. But she
could witness this, mute and still.

It was after. It was after the one army had been
defeated, and the Baron's brother beheaded, that the
slaughter had started in earnest.

"Emily Dontal," the Baron said quietly, calling her
attention back from the bitter recess of memory although her eyes had not left his face. He was older,
and he did not come injured and in triumph to these
halls.

"Yes," she replied, "that is what I was called."

"But it is not, now, what you are. Mother's Daughter, do you understand the gift I gave you when first
we met?"

She did not, could not answer. She could still hear
the screaming.

"I have spoken with the Witherall Seer."

She kept her face schooled. It was difficult.

"And she has told me that my blood-line will
rule these lands; they will fashion not a Kingdom,
but an Empire, and it will stretch farther than
even the lands the Barons now hold." His smile
was slight.

"Why have you come?" she asked, weary now.

"Ah, that. I am not the man I was when I took

the Baronial throne. I have buried three wives," he added quietly.

As it was widely rumored that his first wife had attempted to assassinate him, she expected no open show of sorrow.

"I am in negotiations with Baron Ederett, to the far South. If these are concluded successfully, you may receive an invitation to a wedding."

Again, silence was the only response. It seemed, however, to be the incorrect response.

"My oldest son is much like my brother in his youth. My younger sons are canny." He shrugged. "It is . . . surprisingly bitter, to see them arrayed against each other in such a fashion. They are attempting to become adult in the Baronial Court, and if they survive it—they have sacrificed pawns and slaves in their games—they will emerge stronger for their testing.

"But the Court at this time is no place for a child." And he gestured.

The cloak that he wore fell away, its weave a weave invisible to the eye. When it was gone, a small child stood at his side. She was, to Emily's eye, perhaps three years of age, pale and slender, her hair still blonde, eyes still blue, in the way of children. She did not speak. She did not touch her father.

"This—this is—"

"This," he said, turning to look down upon the child's head, "is Veralaan. She is, as your spies may have told you—"

"I play no games in your Court—"

"Not all spies are paid, Mother's Daughter. Some come to you because they *feel* they are doing the *right* thing. They have hope of you, of your Order. They do not understand that you are content to sit, as dogs, if you are given the appropriate bone."

It was an insult.

She smiled anyway, and the smile was genuine. It annoyed the Baron.

"She is," he continued, "my only daughter. The child of Alanna, my third wife."

The child said nothing at all.

"Your wife—it is rumored that she died in childbirth."

"Ah—that is the word that I was looking for. Rumor. Yes, that was rumored." A shadow crossed his face. It was a terrible thing, that shadow; it spoke of death, in every possible way. And had it been on another man's face, she might have been moved to pity. As it was, she struggled with self-loathing, because there was a part of her that enjoyed his pain.

"It was not, as rumors are often not, entirely true. But it is true now." He put a hand on the top of the child's head. His fist was mailed.

But gentle, she thought, and again she was surprised. "Go," he told the girl. "This woman, she is your new mother. Her name is Emily, but everyone here will call her 'Mother's Daughter.' You must learn to call her that as well."

The child did not speak. But she was, as were any of his subjects, obedient. She crossed the marble floor, her stride small enough that the hall seemed truly grand. Truly empty.

"You are weak," the Baron said to the Mother's Daughter. "It is because of your weakness that I am uncertain of my choice. But it is also entirely because of your weakness that I feel that my child will be safe here. You do not understand politics, Mother's Daughter, and you have been wise enough not to play.

"Therefore no one will tempt you, and I believe

that even were the child my only heir, were the child
a son and of use, you would still protect him with your
life and the resources that I have chosen to leave at
your disposal.

"Do not fail," he added softly. He turned from
the hall.

The child started forward. "Daddy!"

He hesitated. She thought he might turn back, but
the hesitation was his only show of weakness—and at
the risk of exposing even that, he had sent all of his
men away.

She caught the child in her arms, and the child
kicked and screamed, as children will who understand
that they are being abandoned.

Iain was appalled. Amalyn was bitterly, bitterly
angry. Norah was silent, and the silence was chilly.
"Melanna?" Emily asked quietly. She held the child
in her arms, for the child's terrible frenzy had, at last,
given way to an unshakable sleep.

Melanna, wide, round, her cheek scarred from a different life, looked at the child's sleeping back. Her
face was entirely composed; no hint of humor, of desire, of hatred, marred her expression. It made her, of
the Priests, the most dangerous. Hard to deal well with
things that one could not see.

"His men killed my son," she said at last. "When
he was but two years older than this girl." What did
not adorn her face informed her words.

"We have been ordered to protect her," the Mother's Daughter said carefully.

"We serve the Mother," was the perfectly reasonable reply.

The child stirred. Emily began to shift her weight
from side to side, her arms around the child. The

warm child. She, Mother's Daughter, would bear none. Had never thought—until this moment—that she might find solace in the act.

"We have no experience in raising children," Iain told them all. But his eyes were now upon Melanna. "The Mother has not seen fit to grace us——"

"No," Melanna said. "I will *not* do this." She turned from them and strode out of the small common room, her hands in tight fists.

Iain watched her go. "Mother's Daughter, is this wise?"

"Wise? No." Her arms tightened briefly. "It is not wise. But less wise is refusing the Baron's request. Inasmuch as he can be, he is fond of this child. I believe . . . he was fond of her mother."

Amalyn snorted, and Emily frowned. "She is but three years old. If she is her father's daughter, she is also her mother's. We cannot judge her. And she is no son; she is merely a daughter, and without value."

"He has shown himself to be without mercy when the children of others are involved."

She knew. She remembered. "And will we show ourselves to be, at last, a church made in his image? The Mother will turn her face from us, and without her blessing, without her power, what then can we offer the people?"

"Justice."

"We are not the followers of Justice," the Mother's Daughter said firmly. "Nor of judgment."

"Melanna will not accept her."

"Melanna is the only woman here who has borne and raised children. She has served the Mother for ten years. Perhaps this is her test."

But she had not been truthful with her Priests, and this was its own crime. She took the girl to her room and laid her in the small bed, staring at her perfect child's features, at a face which would change, again and again, with the passage of time. Would she be beautiful? It was impossible to tell.

She had prayed for a child. But *not* this one.

What will we do with you, Veralaan? What will you become to us? She understood Melanna's desire. She felt no like desire; death was not her dominion.

But she had in her hands a child born to power, a child born with the blood of Barons in her veins. It was true that the Mother's Daughter had never become involved in the politics of Court—why would she? Between one contender and the other, there was only the difference of competence; there was no difference of desire or ambition, no intent to change, merely to own. What matter, then, whose hand raised sword, lowered whip, signed law?

But here: here was temptation.

It was not only Melanna who was to be tested, but also Emily Dontal, the child who had become woman in the streets of the city, on the day that Lord Halloran had become Lord Breton, Baron of the Eastern Sea.

A child was unformed, uneducated. A clean slate.

And upon such a slate as this, *so much* could be written. She had not told her most trusted servants the words of the Witherall Seer.

Mother, she thought. *Guide me.* And she lowered her face into shaking hands, because it wasn't a prayer for advice; it was a prayer for absolution.

The child would not eat for three days. She would drink milk and water, and Iain informed the Mother's Daughter, with increasing anxiety, that he was certain she shed them both with the volume of her tears. Those tears had ceased to accompany loud wails, desperate flights toward the door; they became, instead, the silent companions of despair. She did not like the robed men and women who ruled the temple; she did not acknowledge the men and women who labored in the Novitiate. She was not allowed to sit when the congregation gathered, but Iain was certain she would take no comfort from the hundreds of strangers who made a brief home of the pews either.

In the end, it was Melanna who took the girl in hand; she was not gentle. Not with the child, and not with the slightly anxious men and women who gathered around her, almost afraid to touch her unless she had finally exhausted herself and lay sleeping.

"You'd think the lot of you had never laid eyes on a child before!" It was custom to lower voices when exposed in the cloisters. Melanna often flouted custom when in the grip of disgust, and as she had come late to the Novitiate, she was often forgiven this flaw. "I can understand her, at least—she's just been abandoned by her only living parent. The rest of you?"

"It's not our custom—"

"And when the Mother grants us *her* child, what then? Will you leave all the cleanup to me?"

"Melanna—" Iain began again. He retreated just as quickly, his hands before his chest and palm out in the universal gesture of placation.

"You're a man," she snorted.

He had the grace to roll his eyes when she wasn't looking, and she the grace to pretend she wasn't actually looking. "Damn you all. I'll take her."

Daughter of the Mother, and not daughter of the god of Wisdom, Emily Dontal observed. It had taken two weeks, a mere two weeks, before Melanna intervened. Emily had intended to allow it, for she wanted Veralaan to feel isolated, and she could think of no better guardian than Melanna in that respect.

And for a while, it worked. But it was a short while.

She came upon Melanna in the smallest of the chambers used by the Novitiates for quiet contemplation and prayer. As Melanna was no longer a Novice, she was surprised to come upon her there, but not nearly as surprised as she was when Melanna looked up, and the dim lights of the brazier shone across her wide cheeks.

Even in the darkened shadows of the room it was clear that her eyes were reddened. She lifted shaking hands and made to rise, and the Mother's Daughter gentled her by lifting her hands in denial.

"Why are you here, Melanna?"

Melanna said nothing.

The Mother's Daughter waited, and after a moment, she drew closer. Melanna was upon her knees; she had surrendered the advantage of height. Of more.

She said, "I wanted the Mother's guidance."

Emily nodded.

"The child—Veralaan—"

"I know it is difficult—"

"No, Mother's Daughter, you *don't*." Her voice broke. "My son was older," she added. "Older than Veralaan. I thought—" She lifted her hands to her face again, callused hands.

"If it is too difficult a task, Melanna—"

But the woman shook her head and rose. "I can manage her. She's just a child." Her tears had dried.

The Mother's Daughter watched her go.

*　　*　　*

But she came to understand, as the days passed, what the difficulty was. It was not in caring for the child of the man she most hated; it was the child herself. Although Veralaan was still quiet, sullen and easily frightened, she understood that Melanna had been appointed her caretaker, and she clung to Melanna whenever they were together. Melanna would extricate herself as she could, bending to free the folds of her robes from the three-year old's fingers.

But she would stop, spine curved, as the child spoke; no one else could hear what Veralaan said. Melanna would speak harshly in reply; harshly and loudly. The child would cringe. But she would not let go; once dislodged, she reached, again and again, for the comfort of this angry attachment.

When Melanna almost missed dinner for the first time—and it would have been a disaster, because the Priestess supervised the chaos that was the kitchen—Emily Dontal *knew*.

Melanna came late to the kitchen, Veralaan in the crook of her right arm. It was the first time that she would carry the child with her in her many headlong rushes from one place to another, but it was not the last. She tossed young Ebrick off his stool without ceremony, paused to criticize him for removing half the potato along with the peel, and then set Veralaan down in his place.

The child started to cry, but the tears were quiet.

"Veralaan," Melanna said, shoving her hands through her hair, "I *don't have a choice*. If I leave this lot to cook, we'll be eating dirt and burned milk for the next three days!"

Veralaan nodded, folding her hands together; they were small and white. But she still cried.

"Hazel, what do you think you're doing with that? The milk will just cake the bottom of the pot! Pay attention! Veralaan, we can go back upstairs when I've finished. I won't forget the rest of the story. But I—EBRICK!"

Emily had never seen her quite like this, and watched in silence from the safety of the door.

Veralaan said something, and Melanna bent to catch the words. Her face froze a moment, and then she smiled, but it was a tight, tight smile.

"Yes," she told the child, lowering her voice. "His mother finds him, and brings him home."

Small hands were entwined in the fabric of the older woman's robes before she'd even finished her sentence. "Veralaan, I've told you a thousand times not to do that. Not where people can see you. These are the Robes of the Mother; they're to be treated with respect." She was busy prying those robes from small fingers as she spoke; it was a losing battle.

In the end, she sighed and hefted the child again in her right arm, lodging the bulk of her weight against her hip. She turned and resumed the marshaling of her beleaguered forces, carrying Veralaan as if she were some sort of precious mascot.

"I don't understand it, Iain," the Mother's Daughter said, over the same dinner.

"What don't you understand?"

Had they not been quite so isolated, she would have guarded her tongue; she was the Mother's Daughter, and inasmuch as she could be wise, she was expected to personify wisdom. Given that there was *already* a god that did just that, she thought it a tad unfair.

"Melanna."

He was quiet for a moment, which was often a dubious sign. At last he put his knife down and pushed his plate an inch forward. "Emily," he said quietly. Her name; a name he almost never used.

She met his gaze and held it. But he did not look away. Had she desired it, he would have. Or maybe not, she thought, as his expression continued to shift.

"Was that not your purpose in giving the child to Melanna to foster?"

"What purpose?"

"She will never have another child," he said quietly. "The injuries she sustained made it certain."

"I know. I was there."

Grave, now, he said, "You have given her the only child—save perhaps one, if we are blessed—that she will ever be allowed to raise in peace."

"I gave her," Emily replied coolly, "the daughter of the man responsible for the slaughter of her family."

"Yes. And so, too, did she see the child."

"And she cared so little for her son that she could—"

"That is unworthy of you, Mother's Daughter. Worse, it is a thought unworthy of the Mother."

Not since she had been in the Novitiate had he dared use that tone of voice on her. It brooked no argument, allowed for none; he was rigidly certain. "I do not know what you intended. I do not wish to know. Leave me with the illusion of your mercy. Melanna will grow, from this. She will remember things that will hurt her, but once she is past the pain, she will remember things that will define her."

"She will love this child."

"In time, Emily, accept that we will *all* love her."

"She is the daughter of—"

"She is a child. Whose child has yet to be determined; it is not in blood and birth that such decisions are made, but in the life itself."

"Iain—" She held out a hand. It shook. "I have looked long and hard at this City, harder still at the Baron who rules it; I have evaluated, as I can, the foreign Barons who bark at the gates. They are of a kind, Baron Breton and the others; if he loses his war, there will be death and slaughter, before and after. I cannot see a way out of this darkness if not through her. If blood and birth matter little to the Mother, they matter to those whose power destroy our people, generation after generation.

"I saw her as a gift. As an opportunity—perhaps our only one. I thought to be a weapon-smith."

He placed his hand across hers. "Have you spoken with the Mother?"

She shook her head. "I know my mother. I *know* what she'll say."

His frown was edged with humor. "There are other ways to fight," he said at last.

"In stories," she replied bitterly. "In song. But in song, the god-born walked freely among the villains, carrying the blood of their parents, and using the power it granted them. Where are their like now? We do not even have a god-born child of our own—" She choked back the words, the bitter fear. "I have seen those who would be heroes. They were not gentle men, and they were not kind, but had they succeeded, they might have been better rulers. If she is soft, if she is weak, what favor have we granted her? What good have we done ourselves? She will be killed by her own naiveté. Had she stayed with her father, she would *be* capable. If we *love* her, will that not in the end make her a victim?"

"Let the definition of weakness be made by men

like Baron Breton, and you have already lost; make of her a woman who can stand against him upon his own ground, and you will simply make another like him. Perhaps she will be beholden to you; perhaps she will kill you, as Baron Breton killed his father. I cannot say."

"If we—"

"But if we have no hope, Emily . . ."

"Hope did not save Melanna's child."

"No," he said quietly. He did not speak again during that meal.

Prayer afforded hope to those who gathered at the Mother's alter; it afforded little to the Mother's Daughter. But in the end, she *was* the Mother's Daughter. She watched as Veralaan grew, claiming, as Iain had predicted, the love and affection of the Priests, the Priestesses, and the Novices. Melanna was her protector and her guardian, and each time the child was introduced to a newcomer, it was by the side of the ferocious Priestess, whose grim and loving demeanor made clear what would happen to those who judged her for her father's crimes.

In a different world, this might have produced a different child. But in this one, not even Melanna—as she had learned so bitterly once—was capable of protecting a child completely.

When she was six years old, Iain began to teach her how to read, how to write, and how to comport herself as a young lady of wealth and power. The former, he had done in the Novitiate for years, but the latter? Not for a lifetime. Melanna hated it, of course. But Emily insisted on it.

"Why?" Melanna demanded.

"Because she *is* the Baron's daughter."

"Why Iain?"

"Because he is the *only* son of a noble family to grace these halls."

"It's no damn kindness to remind him of it. It just reminds him—"

"Of what he's lost?"

Melanna fell silent. It was a mutinous silence.

"Melanna, if he is unable to teach her, he will tell me. Trust him." She paused, and then added, "trust yourself. Trust Veralaan. To understand the odd customs and the graces of the patriciate is *not* to become what they are; if that were true, Iain would never have come to the Mother."

"He cares for Veralaan. Let him do this one thing for her; you have done almost everything else she requires."

"I don't see why she *requires* this!"

No, Emily thought, but did not argue further. You don't want to see it.

Emily Dontal used the excuse of the temple's care to keep her distance from Veralaan, but it was a distance that time eroded so slowly she couldn't say when it broke at last, and she, too, was swept up in the joy—and fear—that came of caring too much for a child.

But she knew the exact moment she became aware of it, and she did not forget.

Iain had, uncharacteristically, bemoaned the lack of a "proper" staircase. The cathedral boasted stairs, but they were subtle, and meant to be traversed with silent dignity; he wanted something that would lead from the heights to the altar in full view of an audience.

And he was embarrassed at the desire.

"She's graceful," he said lamely, "for a child her

age. But she has to practice the stairs," he added, his voice wilting even more, if that were possible. "It's the one time when all eyes will be upon her."

"She's seven, Iain. And at that, a quiet seven. I'm not sure she'd be happy if all eyes, as you say, were upon her. We found the funding for the harp that you requested. We found funding for the dress. But, Iain, the funding to add such a staircase is well beyond our means."

He winced and lifted a hand. "I'm sorry, Emily. She reminds me of my youth, that's all. I see so much potential in her—" He shook his head. She stared at him.

"There was a time," he said softly, "a time in my life when I could see beauty and it wasn't tainted. She *is* that time. I have learned to appreciate beauty in more subtle forms. I see it daily in the struggles of the Mother's children. But this is different.

"And she's the Baron's daughter. She has to know how to make an entrance."

"Iain—"

One of the Novices burst into the room, throwing the doors wide. "Mother's Daughter!" she cried, all ceremony cast aside by panic. "Come quickly!"

"What has happened, Carin?"

"The Baron's men are in the Healerie!"

"What? Why?"

"Three of the injured. They want to take them."

The Mother's Daughter stiffened. "Iain."

But he was perfectly composed now, and he followed where she led. The halls were long and narrow in her vision; the lights were dim. She had seen this many, many times. "Carin," she said sharply, "who is in the Healerie?"

"Edwin. Harald." She hesitated and than added, "Rowan."

Rowan was healerborn. Emily Dontal lifted her robes and ran toward the bend in the hall that would take her at last to the bitter scene she had supervised so often. But as she rounded the corner, Iain her shadow, she saw that the doors to the Healerie had been left open, and in the frame of that door, she saw a broad, bent back that she could not help but recognize. Melanna.

She slowed; a collision and its subsequent lack of dignity would hold her in poor stead. Melanna did not seem to hear her; she had to touch the older woman to get her attention, and when she did, she forgot why she wanted it; Melanna was so tense were it not for warmth she might have been a statue.

"Priestess," the Mother's Daughter said, cloaking her voice with the weight and authority granted the god-born.

Melanna shifted slightly, providing barely enough space that one adult might slide past her. But her hands came up in fists, and as Emily stepped into the Healerie, she saw that Melanna's face was white, bleached white.

And she saw why in an instant.

Veralaan was standing in the Healerie. She wore the deep, dark velvet that had been so costly, and her hair had been gathered above the nape of her neck; were she not so short, she might have been years older.

Rowan was crouched beside one of her patients. The child. Why was so much that was bitter twisted round the lives of children? But the child was unconscious, and Emily thought it unlikely that he would wake before this was over.

And it would be over. The Baron's men were not to be denied. It was the harshest of lessons that the novices learned, and it was repeated over and over again, the birth and death of hope.

Gathered just beyond the door at the other end of the Healerie were the Baron's men. They wore the surcoat of Breton, and carried the swords forbidden to any other citizen of the City. They had lifted their visors, but they did not remove them; they numbered eight. Eight men, to take two who would not wake and one who could barely walk.

But she saw the subtle signs of hesitation in their stance, and she moved forward. Because she did, she could clearly hear Veralaan's voice. The ceilings in the Healerie did it no justice.

"Why are you here?" Veralaan demanded, her arms by her side, her shoulders straight, her chin lifted.

"We've come for those three," the soldier replied. "They are wanted by the Baron."

"They are in the temple of the Mother," she answered evenly, the words so smooth they bore none of the stilted effort that spoke of practice. "They came seeking sanctuary and healing, and we granted it."

We.

"It is not yours to grant," the man said. He shifted his blade.

"It is the Mother's right," Veralaan replied. She lifted a slender arm, a child's arm. "And you are not welcome here if you come to disturb the Mother's peace. You can lay down your arms, or you can leave."

His eyes widened. So, too, did the Mother's Daughter's, but none of the men seemed to notice. Their attention was captive to the girl.

Iain, she thought, *you need no staircase here.* But

she walked forward until she stood to one side of Veralaan.

"Mother's Daughter," the man said, a hint of relief in the words, "we have come to take three criminals to the courts of the Baron."

"But you have not taken them?"

"They can't," Veralaan replied coldly. She did not look up to meet Emily's gaze; her eyes were fixed upon the man who seemed to be in charge. "They are not noble."

"They serve the Baron—"

"And I," she continued, brooking no interruption, "am. I am Lady Veralaan ABreton, and I have ordered them to leave."

"Mother's Daughter—"

Iain had come up behind her, as he so often did. "Lady Veralaan is entirely correct," he said, speaking to her, but pitching his voice so that the intruders might hear him. "The laws of the Barony are quite clear. Lady Veralaan ABreton is a noble, and she has given these soldiers her command."

"Only the Baron may command us."

"Then take the men," he replied evenly, "and offer public disobedience and insult to your master's only daughter."

The moment stretched out. The Mother's Daughter waited. She had meant to put a hand on Veralaan's shoulder, as both warning and protection; she would not have dared now. She saw the indecision upon the man's face, and saw it, inexplicably, shift in a direction that she had *never* seen in all her years of service.

He bowed. Stiffly and angrily to a seven-year-old girl. "We will take word to our Lord," he said, just as stiffly, when he rose. "And you will see us again."

"Send my love and respect to Baron Breton," Veralaan replied calmly, "and tell him that I look forward to his visit."

She stood in the same perfect posture until the men backed out of the Healerie. The silence that surrounded her seemed like it might never be broken again. Not even the one man who was awake could speak.

When the last of the soldiers had left the Healerie, Veralaan turned to Rowan. "Please close the door," she said quietly.

Rowan rose instantly, and tendered the Lady Veralaan a perfect obeisance. She also obeyed.

"Lady Veralaan," Iain said, offering a perfect, shallow bow.

She looked at him, then, lifting her chin to better meet his gaze. "Did I do it right?" she asked softly.

"You were perfect," was his grave reply. "But I think that—"

"They are not allowed to enter uninvited into *my* home. They are *never* allowed to enter my home uninvited." And then she walked over to the unconscious boy who slept in the mat upon the floor. "He's younger than me," she added quietly.

At any moment, Emily expected the child to crumple, to show the strain of the confrontation.

"What could he have done to my father, at his age? There must be a misunderstanding."

No one spoke. They should have. And if they did not, the Mother's Daughter had that responsibility. But the girl's desire for her father, her love for his memory, was something that, bright and shining, not even Emily desired to tarnish. It came as a surprise to her. Bitter surprise.

Melanna ran into the room. But even Melanna hesitated awkwardly on the outer periphery of Veralaan's sheer presence. "Veralaan?"

"Lady Veralaan," Iain said, his tone as severe as Emily had ever heard it.

Melanna glared at the side of his face, but it was a helpless anger. She had watched her charge from the frame of the door, powerless before her power.

"No, Iain," Veralaan said quietly. "She is Melanna. She can call me whatever she wants." And she turned to Melanna. "I'm sorry."

Melanna looked confused.

But Veralaan, clear and confident as children could sometimes be, had no intention of allowing her the grace of confusion. "I'm sorry that I wasn't with you when your son died. I could have saved him. You would be happy, then."

Everyone froze again.

"You loved him," she continued quietly, "more than you love me."

Melanna bit her lower lip. She sank to her knees in the Healerie, and she held out her arms—looking, in her roundness and her sudden pain, like one of the few perfect paintings of the Mother. "Not more than you, Veralaan," she whispered.

Veralaan walked slowly into Melanna's arms, and disappeared as they closed round her back. "Never more than you."

The Baron did not come.

II.

"Lady Veralaan."

The young woman so addressed arched both eyebrows and rolled her eyes in mock frustration. The Priestess who attended her almost snickered. But she didn't speak, and after a moment, the Lady Veralaan ABreton turned almost regally. "Yes, Iain?"

"We have kept the Courtier waiting for as long as we can safely do so. He is, if I recall—"

"Lord Wendham," she replied curtly.

"Lord Wendham, then, and if you know that much, you know he is seldom given to patience."

"He has come to visit *me*," she replied coolly. But she rose, wiping bloodstains from her hands upon the apron that hid her clothing. "And I have duties in the Healerie that I consider to be more important." But for all that, she spoke quietly. "Mother's Daughter?" she said at last, and Emily Dontal, silent until that moment, nodded. The years had aged her. But not unkindly.

"He will wait, Lady Veralaan. Your reputation precedes you, and if you do not tarry for *much* longer, he will pretend not to be insulted." She paused and added, "Rowan is capable of watching the Healerie."

"Rowan," the healer said curtly, "is also capable of speaking for herself, Mother's Daughter." She turned to Veralaan, and offered the young woman a brisk nod. "I can watch the Healerie. But I'd appreciate it if you didn't tarry." Her grim eye fell upon the pallets, the floor, the crowded confines of the room that was her life's work.

Veralaan offered her a perfect bow. An unnecessary one. Rowan accepted it; long years had come and gone in which the arguments about form and necessity had at last been eroded by Veralaan's tenacity. But as Veralaan left the Healerie—by the interior doors—Rowan turned to the Mother's Daughter, her gaze shadowed.

"Do you know why Lord Wendham has come?"

Emily Dontal frowned. "No."

"I believe I do, Mother's Daughter. There will be a funeral that Veralaan will be required to attend."

"Whose?"

"I'm not certain," she replied quietly. "But there has been death in the streets in the past two weeks, and if I had to guess, I would say the funeral of one, if not two, of her brothers."

The Mother's Daughter closed her eyes. But words didn't require vision.

"She's learned more here than we could have taught her had we planned it all," Rowan continued, speaking words that should never have been spoken. "She's seen, every day, what is done in his name, by his men. Or by those who serve him. She knows. No one speaks a word against her father. None of us speak of the wars—not in the temple. But the injured who come to us speak when they dream. The dying? She tends their injuries; she knows how they were caused, and even why. She hears.

"I was against her working in the Healerie," Rowan added softly. "From the beginning, even after she saved those three lives, I was against it. I do not know when that changed, Mother's Daughter. But it has. Her presence here—it does something that my power can't."

"What?"

"It gives people hope."

"Rowan—"

"Hope for the nobility. Hope for Breton. It is a bitter hope—to me—but not to all, and it has spilled from the temple into the city streets, traveling—like hope does—by whispers couched in awe. People know that *if* they can reach her side, they are safe." She paused, and then added, "if she is taken from us, that will no longer be the case."

At fifteen years old, Lady Veralaan ABreton presided at her father's side over the burial of two of her brothers. She wore the black and the white, and it was edged in the color and power of gold; she wore gloves, and a dress so fine it would have fed the temple's beggars for two years. She was tall and straight, slender with youth, and her eyes remained utterly dry.

The Mother's Daughter was allowed to attend her, and accepted the insult conveyed with this permission. No other Priests or Priestesses were likewise allowed to be present. It was just as well. This close to the highest echelons of power, it was almost difficult to breathe. There was no grief offered the dead; their mothers had gone before them to the Halls of Mandaros, and their father? Grim and dispassionate. She offered no blessing; was asked to offer none.

But she saw how the Lords of the Breton court circled Veralaan, and she did not like it. The girl herself, however, seemed above them; if she noticed that they eyed her like jackals, she paid them no heed.

In fact, she paid only one man respect: the Baron Breton. And he was graceful and perfect in his reply. But distant as well.

"It is a pity," he told her softly, but not so softly that Emily Dontal did not hear the words, "that they attempted to prove their power when they had not yet mastered it."

"Lanaris is still heir," Veralaan replied. It was the first time—the only time—that Emily was to hear her speak her brother's name.

"For a while," was his bitter answer.

And two weeks later, when healers had come at the Baron's command, and failed to emerge from the bowels of his dungeons, Lanaris ABreton passed away. Rowan was white with anger, and with a bitter admiration. "I would have healed him," she told Veralaan, as she cut bandages into the long strips that were most useful in the Healerie. "I would have healed him and been damned."

"They didn't."

"No. And they will never heal anyone else as a consequence of their choice."

"What does it mean?" Veralaan asked, in the pause that was wedged by anger between the gentle healer's words.

"It means that Baron Halloran Breton is now without heir. He has a wife," she added, "who has had no issue. This was less of a concern, before."

Veralaan said, with a shrug, "He will find another wife."

He needed one. He had come through war to rule the Baronies to the North, the South and the West; he owned the seas. His armies were like legend and nightmare, and where they traveled, they were not forgotten. While he lived, he held them all.

But not even Halloran Breton would live forever.

As Veralaan had so coldly said, he found another wife. But when she was pregnant, she died of poison. Many, many men perished in her wake.

He came to the temple one evening, with four men. He came on horse; the carriage was slow and noisy, and it afforded lookouts the ability to grant warning. But he did not enter the temple; he waited at the door as if he were simply another supplicant. If he did not wait with grace, he did not wait with ire, and Lady Veralaan ABreton agreed in due time that she might speak with her father, Lord Breton.

He left his men at the doors, and they fanned out, brightly burnished fence beyond which, for the duration of the interview, no one living would pass.

Emily Dontal led him from the door to his daughter. She did not ask him why he afforded Veralaan this courtesy; he did not offer. But he looked aged, in a way that she had never seen him aged. Not with the death of his sons, certainly, nor the death of many wives.

She led him into the small chamber, and when she made to leave, he lifted a hand. It was an imperious gesture, but he did not follow it with words; instead, he met his daughter's level gaze. She nodded.

"Please," he said, with just a trace of irony, "stay, Mother's Daughter. What I say may be of concern to you in future." He did not add, *do not interrupt*. Nor had he need. She bowed to him, and moved to stand beside the wall farthest away.

Veralaan did not run to him; she did not smile or lift arms. She regarded him from a distance. If he noticed, he said nothing—and Emily thought it unlikely that he *did* notice. It would pain Veralaan, but she had grown strong enough over the years to hide pain from all but Melanna and Iain.

"I will be brief," Lord Breton told his only living child, "because your safety is served best by brevity. Your existence here has long been known, but it has never been of grave consequence. I fear that this is about to change, Veralaan. There will be, among the Lords who serve me, men who will offer you much if you will consent to marry them. There are those who would not bother to ask your consent, were you not now in the hands of the Mother. They will not risk her wrath at the moment—if they choose to fight among themselves, they may well need the blessings of the Mother.

"I know them all. I know their weaknesses and their strengths. I have chosen two who I believe are likely to be able to hold what I have built. They could simply take it, but I think they are canny enough not to spend men where it is unnecessary. You are the bloodline," he added quietly. "And, therefore, your presence by the side of the right man will signal legitimacy."

She looked at him. "I am to marry?"

"Not yet," he said quietly. "But soon. You will know. Choose wisely." He hesitated for just a moment, as if he might say something more. But he was Halloran Breton; in the end, he retreated in silence, taking nothing of her with him.

And when the door was closed, Veralaan turned to Emily Dontal. The presence—and the absence—of her father cast long shadow; some hint of the wild fear she had shown as a young child now darkened and widened her eyes. She raised her hands, and they shook, but she did not bring them to her face; she held them out before her, turning them so that she might inspect their palms.

The room was cold and quiet; the thin door was shut. There were chairs around the table, because they had chosen the dining hall for their meeting; it was one of the few rooms that could easily seat then all.

They sat in a tense silence, one punctuated by sudden motion, by words that almost demanded voice. Emily Dontal waited until she was certain that no one would speak.

"This is what we expected, isn't it?" she asked them all. Melanna's glare was tinged with red, although she did not cry. "This is why we trained her. This is why we taught her. She is *the Baron's daughter*. Did any of you truly think that she would spend her life here?"

It was an unfair question, for it had only one answer.

"Iain?"

"I have studied the Lords of the Baronial Court," he said quietly. "My sources—and they are few—have given me what information they can."

"And you trust them?"

"Not at all. They understand why I have requested the information, and they seek their own advantage from the giving." There was no bitterness in the words. "Of the men that consider themselves powerful, I think I know the two of whom he spoke."

"And they?"

"What would you have me say, Emily? That they are *good men*?" Ah, bitterness there. "That they will be *kind* husbands?" And all of Melanna's rage, but cultured, quiet.

"Yes, if it were true."

He rolled his eyes. "In a different story, Mother's Daughter. In a different world." He drew the circle across his chest, a jittery fidgeting motion. "But if she must choose—"

The door that led to the kitchen swung open.

In it, hands by her side, stood Veralaan. "I won't," she said softly.

She had heard everything. "Veralaan—" Melanna rose almost blindly.

"I won't. Do you think I'm stupid? Do you think I don't know? One of them will be responsible for my father's death."

Ah. "Veralaan—"

"And even if they're not, what difference will it make? I know their names. I hear them every day, in the Healerie. I know what they do, in my father's name. I know what they will do. Am I expected to leave the Mother's heart so that one of them may rule?"

"If you do not," Iain said, without fire, "they will

war among themselves. And in that war, there will be more death than even you can imagine. You have some power, Veralaan. If you choose—"

"I *won't*. I will never marry." She lifted her hands; they were fists. "Why didn't you train me to wield sword, Iain? You *know* how. Why didn't you teach me about armies, about strategy? Why did you—*all of you*—let me labor here, let me think I was making a difference?"

"You *are* making a difference, Veralaan."

"And when I leave?"

They did not lie to her. And, because they couldn't, they said nothing.

Six months later, Baron Breton passed away, leaving behind one living child. She was a girl, and although in theory she was heir, it was tenuous theory; no one would follow a woman. But as Baron Breton had surmised, the Court did not immediately fall upon itself, although there were deaths. They decided, instead, that they could wait for Veralaan to make a choice. They signed treaties in blood to that effect: they acknowledged *her* as Breton's only heir.

Word began to arrive in the hands of trusted emissaries from all stratum. Letters were followed by gifts, and gifts by requests for audience.

Iain saw that Veralaan's wardrobe suited her station, but he also demurred when presented with these requests; the Lady Veralaan, he said, was in mourning for her father, for her much loved father, and she could not entertain others until the period of mourning had passed.

It was not—entirely—a lie, although Veralaan did not cry or weep. She refused, however, to meet with these men. And for a year, they accepted this refusal with outward grace. But it was a thin veneer.

* * *

The first girl who came to the Healerie with a message from one of the Lords had two broken arms. The girl could not be more than eight years of age, and she was weeping and frightened—but she was alive. Veralaan was not in the Healerie, and Rowan and Melanna managed to keep this from her for a day and a half.

A day and a half was all it took for the next injured victim to arrive. After that, there were a dozen, and each man, woman or child carried a message for Lady Veralaan of the Mother's Temple, writ in broken bone, in gaping wound: a simple greeting.

Veralaan tended them all herself; she insisted on it. She wept with them, and openly begged their forgiveness. It was the only time she would do so.

Iain said, quietly, "what one lord does, they must all try. But Veralaan, if you accede to these . . . requests . . . they will never stop."

"And if I don't?" she asked. She was bone-white.

"I can't say," he replied at last. "If they kill, the message will never reach you."

"What would you have me do?" She turned to Rowan, hair now gray, skin as white as Veralaan's, and for the same reason.

"I—I can't advise you, Veralaan." She turned away.

"Rowan!"

"I think Iain's right. Start, and it will *never* end. All they will have to do is fill the Healerie with the dead and the dying, and whoever can do the most damage will, in the end, be the one who holds the most power over you." But her hands were bunched fists as she said it, and the cloth around her legs shook as she shoved those fists into her lap.

Melanna tried to drag Veralaan away, as if, for a moment, she were once again a three-year-old child.

Veralaan shook her off without speaking. But her face did not regain its natural color.

"Don't do it," Iain told her. "If you do, they'll know that you're weak."

"And is this how strength is defined?" she asked, staring at the closed doors of the Healerie, her voice very soft.

"In the Baronies, yes."

One day passed.

Melanna wept quietly, her voice shorn of bark, and therefore of strength. Emily put an arm around Melanna's shoulder. "Why are you standing in the hall?"

"Veralaan won't see me," was the choked reply. "She sent Iain away as well. I'm afraid of what she'll do—"

Emily held Melanna tight. "We are all afraid," she whispered. "I prayed. The night she came, Melanna. I prayed to my mother for a child. For the child she has long denied me. I always wondered—I wonder still—if it is because of my weakness, my anger, my inability to simply forgive."

"I don't know. Perhaps the gods do listen to those who aren't born with their blood; Veralaan came after the prayer."

"There is no god of Mercy," Melanna said bitterly.

"No. Only the Mother."

"Where are the *other damn gods*?" Melanna snapped harshly. "Where are the heroes? Where are the men who could stand against those—those—" She lifted a hand to her face.

"You know the answer," was the bitter reply; they were of a mind this evening. "But I—"

"She won't see you."

"She will," The Mother's Daughter said, without stiffness or determination. "Because she sent for me."

"Don't—" Melanna gripped Emily's arms. Her wide fingers would leave bruises there, but it was unintentional. "Don't let her do it."

"She cannot stand to see them suffer because of her. To see them suffer? Yes. Because she has practically lived in the Healerie when she has not been learning how to be a Baroness, she has grown calluses, as we *all* have. But this is new. Until now, they lived *because* of her. She is young, and her heart is not scarred enough. I do not think she will survive this."

"We should have done things differently. We should have—"

The door opened, and Melanna choked in her rush to contain the rest of the words. But she stared at Veralaan's pale face. She lifted her hands to touch it, and Veralaan, instead of withdrawing, lifted her own, catching Melanna's beneath her youthful palms.

"You are my mother," she said quietly.

Melanna, already given over to tears, cried more of them.

"And Emily, you, too. Alayna. Rowan. Even Iain."

"Not father?"

"No. I would never disgrace Iain by calling him that." The words were bitter, but the bitterness was a ripple. "Mother's Daughter?"

"Lady Veralaan."

"I require your presence in the inner chamber."

"The inner—" Emily's eyes widened. "The Mother's chamber?"

Veralaan nodded quietly.

"Veralaan, the Mother is *not* of this world. She cannot offer you guidance, and she cannot protect you. She—"

"She cannot even hear me, if you will not intercede," Veralaan said. "I know. I know all of this,

Mother's Daughter. And I know that Rowan is also right. But I can't—I can't go into the Healerie again. I can't—" She stiffened. "It won't end with strangers, even the strangers to whom you've dedicated your life. If injuring—and disfiguring—outsiders won't work, they'll try insiders. We'll lose Novices. I might lose—" For a moment, the younger Veralaan was *there*, in the wide eyes, the frightened eyes, of a child who had been abandoned by her father. "I've made my choice."

"What choice, child?"

"I am not a child, Mother's Daughter. I *am* the Baron Breton, by the acknowledgment of the Lords of the Baronial Court. And in the end, it was not a request. You will accompany me to the inner chamber."

"There is no magic in the inner chamber, Veralaan."

"No, Mother's Daughter."

"Then why?"

"The Mother will hear you. And when you call her—if you call her—she will come." She turned to Melanna and hugged her tightly. "Tell Iain—"

"I won't. I won't tell him anything. You want to tell him something, you *have to be here to do it*."

The inner chamber. The room in which the prayers of the Mother's Daughter were made. It was a small room, with a modest ceiling, stone walls, and a small altar. Upon the altar was an empty bowl, an empty basket, a small candle; things that were entirely modest and ephemeral.

"It is not a very fine room." The Mother's Daughter came to stand by the altar; she did not kneel.

"What need have gods of finery?"

"Ask men who envy the gods the power they think gods possess," was the bitter reply. "What do you wish me to ask of my mother?"

"I don't," Veralaan said evenly. "I wish to ask it myself."

The Mother's Daughter was silent for a long moment. "Veralaan—I can summon my mother. And in reply, she will summon *us*. We will walk in the world that is neither man's nor god's. It is . . . not an easy place to endure."

Veralaan, however, was young; she would not be moved. "Call her."

And Emily Dontal did.

The mists ate away at the floor; they severed the walls from their moorings, until only the mists themselves remained. They were not gray, not black, not white, but all of these things, and interspersed with them, colors, muted and moving as if at the behest of strong breeze. But none of these things moved Veralaan; she endured them as if they were simply a matter of fact.

Emily was impressed.

But when the Mother came, Veralaan lifted chin and looked up, and up again, for the form the Mother chose was not comforting, and not small; she was tall as the skies of mist, her arms long, her shoulders wide. She came carrying no baskets; she came attended by no beasts of burden, no emblems of unearthly authority. She wore the workaday robes of a field laborer, and her face was lined by sun and wind.

"Daughter," she said to Emily. "Why have you summoned me?"

"At the behest of one of your Novices," was the quiet reply. "And no, Mother, I do not know why."

"Ah, daughter," the Mother said quietly. But she spoke not to Emily, but Veralaan. "I have long watched you, through the eyes of my only child. What do you wish of me?"

"This world, this place," Veralaan replied. "It is said that time moves strangely here."

"It is true. Time is of passing consequence to my children, but it does not touch me."

"And if I spent time here, would I age?"

"You are mortal."

"If I were willing to age, would time pass beyond this place?"

"In the mortal lands?" The Mother frowned. Emily could feel it as if it were weather, a storm. "Why do you ask this, child?"

If Emily's use of the word had caused offense, the god's use did not. "Because I have no time. Beyond this place, your followers are dying because men with power seek my attention."

"They seek more than that."

"Then you already know why I ask."

"I wanted to be certain that you did. What would you have of me? I am no warrior, and I am bound to my lands, as you, in the end, must be bound to yours."

"I want a son," Veralaan said.

Emily almost stopped breathing.

"I want a golden-eyed son, a god-born child. I was not trained to war," she added bitterly, "because I am a daughter. I cannot fight. I cannot lead armies, even if there were any willing to follow. Everything I am, I have become in your service.

"But I am not without strength. I am willing to bear such a child, and to raise him as I can—but only in the lands between; if I bear him here, he will die."

"If you bear him in the lands between, you might, child."

"I am willing to take that risk."

"I cannot give you the child you seek."

"I know. But you are sister to many gods, and I—"

She struggled now, with the words. "And I wish you to intercede on my behalf with one of your brothers."

"Which one, child? The fate of the god-born is death in your lands, and there is not a god who easily surrenders his child to death."

"I know," she whispered. "Not even a man as monstrous as my father could do that."

The Mother was silent a long moment. "If you ask it, and if you are willing to live in the half-world, there may be those among us who are willing to offer what you ask. But child—those born to the blood are driven by it. Which god would you choose?"

Cartanis, Emily though. Surely Cartanis, god of just war. But Veralaan was silent. After a moment, she said, "Which god would you choose for me?"

And the mother laughed. It was a low, rich sound, a sound carried by a host of voices, a multitude of emotions. "It is not a question that I could answer," she said, when she had stopped. "But think long on what is missing in your world, and perhaps you will find the answer you seek." She held out her arms, her huge arms, and gathered Veralaan in them, as if she were a babe.

"Emily," she said, when she had pulled Veralaan from the ground that the mist obscured. "You have done well. You have struggled, and you have chosen to love this child as if she were your own."

"No, Mother," Emily said, bowing her head. "I had no choice. But the others? Melanna, Iain, Rowan— they are worthy of the praise you offer me. They love her. And they will be grieved indeed to lose her."

The Mother's smile creased; it blended with sorrow. "Loss defines us," she told her only blood daughter. "But more than that, what we choose to lose defines us. I will go. But wait here, Emily."

* * *

Emily Dontal knelt by the altar. The mists had parted and dispersed, and in the absence of her mother, she felt the world as the grim, dark place it was. No dint of labor could lift that darkness. It was said that the gods had once walked the world, and she bitterly regretted the fact that she had not lived in those times.

But one could not choose.

Mother, she thought, as she pressed her forehead to stone. Her vision was skewed by a thin sheen of water; there were tears there that she could not shed. She had been bidden *wait*, and she was dutiful. She waited. Feeling, now, the cold of stone in her bones, the ache of age.

She did not see the mists as they came again, until they had all but covered her. But she stood as they did, so that she might see her Mother again.

It was not her Mother who stood before her.

It was a young man. And beside him, another. Two. They gazed down upon her, for they were tall, and their eyes were bright, golden. That light seemed to burn the mist away, and she was captive to it, although—had she been vain—she would have known that those eyes were kin to her own.

"Mother's Daughter," the man to the left said quietly. He offered her a hand, and she stared at it for a moment. Then she took it.

"I am Cormalyn," he said quietly. "And this, my half-brother, Reymalyn. We have heard much about you, and we are honored to meet you at last."

She shook her head, almost in wonder. "You are the son of Cormaris, Lord of Wisdom."

"I am."

"And your half-brother, the son of Reymaris, god of Justice."

"I am," the second man said, speaking for the first

time. "And I am capable of speaking for myself, although my brother is the better with words." He, too, offered her a hand.

She felt her throat constrict.

"We are the sons of Veralaan," they said, in unison, "and as she is, by acclaim, Baron of Breton and therefore the Eastern seas, we are her heirs, and between us, the legitimate claimants to the Baronial lands."

But she could not speak. *Veralaan*, she thought, staring at the two.

Cormalyn's smile was gentle. "It is hard, for my mother," he told her. "But hard, as well, for you. Or it will be. She is coming, Mother's Daughter. But she is not what she was, and you must warn the others."

"I—"

But they stepped to the side, and between them, as the last of the mists left, she saw Veralaan. No: she saw through time, down a stretch of more than a decade and a half, to see the woman that her Veralaan might become: Stronger, wiser, but almost silent in her isolation. Her hair was still blonde, and it was longer, and the features of her face were unmistakably her own; she did not look old, but she was no longer a fifteen-year-old girl.

She was a woman.

She had borne these two, and she had raised them.

"Mother's Daughter," she said quietly, as if speech were foreign to her. She held, in her arms, a blanket, but she wore the same dress that she had worn on the day—this day, some half an hour past—she had left.

"Veralaan!" Emily said, pushing past the two men who had at first seemed miracle and were now merely adornment. She held out her arms wide, but Veralaan stepped back. She smiled, to show that it was not an act of rejection.

"My sons," she whispered.

"You were always an ambitious child," Emily said with a wry grin. "Two?"

"Wisdom. And Justice. Because we need both." She added, with a rueful grin, "I was never really good at making choices unless they were obvious."

"What will you do?"

"I will summon the Baronial Court, Mother's Daughter. They will come, and they will meet my sons and their fathers."

"You would—you would summon your fathers? In the Court?"

The two men said nothing, but they looked at their mother.

"I speak too freely," she said with a pained smile. "I am accustomed to company of those for whom silence is no barrier. I . . . have to learn again, Emily. Will you . . . will you let me stay here, when I abdicate my throne in favor of my sons?"

"Veralaan—they are two men."

"Yes. But they were raised by their fathers, and they know things that not even you, Mother's Daughter, can know. They will build an Empire. The Witherall Seer foretold it; my father went to the Seer before he brought me to your temple, and I listened to what she said, although I didn't understand it at the time. But it has to be the *right* Empire, or else, what's the point?" She took a step forward, and then stopped. "I almost forgot." And she held out the blanket to Emily.

"What is this?"

"It is a gift from the Mother, although she wept to part with her."

And Emily Dontal closed her eyes. "I do not think my arms are strong enough," she whispered, afraid to open them.

"I do. There is work to do, Emily. I cannot promise

that it will be without bloodshed and death. But you've always done what needed to be done, and if my sons are driven by Justice and Wisdom, they will *always* need the mercy of the Mother, the compassion of her Daughters. Take your child. I want—I want to see Iain and Melanna. Because they haven't changed.''

And Emily's arms closed round the infant whose eyes, golden, were a reflection of her own. Mother's Daughter.

THE CAPTAIN OF THE DEAD

Fiona Patton

Fiona Patton was born in Alberta and grew up in the United States. In 1975 she returned to Canada and after a series of unrelated jobs including electrician and carnival ride operators, moved to rural Ontario with her partner, one tiny dog and a series of ever changing cats. Her "Branion" series, which includes *The Stone Prince, The Painter Knight, The Granite Shield,* and *The Golden Sword,* have all been published by DAW Books and she is now working on the first book of a new series tentatively entitled *The Silver Lake* for DAW as well.

THE SCREAMING had never bothered him; not as a newly uniformed soldier drafted to restrain the wounded for the army physicians in their hot and fly-filled tents on the edge of battle; nor when he'd taken up the saw himself in those same tents; drafted once again because his empire needed physicians as badly as it needed soldiers. It was an age of expansion and of conquest and in those tents he learned herbcraft and spellcraft, how to knit bones and heal wounds, how to magic a man back on his feet to carry on the battle, and how to sew up his shroud. Cutting and sewing and stitching and spellcasting, he served the Imperial armies year after year. As his back bent and his hair thinned, the red-and-golden wyvern standard came to cover half the world; no principality or kingdom, no loose conglomerate of city-states or independent tribe of horsemen could stand against them; their magics were too powerful and too terrible to be repulsed.

Until they came upon a small mountain kingdom with magics both powerful and terrible of their own.

The fighting raged for months, in the valleys and in the glens, as the rains washed out the passes in spring, and the snows blocked the supply lines in winter. The Empire called for reinforcements, drawing soldiers from every corner of their realm. The mountain kingdom called as well and their allies poured over the passes in a river of brilliant flags and flashing weapons.

In the physicians' tents the wounded flowed like a river of a different sort. Bent over his table, he stitched and sewed, ignoring the flies, the stink, and the screaming as he always had as, inch by bloody inch, the Imperial soldiers drove the Mountain troops back by sheer weight of numbers. They took stronghold after stronghold until talk was that one more push would see it done.

Then the Mountain troops struck back.

A dozen men slipped into the Imperial camp one moonless night. As silent as shadows, they passed the picket lines and the sentries on duty before the officers' tents and came upon the physicians as they lay, too exhausted from their labors to raise the alarm. They took five of them that night to a dark and frightening place and gave each of them a choice: death or aid them in one tiny chance of their own, one desperate chance offered up by a man imprisoned for terrible crimes, a physician gone insane but possessing a magic long denied and feared, a magic to reanimate the dead. They spoke of the decision their leaders had made in the last of their strongholds, to once, just this once, sacrifice whatever they had to: beliefs, idealism, even honor, to emerge victorious over their enemies. They needed physicians to work this magic and they did not have enough of their own. A simple choice.

Even then the screaming hadn't bothered him. Not when, one by one, the Imperial physicians broke and gave them aid, nor when his own screaming destroyed his voice, changing his soft, pleasant tenor to the harsh, ragged cry of a battlefield crow. The screaming hadn't bothered him, nor the stink, or the darkness, or the terror, or even the pain. It took a much softer attack than that to break him.

It came in the form of a man wearing the symbol of the mountain kingdom's royal guard: a flock of birds flying high above a silver cloud. A captain. He came to him in his dark prison and he spoke of the pain and suffering of the people he'd sworn to protect, a people who only wanted to live free and live safe. And he spoke of life; of tiny remote villages where the children played without a care, of the warm sun on the green and growing valleys dotted with sheep and goats, of mountain slopes strewn with flowers. Of laughing and loving, and drinking and singing. It was that and not the screaming that finally broke him, that caused him to look around at the stink and the darkness, and allow the captain to bring him back into the light. Here, under a banner of flying birds and the tutelage of a madman, he labored as he had before in fly-filled tents on the edge of battle. But there was no warm sun and no green valleys here, only blood and deep, cloying mud, and the cold, hard bodies of the dead. He cut and sewed and stitched and stuffed the red-hot herbs into eviscerated cavities until his hands were stained and numb, drawing the dark red symbols on their bodies in their own blood, setting the mountain kingdom's small and shrinking army back on its feet to fight again, and again and again.

And slowly the Mountain troops gained back the ground they'd lost.

Their soldiers gave him what service they were ordered to. They supplied him with barrels of herbs, spices and ink, thread, and needles and brushes. They fed him: jug after jug of a vile, brown syrup at the madman's command, a drink that kept him on his feet for days, then weeks, then months at a time, a drink that made him feel numb and dead inside like the river of bodies they brought to him, piling the corpses to either side of him when his tables grew too laden.

He no longer needed them to restrain the wounded; the dead did not struggle—not as the living knew struggling to be—although they fought in their own way with stiffened limbs and resentful, unwilling hardness. The newly dead were the worst, their bodies seemed to shrink away from his needle and his brush. And why wouldn't they, he thought when he thought about it at all. But that wasn't often. He cut and sewed and stuffed and drew the terrible glyphs on their bodies, muttering the death magics he'd been taught, and sent them back into the field.

The orderlies who served him carried out their orders, but they didn't speak to him. They did their service and they fled. Sometimes they came back to him as corpses themselves, but he scarcely noticed, for he didn't speak to them either. As the rains washed out the passes in spring, and the snows blocked the supply lines in winter, he forgot he had a voice, or even a name. He forgot about remote villages full of children, of the warm sun on green and growing valleys, of mountain slopes strewn with flowers. Of laughing and loving and drinking and singing. Even of herb-craft and spellcraft and healing wounds and knitting bones. He forgot about shrouds because the dead no longer needed them. He forgot how to speak and even how to sleep. He bent his head over his task and he worked, ignoring the screaming as he always had.

He barely raised his eyes when they put chains on his ankles and guards on his tent the night the empire raided the mountain physicians as they themselves had been raided: to service a new army of the dead. The guards never spoke to him any more than his orderlies did. And when the living sentinels and the living orderlies were replaced by his own dead; the dead to guard the dead and the dead to carry the dead, he wondered if there was truly anyone left alive. And then he'd hear the screaming and he knew that a few still lived and fought.

But most of them died.

The uniforms changed as the seasons changed, the birds became wyverns, became mud and blood-encrusted rags sewn together with his own dark thread and that of the other necromancers laboring on both sides now to keep the armies fighting. But he sent they all back regardless. The screaming never bothered him, even now when there was so little of it. The dead were all he knew and the dead never screamed.

Wild, undulating howling filled the air over the battlefield day and night.

Except when they were ordered to, he amended.

But the screaming never bothered him, nor the stink, the darkness, the terror, nor even the pain.

Until the captain was laid before him.

Then he checked, and a deep and terrible sadness began to radiate up from his chest, a sadness and a despairing weariness that he hadn't felt in years. He remembered the captain's words: the warm sun on the green valleys and the mountain slopes strewn with flowers. He looked up from his table then, his dull and nearly lifeless eyes seeking the captain's vision, but he saw only death. He swayed, suddenly dizzy and sick, but something in the captain's still face kept him on his feet.

Laughing and loving and drinking and singing.

It might be somewhere.

A new light began to shine very faintly in his eyes and he bent to his task, slicing open the captain's chest through his leather uniform with its blood and gore-encrusted flock of birds. The birds hadn't flown in a very long time, he noted, but they might again. Catching up a fistful of herbs, he spoke a different spell this time, then thrust the herbs into the captain's chest, and took up his needle and his brush once more, hardly daring to hope. He was the best the madman had ever trained and so the officers always came to him. He didn't bother to wonder why they were needed anymore since the dead didn't make decisions.

Not yet.

Laughing and loving and drinking and singing.
Mountain slopes strewn with flowers . . .

The captain came back to him again and again and again, each time shocking him a little farther from his lifeless stupor, each time fueling the tiny spark of hope that had begun to burn inside him, the hope that he might once again know those things the captain had spoken of so long ago.

Laughing and loving . . .

The second time he changed the herbal mixture, the third time the spices, the fourth time the painted glyphs upon his chest, the fifth time those upon his limbs. The sixth time the captain's mouth and tongue moved as if he might speak, the seventh time he shuddered violently, and finally the eighth time he opened his hazy, yellow eyes and stared up at the necromancer who had brought him back into the world.

Slow, soft, falling darkness, peace, then light and pain and screaming, then the darkness once again . . .

The first thing he remembered was light, the second, sound—screaming, yelling, and the clash of weapons. Then came the memories: a sword in his hand, standards fluttering in the breeze, lines of pike men on the field, death, the slow, soft, falling darkness, peace. Over and over again.

He remembered pain, felt pain, felt the cold in his limbs and the heat radiating up from his chest where a great pressure threatened to split his skin. When he finally managed to open his eyes, he wondered at the misty, yellow fog that covered his vision. He remembered fog, and rain and snow and hail. And he remembered the man looking down at him, filthy, dirt-encrusted hair strangling over a gray, lined face, empty, nearly lifeless eyes staring inward to a horror he could barely face. He remembered his own name, made to speak it, but his jaw seemed frozen. He tried to move and found his limbs responding. He stood, and looking down, he saw his hands, yellowed and cracked and covered in blood, long dried and black. He knew his first thrill of fear˘ and that was all he knew for a long time.

Slow, soft, falling darkness, peace.
Light and pain and the clash of weapons, then the darkness once again . . .

The man stared down at him, his nearly lifeless eyes haunted but . . . hopeful. And he spoke to him. In a harsh and ragged voice, he spoke of life, of the warm sun on green valleys dotted with sheep and goats, of mountain slopes strewn with flowers, of children playing in remote villages. Of laughing and loving and drinking and singing.

And he remembered. He remembered the faces of his men, his children, his wife, and his kin. He reached out and nearly fell into the man's arms as his legs gave way beneath him. They hung there for a moment; each gaining some small, surprising, unlikely and unfamiliar comfort, then the man turned him to face a vast field of battle.

Thousands of soldiers struggled and died, ragged banners rising and falling and rising again, lines of corpses carrying corpses, trundling like ants back and forth from the tables of the necromancers. And, as the glyphs took him and he returned to the field, he saw the man sway, then draw himself upright once again, his face drawn up into a grimace of fear and hope. The hope seemed the more terrible of the two.

Light and the clash of weapons and the soft falling darkness. Peace.
And light . . .

"They're all dead now, or most of them anyway," the necromancer said, catching up an earthenware flagon and downing the contents. The captain watched as his wrinkled throat worked and rivulets of brown syruplike liquid trickled down his gray, matted beard.

"All dead." He returned his attention to a nameless corpse too battered to show any signs of rank or allegiance anymore. "Life," he muttered as if it were an incantation. "Laughing, loving, drinking, and singing. You said those words to me, long ago," he noted as he scooped the old dried herbal mixture from the body's chest. "Do you even remember what they are?"

"Do you?" the captain replied, his voice as ragged and harsh as the necromancer's; he'd only just begun to use it and it still seemed alien to his ears.

"No," the man confessed tiredly as he reached for a fresh handful of spices. "I hold onto them, however, as if I'd seen them in a beautiful dream once. But they weren't in my dream, were they? They were in yours." He turned, his eyes bright with unremembered tears. "Can you dream anymore?"

The question made the captain feel angry and the anger made him feel good, made him feel . . . almost alive. Almost, but . . . not. He thrust the necromancer aside without answering his question and returned to the battle and the soft, falling darkness and the light. Again.

"Do you even remember what you fought for?"

The captain was standing at the opening of the tent, staring out at the field while the necromancer worked. The clash of weapons was a constant roar all around him, but there was little screaming now. Even the dead had fallen silent; like the necromancer they were bent and bowed, but they fought and struggled on. He turned and nodded tightly—this last death had snapped his neck; it felt hard and stiff as if the bones had fused in death. He supposed they had.

To live safe and live free . . .

"Freedom," he said simply, remembering that the word had meant something vitally important to him long ago.

The necromancer shrugged emaciated shoulders and the captain could see the bones move through his threadbare shirt. "Does that mean anything now?" he asked. "Are you free? Are they? No, there is no freedom left," he said, answering his own question. "Your leaders sacrificed your freedom and theirs along with everything else for their *one desperate chance at victory.*" He spat bitterly. "Their one sacrifice." He shook his head wearily. "Some sacrifices should never be made. Some sacrifices corrupt and destroy everything you're trying to save."

"They had no other choice," the captain said, but even to his ears the protest sounded weak. "Your people gave them no other choice."

"There is always another choice. You could have surrendered, you could have run, you could have magicked the mountains down on their heads."

"*You* could have left us in peace. *You* came to *us*. *You* made war on *us*. We simply defended our homes."

"Defense is only defense so long as it does not destroy what it defends and a decision is not truly made once if it must be remade over and over again."

His words unsettled the captain and he turned his yellow eyes on the man's face. "Some things are worth sacrificing everything for," he said, "they're worth dying for." He turned back to the battle, feeling what was left of the necromancer's original glyphs drawing him back. "And worth killing for."

"Some *things*?" the necromancer asked, his voice finding new life in his indignation . . . "What things? Victory?" His voice was demanding now, sarcastic, the voice of a healer, the voice of a prisoner.

"Life," the captain answered simply.

"And when there is no life left but the killing goes on and on and on. What is worth killing for then?"

The captain had no answer. As he felt the pull of the glyphs calling him back to the battlefield, he heard the man speak again as if from far away.

"What is worth living for?"

The answer hovered just beyond his reach and then he stepped onto the field and it was gone.

Life and love and the warm sun . . .
And the soft, falling darkness and the light.

"When you take on the actions of evil, you become evil," the necromancer said, his breath misting the air before his face. It was winter now, but he didn't seem to feel the cold. The captain had seen him paint some of the glyphs he carried on his own chest that morning and wondered at how he could live with the heat, but then he supposed that was the point of drawing them in the first place. Heat. Warmth. Life. He wondered if he'd used his own blood, then supposed he'd have had to; there was precious little fresh blood anywhere else these days

"Is it that simple?" he asked, pulling himself from his reverie with some effort.

The necromancer shrugged. "I used to think it was, long ago when I was young. I believe I think so again now that I am old. Good and evil are simple concepts.

And I suppose it was simple in the beginning, a small mountain kingdom struggling against a cruel empire. But not now. Both sides are so steeped in blood and death now, they couldn't wash it away if they bathed in a thousand clear and running rivers. Besides, there are no running rivers left either. They're all choked with death."

"So what is good and evil, now then?" the captain asked, feeling truly curious and enjoying the sensation. His eyesight seemed clearer these days, his hands, though still yellow and cracked, seemed to work a little better and that made it easier to accept the feelings the necromancer's words invoked.

"This is evil," the man answered, gesturing at the battlefield. "Waste. Destruction. Killing for no purpose."

"So what is good? *Is* there any good left?"

The necromancer shrugged. "*We* are all that's left."

The captain felt a smile build on his lips and was surprised; he couldn't remember the last time he'd smiled. "So, are we good?" he prodded.

"We might have been once, when I was a healer and you a protector and not purveyors of death."

"Could we be again?"

"I don't know." The man squared his thin shoulders. "But since we are truly all that's left, we will have to do." Looking up into the cold, winter sky, he shivered. "I'm old, captain," he said suddenly. "Old and tired and I'm afraid to die in this place." He turned, his eyes filled with longing. "Take me to your green valleys and your mountainsides strewn with flowers. Take me to find life."

And the captain broke the power of the glyphs at last as he broke the chains about the necromancer's ankles, wrapped him in an old blanket, and carried him away from the fly-filled tent. Turning their backs on the battlefield, they headed up into the mountains, searching for life.

They walked by day and by night, pausing only for the man to drink from the jugs the captain carried lashed to his back, then moving on, the faint noise of battle in the distance the only sounds around them.

But there was no life to be found. The armies had come from every corner of the world it seemed, burning and looting and destroying everything in their path before they'd even reached the battlefield and all they found was empty village after empty village.

They kept moving, the captain trudging through waist-deep snowdrifts in some places, keeping the man warm with the burning magics in his chest. When the snows finally gave way to rain and the rain to sun, they began to descend to the other side of the mountains and finally passed through the wasteland to the valleys and forests awash with fragile new growth on the other side. There the voice of battle finally gave way to the sounds of birds and insects reclaiming their world and the man wept to hear it.

But the land was still empty of people.

They kept walking, day after day. When they ran out of the madman's brown syrup, the captain caught small creatures and rendered them into broth, sitting the man before the fire and feeding him with a spoon he carved from a piece of wood. The man grew ill and the captain feared he might die but, as the summer breeze slowly warmed the land, he rallied. The captain began to add tiny pieces of boiled rabbit and squirrel to the broth, then herbs and roots he found growing wild along the way. As they headed deeper into the valleys, they heard the sounds of wolves in the distant hills and their song lulled the man to sleep in the captain's arms for the first time in years.

In the height of summer they found a running stream both warm and clear. They wondered at it and, kneeling, the captain washed the man very gently, slowly wiping the blood and dirt-encrusted gore from his body. In an abandoned shepherd's hut he found him clean, warm clothes. Then he caught a sheep gone wild in the mountains, and the man ate meat again. Then one day as the sun shone down upon his cheeks, he pulled his hair back from his face and tied it with a bit of twine. The captain trimmed his beard for him and he began to look out at the world without fear.

Then one day as the leaves on the trees began to show a hint of autumn color, they found what they were looking for.

It was the screaming that drew them. The man shuddered at the sound, but as they came closer, they found a young boy, fallen, his leg torn and bleeding from a ragged piece of rock. A few gaunt adults crouched nearby trying to give him what aid they could. They fled as the dead man and his strange burden approached, but the captain tracked them to a small cave and, laying the man down before the entrance, peered in at the huddled men and women as they stood guard before the injured child.

"I won't hurt you," he said as gently as he was able in his harsh, dead voice. "This man is a physician. He can help him."

He withdrew to a distant ledge and waited and after a long time the people crept outside.

And the man remembered how to knit bones and heal wounds.

*　　*　　*

The captain stayed with them throughout the winter, helping them catch the few remaining sheep and protecting them from the larger predators that were beginning to return to the lower slopes. The people called him Captain and they called the man Grandfather. The man cried at the word, but grew stronger in their company. But he was old, terribly old, and the memory of the battlefield still haunted his dreams. The captain knew it, and so, when the snows began to melt in the warmer air of a new spring, he came to him.

"We found life," he said.

The man nodded.

"But that isn't enough, is it?"

"No, we have to end the battle. End it and life will return, not just here, but everywhere."

Glancing past the man's shoulder, the captain watched the boy they'd saved darting through the meadow grasses. "No, Grandfather," he said gently. "We don't have to end it. I have to end it."

"You cannot break the power of the glyphs," the man insisted. "You need me for that."

The captain smiled sadly. Crouching down, he took the man's frail hand very carefully in his own. "I don't intend to break the power of the glyphs," he said. Pressing the man's fingertips to his chest where the ancient symbols still gave off a faint, pulsing warmth, he shook his head. "This isn't life, Grandfather, and it isn't death. You said once that waste and destruction and killing for no purpose was evil. Well, eternal struggle without rest is no better. It leaches what good may be found in the sacrifice of battle." He stood. "Some things are worth living for, and some things are worth killing for. You will live, and I will kill, and when all the dead are finally laid to rest as they should have been so long ago, there will finally be an end to it and life can return."

The man looked up, his face pained but resigned. "You will have to kill the necromancers first," he said. "But I think that they long for rest as deeply as the dead. I know I did."

"And now?"

The man smiled as the boy ran up to him and laid an armload of spring flowers in his lap. "Now I have something to live for, at least for a little while longer."

They embraced then as they had long ago and the captain turned and made his way back to the dead. As the summer gave over to winter and winter to spring and with the heat from the ancient glyphs upon his body slowly fading, he crossed over the mountains and went down into the wasteland once again.

He heard the battle long before he saw it, but eventually he crested a rise and looked down upon a massive field writhing with struggling bodies. There was no more screaming now, no more keening; only the methodical sounds of combat. On the edges the dead still guarded the ragged tents where the necromancers still worked feverously stitching, stuffing and sewing, and drinking the brown syrup that kept them on their feet. The dead orderlies still carried their own back and forth like demonic mothers, piling them beside the overladen tables and the dead soldiers still shambled back to the fighting when the necromancer's work was done. Most of them had no armor, some no clothes; those without weapons tore at each other with stiffened, lifeless fingers. But there was such a deep abiding weariness in the air that the captain almost fell to his knees from the force of it, but strengthening his resolve, he rose and went down into their midst again.

He began on one side, he didn't know or care what

side it had once been, and he brought death to the necromancers, one by one. Most did not struggle. One even held his thin, emaciated arms out to him in gratitude before he fell. When the captain found the madman, he was already stiff and lifeless, still bent over his table, long dead. He left him there.

He killed the guards on the tents next and then the orderlies. Now that there were none to carry the soldiers from the field, they lay where they'd fallen, finally giving themselves up to the earth. The sounds of battle grew quieter and the stench of true death began to shimmer in the air.

Then he turned to the combatants. As the snow began to cover the bodies of the fallen, he called his people to him and they came, Imperial and Mountain forces alike, all his now, laying their weapons aside before giving themselves over to the final death.

And after the last man standing in a uniform so rent and tattered he could have been from either side or none at all, had finally fallen, there was silence on the field; no screams, no keening, no sounds of battle, or clash of weapons and no movement at all except the wind blowing through what was left of his own uniform.

And, standing in the midst of death, the captain remembered life. He remembered tiny remote villages where the children played without a care. He remembered the warm sun on the green and growing valleys dotted with sheep and goats, the mountain slopes strewn with flowers; the laughing and loving, and drinking and singing. He remembered the people he had sworn to protect, his people who only wanted to live free and live safe. And might again. Then raising his sword toward the west and the man who'd brought him back to life, he drove the point deep into his

chest, through the crest of flying birds long ago torn
and faded away, through the last of the glyphs that
had kept him struggling for so long. And fell.

Slow, soft, falling darkness.
Peace.
And rest.

Tanya Huff

The Confederation Novels

VALOR'S CHOICE
0-88677-896-4

When a diplomatic mission becomes a battle for survival,
the price of failure will be far worse than death...

THE BETTER PART OF VALOR
0-7564-0062-7

Could Torin Kerr keep disaster from striking while escort-
ing a scientific expedition to an enormous spacecraft of
unknown origin?

To Order Call: 1-800-788-6262

DAW 19

Tanya Huff

The Finest in Fantasy

To Order Call: 1-800-788-6262

Tanya Huff

Smoke and Shadows

First in a New Series

Tony Foster—familiar to Tanya Huff fans from her *Blood* series—has relocated to Vancouver with Henry Fitzroy, vampire son of Henry VIII. Tony landed a job as a production assistant at CB Productions, ironically working on a syndicated TV series, "Darkest Night," about a vampire detective. Except for his crush on Lee, the show's handsome costar, Tony was pretty content...at least until everything started to fall apart on the set. It began with shadows—shadows that seemed to be where they didn't belong, shadows that had an existence of their own. And when he found a body, and a shadow cast its claim on Lee, Tony knew he had to find out what was going on, and that he needed Henry's help.

0-7564-0183-6

To Order Call: 1-800-788-6262

DAW 46

Tanya Huff

Victory Nelson, Investigator:
Otherworldly Crimes a Specialty

"Smashing entertainment for a wide audience"
—*Romantic Times*

"One series that deserves to continue"
—*Science Fiction Chronicle*

BLOOD PRICE
0-88677-471-3

BLOOD TRAIL
0-88677-502-7

BLOOD LINES
0-88677-530-2

BLOOD PACT
0-88677-582-5

To Order Call: 1-800-788-6262

Tad Williams

THE **WAR** OF THE **FLOWERS**

"A masterpiece of fairytale worldbuilding."
—*Locus*

"Williams's imagination is boundless."
—*Publishers Weekly*
(Starred Review)

"A great introduction to an accomplished
and ambitious fantasist."
—*San Francisco Chronicle*

"An addictive world ... masterfully plays
with the tropes and traditions of
generations of fantasy writers."
—*Salon*

"A very elaborate and fully realized setting
for adventure, intrigue, and more
than an occasional chill."
—*Science Fiction Chronicle*

0-7564-0181-X

To Order Call: 1-800-788-6262

DAW 45

MICHELLE WEST

The *Sun Sword* Novels

"Intriguing"—*Locus*
"Compelling"—*Romantic Times*

THE BROKEN CROWN	0-88677-740-2
THE UNCROWNED KING	0-88677-801-8
THE SHINING COURT	0-88677-837-9
SEA OF SORROWS	0-88677-978-2
THE RIVEN SHIELD	0-7564-0146-1
THE SUN SWORD	0-7564-0170-4

and don't miss:
The Sacred Hunt

HUNTER'S OATH	0-88677-681-3
HUNTER'S DEATH	0-88677-706-2

To Order Call: 1-800-788-6262